The

Treasure
of
Pawley's Island
Pawley's in the Spring, 1893

The Treasure of Pawley's Island
Pawley's in the Spring, 1893

― Celia Childress Halford ―

SANDLAPPER
PUBLISHING, INC.

THE TREASURE OF PAWLEY'S ISLAND
Copyright ©1987 by Sandlapper Publishing, Inc.

All rights reserved. This book may not be
reproduced, in whole or in part, in any form,
(except by reviewers for the public press),
without written permission from the publisher.

2 4 6 8 10 9 7 5 3

Published by Sandlapper Publishing, Inc.
P.O. Box 1932, Orangeburg, S.C., 29116-1932
MANUFACTURED IN THE UNITED STATES OF AMERICA

Illustrated by Celia Childress Halford

Library of Congress Cataloging-in-Publication Data

Halford, Celia Childress, 1942-
  The treasure of Pawley's Island.

   Summary: 1893 twelve-year-old Bessie and a new friend go in search of pirate treasure on Pawley's Island, off the coast of South Carolina.
   [1. Buried treasure—Fiction. 2. Pawleys Island (S.C.)—Fiction.] I. Title.
PZ7.H1387TR 1987   [Fic]   86[25997
ISBN 0-87844-068-2 (soft)

*This book is dedicated with love
and gratitude to my sons,
Jonathan, Blair, and Spencer.*

Acknowledgements

Ten years ago I began writing for fifteen minutes a day on a short adventure story for children because that's where I was—surrounded by three boys ages 8, 5, and 1 who climbed roofs without using ladders, hauled their baby brother up to treetops in a bucket, used pounds of rubber bands in glorious rubber band fights on rainy days, sleepwalked all over the house, built hideouts in attic rooms, climbed out of windows in the dead of night, tied balloons to the dog's tail, and chewed on the same piece of gum for ten straight hours. They dragged me through motherhood then, and they are still doing it now. How could I not write about them and for them! During all ten years while I wrote, they never tired of asking, "How's the book, Mom?" Although they never expected me to finish it (I believe they have grown up with a perpetual state of one-bookness), I did complete the thing with their help and with the help of several people who miraculously appeared at just the right moment; Dr. James A.W. Rembert of The Citadel read and advised several times, Harriet McDougal worked with structuring, Mary Anne Spivey read and corrected, Barbara Allen of The Citadel helped with revisions over a three year period, Kathryn Childress (my mother and a coastal expert) gave unerring suggestions, and Beth Littlejohn worked with the final draft. These people were friends whose judgment I could trust.

"Fair the day shine as it shone
    on my childhood—

Fair shine the day on the
    house with open door;

Birds come and cry there and
    twitter in the chimney—

But I go forever and come
    again no more."

—Robert Louis Stevenson

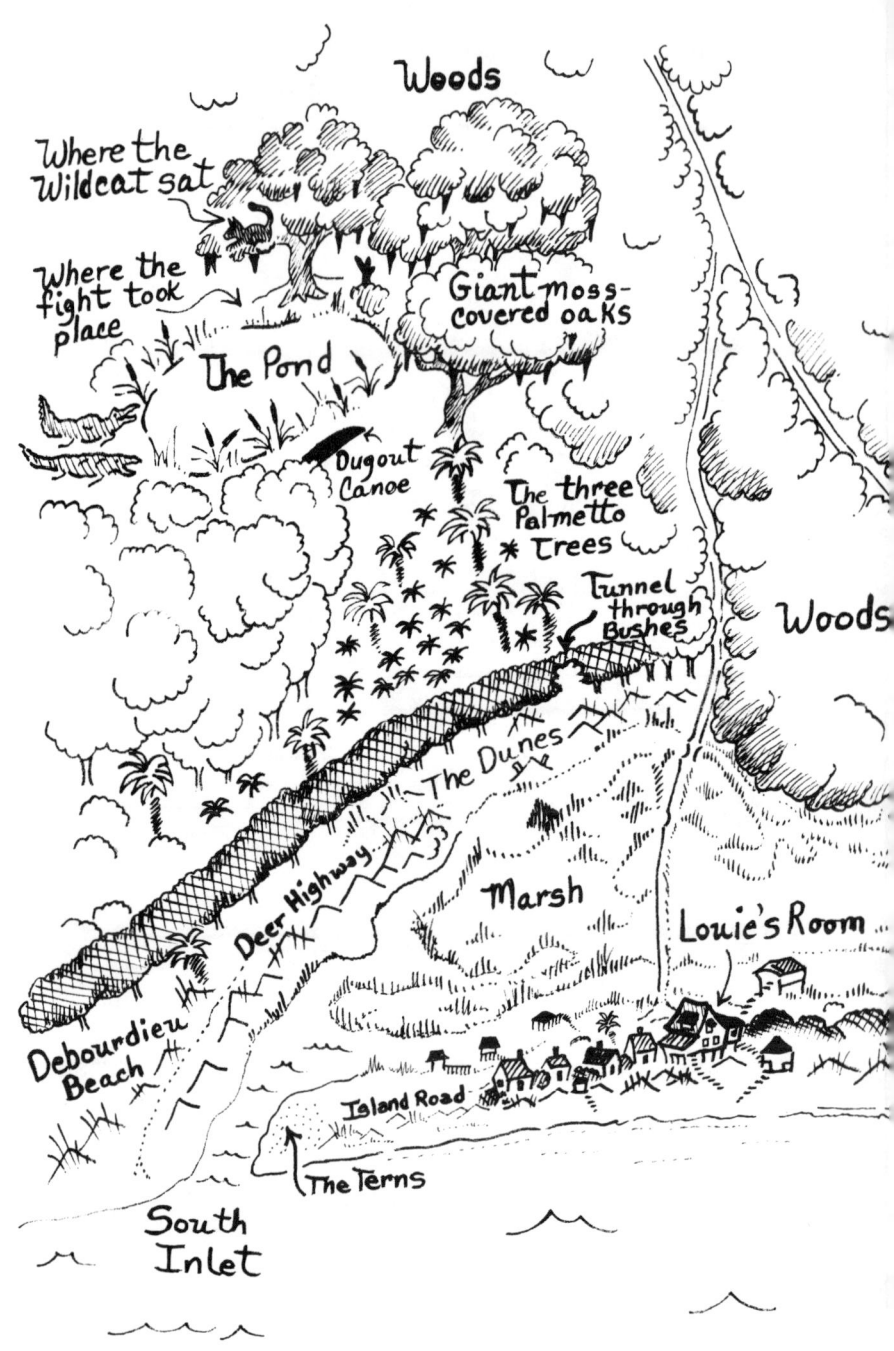

Introduction
Shadows and Sunshine

1

On April 1, 1893, my family and I traveled with our Negro servants on our annual migration from our rice plantation to Pawley's Island, a small sea island on the coast of South Carolina. Almost thirty years after the War Between the States and immediately after a cold and long winter, we yearned to see our old beach home. I was twelve going-on-thirteen in 1893, at the peak of my childhood, a child of the plantation and a child of the seaside. I was ready for spring to unfold.

Looking back, I smell the fragrance of those adventurous and perfumed days, and I am unsure which meant the most to me, the special quality of life at Pawley's Island or my encounter with events and people that would unsettle even a brave boy who became my friend. That was the spring when I began to grow up, leaving behind the life of a sheltered girl living in a more gentle time in our history, to enter the world of danger in the marsh and woods behind Pawley's.

I have written this story, taking it from a journal written by candlelight in my attic room, so that my grandchildren can see that world. Those pages, a journal more flavored by salt air than I then knew, were used as a basis for this story, with descriptions and history not only from childhood memories but from my growing store of knowledge after living on Pawley's these many years. The "old Pawley's" that you will read about is gone forever. I am reminded, however, that it lives anew with each generation of shore lovers, those enterprising and daring Pawley's youth.

Just as it is when we move from shadow into sunshine, so it was that Elizabeth Lois Duvall moved from childhood toward maturity in the spring of 1893.

I looked over at my playmate, and I knew she had outgrown me.

Chapter 1
At The Plantation

When I first saw the strange old man—with his Negro helper and his black cur—I did not know that he would be part of a mysterious treasure hunt on Pawley's Island, a hunt which would satisfy my longings for friendship and adventure.

He stood at one end of a great cypress dugout canoe, poling it down the Waccamaw River; we slowly passed him in our steamboat, going up the river as he went down, past Butler's Island. Yellow teeth dangled from a deerhide string hung around his neck. His hat, clothes, skin and beard seemed the same color, yellow-brown.

A dog's nose appeared over the edge of the canoe. The black cur eyed us intelligently as we eased by. He was more interested in us than was his master, who only acknowledged our presence by a curt and formal lifting of his greasy, wrinkled hat. Grandpa, in the wheelhouse, and Uncle Sumter, standing at the rail by my side, lifted their hats in return; Mama, Grandma and Aunt Alberta nodded to him. The Negro servants glanced up but paid him little attention. Cousin Jane Anne, who was sitting by my mother on one side and her mother not far away on the other, openly stared at him. Leaning over the rail, I stared hard at him, too.

Then I noticed two boots sticking up stiffly in the other end of the canoe. "A dead man!" I exclaimed, startled at the bizarre sight. But as we looked back, the dugout rose and fell in our wake, and I saw a Negro man lying in the shallow bottom, casually smoking a cigarette beneath a tattered hat. Two shotguns were propped near him in the rough canoe.

Uncle Sumter's shoulders heaved with his rasping, high-pitched cough. I turned to his butler, who was leaning on the rail with us. "Daddy Buck," I asked, "who are those men?" I pointed back at the dugout. The yellow-brown man was languidly poling the dugout closer

Chapter 1

to Butler's Island.

"Dey hunt an' dey fish," he answered. "Dat's all. Dat man ib *Old Dirty*. He ib po' buckra—trash!—an' dat ugly man lyin' in de bottom is his help. Huh, he lyin' down lak he de boss."

Daddy Buck had a look of disgust on his mahogany face, a look of disdain for men he considered to be of low type. He himself, with a fine reputation as a house servant, was particular about people. But when he turned away from the disreputable men, he smiled at me. He was glad to see me again after six months, and I was glad to see him.

"Missie," he cried, "yuh goin' t' land in dat black water ober de side! Yuh half fallin' in now. Ah gotta say git back!" He grinned when I complied, showing me his broken, yellowed teeth. "He! Hee! Missie soon be de *lady*."

Uncle Sumter coughed even more violently, bending nearly double over the railing. Daddy Buck took his attention from me and led him to a bench beside the little wheelhouse. Uncle Sumter fell onto the bench and fumbled around in his pockets for his carved silver flask, tipping it to his trembling lips for a big gulp of the cough medicine he had been taking for years. "Black cherry," he mumbled to my mother between coughs, "black cherry..." It seemed to quiet his cough as he drank from the flask.

When I looked back down river, I could not see Old Dirty poling his dugout. He and his crew were out of sight around the bend of the island.

"Jane Anne, did you see those two men?" I asked, settling myself between my cousin and her mother, Aunt Alberta.

"No," she replied. "I only saw the filthy man with the beard."

"Did you see the dog? And the dark little man lying in the bottom?" I asked her insistently.

"Now, Bessie, there you go making up stories in your head again. I thought you would have grown out of that this spring." She patted my shoulder like I was a poor thing and turned again to talk to Mama.

I listened to family and servants chatter above the sound of the engine. The rice fields slipped by. Crows were circling over them here and there.

I thought to myself that I would probably never see those men again and Jane Anne was right, that they were part of a story I was never to know.

But she was wrong. We were to see Old Dirty and his helper again, within a few weeks.

My adventure had begun.

The Treasure of Pawley's Island

✦ ✦ ✦ ✦ ✦ ✦ ✦

On the rice plantation before dawn that very day, Mama's cool fingers had stroked my forehead. "Wake up, dear," she had whispered. "Put on your blue sailor suit—Tassie ironed it and laid it on the foot of your bed. I've told Maum Polly to keep a hot breakfast for you in the kitchen. We've eaten already. Now dress and run down there. Your trunks are all packed—all you need to do is pack your cloth bag."

I lay quite still, trying to wake up and enjoying the smoothness of her fingers on my forehead and hair.

"Isn't it still dark, Mama?" I asked, feeling cold. I struggled to pull more comforter over myself.

"It's an hour before dawn," Mama replied, quietly, and helped me tug at the covers. The ecru lace falling over the top of the canopied bed was dark. The coal in the fireplace grate had burned away. I rubbed my eyes, barely able to see.

"Bessie, look who's asleep over on her pillow—you've waited months to see her," Mama whispered, gently turning my head toward the other side of the big double bed.

I sat bolt upright. There was Jane Anne, snuggled deep in the pillows and almost entirely covered by the down comforter. No wonder I had felt cold.

"Now awaken her slowly, Bessie," Mama whispered. "She had a miserable, wet trip up from Charleston. I guess it was a couple of hours past midnight when she arrived. Didn't you hear her come in?"

I shook my head in disbelief. I had tried to stay awake as long as I could, waiting for her with great anticipation.

"She came in past midnight? What happened, Mama?" I was shocked to think of Jane Anne traveling on the dark, wet roads so late in the night.

"One of the horses broke a leg. The driver finally had to put him down," Mama whispered back. "Dress yourself. Let Jane Anne sleep a few more minutes while you dress. Her mother will be in any minute to awaken her. You know Aunt Alberta. Hurry now."

Mama drew her shawl more closely to her. I could not see her sweet face in the darkness. She turned slowly, with tired movements, to the door. I slipped out of the bed and crept around to Jane Anne's side.

"No, Bessie," whispered Mama, catching me. "Leave her alone. I'll send Tassie up with coals for the fire."

"But I want to talk to her, Mama."

"Shhhh. You will will have all spring and summer to talk," she whispered firmly. "You must be ready to go in less than an hour—dress

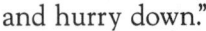

Chapter 1

and hurry down."

As she tiptoed from the room, I could hear the servants scurrying through the wide central hallway, their heels clicking softly on the wide pine boards.

I pulled off my flannel gown and hurriedly, because of the cold air, jerked on my underclothes, again slipping closer to take a look at Jane Anne. I moved the candle from a table to a nearby bureau.

Although her face was half-covered by the linen pillow slip, I could see she looked older than when I had last seen her in the fall as she excitedly waved good-bye to me to travel to her boarding school in Charleston. I hurriedly lit another candle and held it closer to her face. Some of the baby fat had melted from her cheeks, and her curved lips were even more rosy than before. Long dark lashes lay gently on creamy cheeks. A natural and perfect blush colored them, even in sleep.

She looked too old now to play pirate with me. Would she fish for crabs on the inlet pier, or race me down the beach any more? Would she still want to collect shells, or build drip castles at the edge of the water? I looked over at my playmate, and I knew she had outgrown me.

Perversely, I chose my longest fingernail and used it to scratch her pillow with long slow scratches, our old secret signal for awakening. Scratch, scratch, scratch.

She slept on, with her pale blonde hair scattered in curls over the pillow.

Scratch. Scratch. Long irritating scratches.

"O-h-h-h, Bessie."

Scra-a-a-atch.

"Oh-h-h, let me sleep."

Scratch, scratch.

"My head. Bessie, please—we'll have weeks, months to talk. Let me sleep." Her voice was the same babydoll whisper. That had not changed.

I felt she definitely needed another scratch and proceeded to make it the best one.

"Well, you haven't changed, Bessie. You still like to torment me." She sounded resigned to awakening.

"No, no, I know you need to wake up. It will take you longer to get dressed and packed than Methusela." I rustled around, making noise, trying to help her wake up. I slipped the sailor suit over my head, muttering noisily, buttoned it, tied the bow and drew on my itchy wool stockings. "Your mama will be here in a bit. You better jump up."

Jane Anne spoke from under the comforter, "No doubt she will. And those maids will too. Mama was out on the porch last night with a lantern waiting for me. She was about ready to jump in a carriage—at

The Treasure of Pawley's Island

midnight—and come searching the roads for me."

I lit a third candle and saw that Jane Anne's small traveling cases and a couple of larger ones were scattered about the room, some opened, some stacked. Her clothes were thrown everywhere, untidily. The mess was distasteful.

"Every bone in my body aches. The rain started a few hours out of Charleston, and we couldn't half see the road. That old carriage driver had no consideration on that bumpy road. Why, he whipped those horses," Jane Anne declared. "And all he could say was 'Dat Miz will skin me alive fo' bringin' yo' in late, Missie.' " Jane Anne laughed. "And she just about did when she saw us. When she spotted us driving up to the house in the rain, she started blessing him out."

She sounded then like the old Jane Anne. Pleased, I poured cold water from the pitcher into the wash basin and made hasty motions at cleaning my face.

"I want to hear all about your school year," I pleaded. "Tell me about the *balls*, the teas, your friends, the classes. Sit up!"

"No, you go on. Call the maid—I need a bath. Why, I'm filthy."

"Ha!" I replied, "You'll never get one drop of hot water for a bath this morning. We're leaving in a few minutes. If we ask now, you might get enough hot water for tea. I'll send Tassie to the kitchen for some." Then I added softly, "Hot tea will make you talk." I went to the door and flung it open, calling, "Tassie! Tassie! Are you out there? Bring Miss Jane Anne some hot tea with fresh cream. Tassie, do you hear me?"

"Yes'm! Ah hears. Ah knows she need dat tea. Po' lil thing." Tassie scurried down the stairs, clacking her tongue.

"Hurry! Hurry!" I urged again and ran back to the bed. Jane Anne's eyes were closed again.

"Which clothes can I hand to you?" I yelled at her, causing her to flinch. "Wake up—Grandpa is going to start that steamboat engine in a few minutes. Here, let me dip a cloth in water for you."

I stumbled over her baggage and her expensive but disheveled clothing to the pitcher of icy water. "Put this on your forehead," I suggested, wringing out the cloth and then offering it to her. She took the cloth as I imagined a princess would and laid it gently over her eyes.

I wandered over to take a peek at her luggage. She had not learned neatness this year, either. One Saratoga trunk was slung open to reveal the gleam and profusion of pink opaque bottles and jars of fascinating toiletries, a jumble of expense.

"Why do you need all these jars, Janey?" I inquired.

"Jane Anne. Call me *Jane Anne*. Miss Lilly said I must be known as Jane Anne from now on." She sighed again, pressing the cold cloth

Chapter 1

to her face.

"Jane Anne, Jane Anne. I'll try to remember. Would I be known as 'Elizabeth Lois' if I were to go to school at Miss Lilly's?" I asked.

"Yes, I guess so, but you'll never go there," she replied from under the cloth. I could not reply, for I knew it was true. My schooling would consist of Grandma teaching me from Grandpa's enormous library. My family could not afford to send me to an expensive boarding school in Charleston.

"I'm feeling a bit stronger, Bessie. Would you please pick up my clothes? Mama will pitch a fit if she finds that suit on the floor. Put them over there. No, there. Don't speak. I need a bath. Why can't they warm enough water for a small bath?" Jane Anne finally sat up. "Hand those underthings to me . . . no, those!"

I laid the underclothes, a fancy lacy corset included, neatly on the bed. My underclothes, beneath my plain sailor suit, were of plain cotton. I finished picking up her clothes from the night before.

Jane Anne climbed off the tall bed, moaning, and washed her face. Then she opened a dainty jar and rubbed her cheeks with rosewater and glycerin.

My cousin had acquired gracefulness during the months she had been away at school, or perhaps it was just that I had never noticed it before. I thought of birds dipping their wings as she brushed back her hair to reveal the white-blonde baby hairs that swept up from her forehead. With her delicate features, those almond-shaped blue eyes, and that hair, that pale and silky hair, she was now beautiful. I guess she knew it.

I watched her, fascinated, as she moved about the room, brushing her pale hair. She leaned over like a willow, her tortoiseshell brush rhythmically moving through her floating hair like the wind moving through long leafy strands. I felt like a little girl, a plain little girl.

"Bessie, Bessie," she sighed, "I'll never live through another ride today. You know I need twenty-four hours in this bed. You know how my head aches when I haven't had enough rest—now, you are staring, Bessie. Go sit down on that chair," she ordered, sounding pleased.

I meekly sat on the upholstered chair while she continued brushing and weaving about the room. "The noise of that old steamboat will throb right through my head," she said. "Just you wait—in an hour you'll see me faint dead away on the deck of that dirty old steamboat. And Aunt Hagey will be pickin' at me and screaming. And Mama will be horrified."

"I have never seen you faint a single time," I observed. "You sound too strong to faint this morning."

The Treasure of Pawley's Island

"Well, I fainted several times in Charleston this winter," she answered firmly. "It comes upon me suddenly, and down I go."

There was a knock at the door, and two maids entered with Jane Anne's tea tray.

"Missie Janey, Missie Janey!" they cried, grinning, "Yo' back heah safe—wel-ky home, wel-ky home!"

"Now, you must call me 'Miss Jane Anne.' Miss Jane Anne, I want to be called 'Miss Jane Anne.'"

Tassie murmured the new name while settling Jane Anne into a comfortable chair and pouring her tea, complimenting the brew to high heaven for its hotness and flavor and recuperative powers. Then the maids proceeded to strip the bedding off the bed, bundle it up, roll up the mattress and tie it with stout string. Finally they pushed it into the hallway with loud grunts in proportion to the labor involved.

Jane Anne sat in her blue taffeta robe, sipping her tea and rubbing her temples. I sat watching her, trying to grow accustomed to the changes in my cousin during the winter.

Tassie stood in the doorway and gave her voluminous skirts an emphatic swish. She said, "Missie *Jane Anne,* y' turned into de lady in de winter. Ain't dat so?" She looked at me and then the other maid, who chirped, "Ain't dat so?"

Tassie was so pleased that she continued, "Yo' mama be proud. Yo' papa be proud. Yo' hair ain't stringy dis heah year, an' yo' shape dun growed out, an' yo' papa hab t' beat de beaux off wid de stick!"

"Yes, Tassie," said Jane Anne, "everybody grows up. Now isn't that so?" Then she waved her hand impatiently, "You two go finish packing or whatever you are doing—wait, send Aunt Hagey up here to pack these clothes and things. And have her bring me a hot, hot biscuit from the kitchen. I'm hungry. If I can't have a bath, I'll have a biscuit. Go find her. Look in Mama's room."

"Yes'm." Off they went, closing the door behind them.

At that moment Teaspoon, our houseboy on the plantation and pier boy at the shore, called from down the hallway. "Ah'm heah! Collectin' de mattress an' de trunk, an' de box an' de bag an' de ober anythings!"

His squeaky voice was full of excitement. I knew he could not wait to see his beloved pier, his station of action for the next half year. There he was ruler, in charge of fishing and crabbing from the pier which stretched over the marsh behind our cottage. Often times Teaspoon was my playmate as well.

His black, diminutive fist thundered on the door like a woodpecker,

Chapter 1

ratta-tat-tat.

"Ah'm here! Ib de *mattress* dun tied?" he yelled at us from the hallway. "Oh, dere dey be! Ib de *trunk* dun ready? Oh, dere dey be!" he exclaimed, spying my luggage in the hallway. "Ib de *box* ready? Ib de lady ready t' hop de wagon?" Again his fist thundered on the door.

I opened the door a crack to see him dancing around the trunks and other luggage in the hallway. "Hush that noise, Teaspoon," I scolded. "We'll send for you when we're ready. That's my luggage out there. You send it on down. No, go on. And hush your voice."

"Dis not de mornin' fo' de hush!" he yelled, his voice going even higher. "Uncle Zeke gib de order t' yank de box an' de mattress an' de trunk an' de ober anythings outta de house, an' straightaway ah yanks! Come an' gettum," he called over his shoulder to a field hand who was climbing the stairs to fetch the luggage to the wagons lined up in front of the house.

"Take dese an' hop up back fo' mo'," he told the hand and then turned to me. "See, Missie, ah dress fo' de trip."

I opened the door to take a closer look at his costume. It was a bit more unusual than his ordinary clothing. He wore an old gray wool Prince Albert—a cast-off from better days, from an elegant wardrobe—with black velvet cuffs and lapels. He had prevailed on someone to alter it to his small stature, but it still hung on his thin frame nearly to the ankles. Its fanciness pleased him enormously, and he danced around in the dark hallway, showing it off because he knew I would appreciate it.

"An' see de trouser," he crowed, pulling back the coat to show his unusual striped trousers, which were tied together with a rope.

"An' de hat," he pointed out. "See de pin?" Teaspoon had pinned several long feathers on the front of the bowler, white and gray egret and heron feathers, nearly a foot in length. He was a remarkable sight.

"My goodness!" I exclaimed, trying to sound like Grandma. "You have outdone yourself this time with fashionable polish and amazing attire!"

My vocabulary choice appeared to be satisfactory. He beamed. Teaspoon always appreciated high-flown phrases, the more un-understandable, the better.

He peered around me, spying Jane Anne's baggage. "Ho—ah see dose trunks! Bring out dose trunks," he called, proud and confident in his new clothing.

"Miss Jane Anne has a rotten headache, and you are making it worse!" I scolded sternly. Then, because he was dancing around again, I yelled, "Send the rest of these down, please, but you'll have to wait

The Treasure of Pawley's Island

for Miss Jane Anne's bags. And it will be a while. Do you hear? A while!"

Tassie sailed around the corner. "Git dat jumpin' boy outta heah! Ah heah him yell downstair. Missie Jane Anne still be in de night clothes, an' de pearly face not dressed eber, you loud blabber. Po' thing she hab de head ache—git outta here!"

She pushed him down the hallway, with him squealing all the way. "Git, Git!" she hollered.

Jane Anne, drawn to the door because of the noise, called to her, "Tassie, do I have to wait all day for Aunt Hagey to bring me a biscuit? I want it right now!"

She closed the door, peeved. "Bessie, it seems to me that on my first morning back Aunt Hagey would be right up here. How can I be expected to dress and pack at the same time? Well, I just won't do it. And you know that Teaspoon should be put back in the fields. He's too loud to be in the Big House."

She began pulling a rainbow of shirtwaists from one trunk, holding them up to her and tossing them aside, muttering about Aunt Hagey's unfaithfulness and Teaspoon's volume. She scrambled through another trunk of traveling suits. Finally, out came a cream-colored suit. It was a most unsuitable garment for traveling, I thought. I looked down at my practical blue sailor suit. Even though I felt inadequate, and even though I was amazed at the change which had taken place in my cousin, I was enjoying all the excitement Jane Anne had brought to our usually quiet house. I knew she had not caused all of the noise, yet our plantation house had been terribly quiet since the very day she had left for school in Charleston. Many times Mama had told me that Janey—Jane Anne—brought excitement with her, that things happened when she was around, and not all of them pleasant.

But at that moment I forgot her words in the pleasure of being around noise and excitement, around a girl only a few years older.

She laid the cream suit on the bed and chose a pale silky shirtwaist with a high collar of ruching, tiny pleats up to her chin. With approval she laid the blouse beside the suit. "How do you like these old things?" she asked me.

"Beautiful," I replied timidly, then with a rush of words I said, "but you'll have spots all over that before we arrive."

"Hush your month! I will not!" She deftly began to put up her hair with long golden pins, almost the same shade as her hair. "Go eat your breakfast before you make us late, little girl."

"I have plenty of time," I answered serenely. "Did you ride the trolley cars in Charleston? Did you walk through Whitepoint Gardens? With a beau on each arm? Did you take tea with lemon in the afternoons

Chapter 1

with friends? Did your headmistress let you read *novels*? Did a beau call for you in a silver cab pulled by matching greys?"

My mind had been filled all winter with visions of Jane Anne living a gracious, scholarly life in beautiful Charleston, with parties, laughing friends, balls, adoring beaus, and wonders beyond my comprehension.

Jane Anne pranced about the bedroom, slinging clothes right and left, even kicking a few.

Then she began to dress, ordering me to lace her corset.

"Just a week ago," she said in her airy voice, "Mr. Thomas Legare Bailey escorted me to a concert at a theatre. Of course, we were chaperoned by Miss Lilly and two other students. He begged Miss Lilly to be able to escort us." She laughed gaily, and I laced her corset tighter and tighter.

"I believe a string quartet played at the Dock Street Theatre. And someone did a reading. I don't remember the title—lace it tighter. Miss Lilly said the music was glorious. Of course, *my* favorite music is on Sunday afternoons at Whitepoint Gardens, when we walk around and talk as the music plays ... I like to *promenade* on a gentleman's arm—that Miss Lilly interposed herself between Mr. Bailey and me at the concert at the last moment, and there was absolutely nothing I could do about it. I could not ask her to move, and of course he could not—hand me that shirtwaist—I felt like telling her to get her bustle into the next seat, but I only hinted. I said, 'Miss Lilly, perhaps you would be more comfortable here in this seat near the aisle. There's more air circulating here.'"

Jane Anne was an excellent mime. I could see the entire scene in my mind's eye as she acted it out while dressing, no small feat.

"Mr. Bailey understood my meaning. You should have seen the look he passed me. But Miss Lilly only looked away. Charleston is much more civilized than Georgetown *ever* was, Bessie—look at these old shoes! I can't wear these!" she declared, tossing them into a corner. "Time is passing this old place by, just passing it by. Charleston is where I will live when *I* marry."

I buttoned the back of her shirtwaist. It closed with twenty-five tiny covered buttons.

"Are you going to marry Mr. Thomas Legare Bailey?" I asked.

"No, of course not, silly. He couldn't provide for me, not at this time at least. But Mama advised me to practice *repartee* with many young gentlemen, and Mr. Bailey does repartee very well, even with his eyes, his velvet brown eyes. But he has no money—Julia told me last week he might inherit from an aunt, but that is only hearsay. My

The Treasure of Pawley's Island

future husband must have means, Bessie, substantial means."

"He *repartees* with his velvet brown eyes?" I asked. I could see those eyes.

Jane Anne was drawing on her cream-colored stockings and didn't appear to hear me.

"I'll walk with you to visit your friends at the shore so that you won't have to walk alone," I volunteered. "And we can take horses and ride under the oaks over on the Neck, if you like." Then I demanded, "Are you going to collect shells with me this year?"

"Don't be silly, Bessie. Now, come over here to the glass. Look. Just look at yourself." I looked in the mirror.

"Look at your hair—yes, it's thick and golden brown. But it's like wet straw. Thank *goodness* for my hair. You must do something about *your* hair. Too bad it's so straight and the ends are all split." She looked at it in disgust.

"Should I cut it?" I asked eagerly.

She ignored me. "Well, at least you have arched eyebrows and a widow's peak," she said. "I'd like to have those myself. When you reach sixteen like I am, you will *have* to use a bit of rouge on those cheeks. I've not had to use any. See—your cheeks are pale like your mother's—absolutely white."

She held out her wrists for me to button the six tiny buttons there.

"I will only walk or ride with you this year if I have time. And I may not have a minute free. Mr. Bailey admired my hair greatly and said my complexion is like a pink camellia japonica. *Your* complexion is like a white daisy. I had coiled my hair up at my neck, rather like today." Jane Anne waltzed to the mirror to take another look at herself.

"See this dimple in my chin? When my hair is up, my chin shows to its best advantage, don't you think? I pinned in silk flowers from the Orient, touched with French perfume. Bessie, just look at your hands."

Jane Anne measured her hands against mine. Mine were an inch longer. I wondered when they had grown that long.

"Well, perhaps your hands are growing first and then your little body will follow. You have your papa's hands—that's what they are. But your voice is, uh, pleasant, and your nose is fairly straight, even if it does have a high bridge. Now, if you learn how to dress, those will stand you in good stead. Small and thin, with big hands and white skin, perhaps even a bit yellow."

A sick feeling swept over me. My hands were large. My skin was sickly. My hair felt heavy and broken to its very roots. I felt as low as a plantation dog, slinking its way around from place to place.

Chapter 1

"Mama said my hands are artist's hands," I whispered faintly.

"Huh," said Jane Anne, admiring her fully-dressed self in the mirror. "Where is Aunt Hagey? She has to clean up this mess."

I put my hands in my pockets. Through the window I saw that darkness still hung over the plantation.

"I better go eat breakfast now, cousin. Perhaps we can talk more on the steamboat?" I walked to the door.

"Perhaps. Oh, I hear Mama's step in the hall. Where *is* Aunt Hagey—look at these clothes spread everywhere! You were supposed to pick them up, Bessie."

I escaped out the door as Aunt Alberta entered. "Good morning, Aunt Alberta," I said, skipping past her.

"Good morning, Bessie," replied my aunt, sweeping past me. "*Good morning*, dearest Jane Anne. Did you rest?" She flung her arms wide, rattling her strands of pearls, and exclaiming, "This room, *this room!*"

Aunt Alberta was magnificently dressed in a mauve traveling suit covered with tucks and gathers and bits of lace. "Where is Aunt Hagey?" she bellowed, clasping her hands together and then swinging them wide. "We must organize these cases. Organize, organize!"

I ran for the kitchen.

The Treasure of Pawley's Island

I remembered how for weeks the entire household had been preparing for our great migration to the sea island.

Chapter 2
I'll Find My Own Mysteries

The waxed and glossy heart-of-pine boards of the old plantation house's wide central hallways reflected candlelight. Light flickered on the old gilt-framed oil paintings lining the walls. Servants and field hands were busy carrying luggage of all shapes and sizes from the second floor bedrooms into the drafty hall and then downstairs. As I passed Aunt Alberta and Uncle Sumter's room, I saw why Aunt Hagey, Aunt Alberta's maid, had not arrived to pack for Jane Anne; she was too busy with Aunt Alberta's luggage, organizing and folding, packing for her demanding mistress' trip to the island. Daddy Buck, her husband, shouldered a heavy trunk to be carried down the curved stairs, past the carved French table, past potted plants, to be deposited under the crystal and silver chandelier.

As I sped past Daddy Buck, I remembered how for weeks the entire household had been preparing for our great migration to the sea island twenty miles north of Georgetown. Not only had our clothing been washed and mended, but down from the attic had come a summer wardrobe for the shore house—white linen and dimity curtains, both trimmed with generous borders of tatting, a delicate handmade lace, and white bedspreads decorated with the same. The plantation's rugs had been carried out to the line and beaten by the maids until clouds of dust covered the dusky women. Then several colorful rugs were selected for the trip and rolled up in newspaper that had been dipped in turpentine; most were stored in the attic, and a few were packed for the journey. Large pieces of canvas and equally large squares of rush matting were rolled or folded up; these would finally be tacked to the bleached floor of our beloved Pawley's Island house. The rugs would be laid over them in several rooms.

The winter curtains, excepting the blue velvet ones in the parlor, had been seized from the windows, cleaned and packed up to the

Chapter 2

cedar attic. The plantation furniture was covered with muslin sheets to await our return, with only a few chests and chairs selected for the journey to the beach cottage. Mosquito netting had been bleached, mended and packed in boxes to take along.

Many hours were spent in organizing and preparing foods for the move. Grandma and Maum Polly, our cook, had counted out barrels of flour and bag after bag of our very own golden plantation rice. Grandpa and Papa could not eat dinner at the shore without their rice. (Truly, serving a dinner or supper meal without it was unthinkable in our family.) Winter vegetables were jerked from the cold ground and bagged. Jugs of honey and molasses, jars of figs and pears, tomatoes and corn, barrels of apples and bags of dried beans—all were neatly listed and packed.

"Heaven is orderly," said Grandma, "and life must imitate heaven, or the angels will not want to come here."

The four black housemaids were as busy as Mama, Grandma and Maum Polly. And Grandpa and Uncle Zeke not only carried out their regular duties—which were heavy enough—but they also worked and planned for the trip, repairing the steamboat, seeing to the animals that were to accompany us, gathering a thousand and one tools, bags and barrels of foods, and furniture. These were all men's duties.

The servants had carefully polished, rolled in flannel, and gently packed the silver flatware, pitchers and candelabra. An infinite number of bowls, pots, pans and other kitchen impements had also been packed, along with the snowy bed and table linens. Mama's rosewood rocker was lovingly set aside to take—for how could she rock a new baby at the shore house without it? As Grandma and Mama had organized, the housemaids had packed sewing boxes and cloth, soap, home remedies, textbooks for me, and everyone's special books and games, to break the monotony on rainy days. They had packed lanterns, oil lamps and candles—these overseen by Grandpa, who knew their importance. The hurried packing had continued with summer clothes and some fresh woolens, including coats and capes for the cool spells; all these were laid carefully in the trunks, bags and boxes from the trunkroom under the house.

◆ ◆ ◆ ◆ ◆ ◆ ◆

Downstairs, I heard Mama walking from room to room, calling out orders to the servants. I knew she had been up a good part of the night checking over our trunks, bundles and rope-tied boxes. As I descended the wide staircase, Grandma was cautioning her to slow

The Treasure of Pawley's Island

down, but Mama said she would rest tomorrow. "The day has just begun, Mama Belle," she said, smiling, with love in her gentle eyes.

Grandma replied that *now* was the time Mama should take care of herself. She didn't want her son to have another woman raising her grandchildren, Grandma said, and childbirth was the surest way yet to shorten a marriage and make way for a second wife. Why, she had seen it a hundred times. Besides, she was quite happy with the daughter-in-law she had and was unwilling to give her up to exhaustion and an early grave. "The family has waited too long for the birth of this baby," she concluded, giving Mama an affectionate hug.

I said good morning to them both and kissed them. I looked at Mama's wan face and swelling abdomen and thought of how determined she was to have another baby, to finally bring one to full term. Yet she was energetic and could seldom bear to sit still unless she was reading, doing handwork or playing her beloved piano. "I'm like that, too," I thought. Grandma called me a hot worm.

I heard Grandpa's voice on the porch, directing field hands to begin carrying the baggage from inside the house out to the wagons. In they trooped, each stopping to carefully clean his heavy shoes at the door. With eagerness, I made my way through the commotion and out the door, weaving my way past baggage and scores of household items to the kitchen house which sat under the swaying dark arms of an old oak.

The brightly-lit little building was in pandemonium. Kitchen maids were in a dither; Maum Polly was waving her wooden spoon in the air. With dispatch the maids jumped in every direction as their general spoke. In the midst of it all I ate a hasty breakfast at the tiny table Maum Polly kept for me near the brick fireplace. I watched the hubbub, excitedly thinking of our new baby and the wonderful changes it would make in our household, imagining the stories Jane Anne would tell me of Charleston, and thinking ahead to Pawley's Island.

When I finished my oatmeal and buttered boiled egg, I ran back to the front piazza with its swaying lanterns. It looked down on a dark grassy slope to the river below. That river at the end of the driveway was to be our highway to Waccamaw Neck and Pawley's Island. I peeked through one of the long porch windows into the drawing room. Mama and Cousin Jane Anne were sitting together near the fireplace. I decided to go inside and listen at the drawing room door. Mama was resting in a comfortable chair, as Grandma had urged her to do. Jane Anne must have left her mother and Aunt Hagey upstairs to do battle with the chaos of her clothes and trunks so that she could partake of tea with Mama in the parlor.

Their voices mingled, tinkling above the scurrying noises of the

Chapter 2

servants. One candle lit the darkness of the large, graceful room.

I poked my head in the doorway to hear what they were saying. The subject was Governor Tillman *again*. Everyone seemed to be discussing our South Carolina governor. Wherever people gathered, the conversation gradually turned to Tillman. Grandpa, like other plantation owners, did not approve of the governor of South Carolina, thinking him common. Our governor was supported by the small farmers of the state, the "Wool Hat Boys," who said they were tired of being ruled by the "aristocracy," the plantation owners and formerly wealthy families from before The War, those men who formerly wore "top hats."

"And you sat behind Governor Tillman at the concert?" Mama was asking Jane Anne as my cousin was adding more sugar to her hot tea. "You say he kissed your hand? Rumor has it that he never kisses anyone's hand." Mama was warming her own hands around the tea cup. The delicate fragrance of it drifted my way.

"He kissed several hands, Sis Mary. And his voice is loud enough to deafen, like he wanted everyone in the concert hall to hear his every word, and he was bored in the concert. Miss Lilly observed him looking about and even sleeping. *Bored,* she said. And he fidgeted," continued Jane Anne disdainfully. She adjusted the lace at her wrists and sipped her tea.

"Were you bored?" asked Mama.

"No, I'm never bored—the Governor wiped his nose on his cuff and didn't even notice it. Sis Mary, some people don't care about concerts, or culture. And Ben Tillman is one, I guess," she sighed. "Oh, he came to be seen all right, so said *Mr. Bailey* to me the next afternoon as we sat in the parlor at tea."

"What was the concert?" Mama asked. She loved music and was a skilled pianist.

"Oh, I don't remember now. Strings, I believe. Strings are too shrill. I'll take the pianoforte anytime. I wore my green velvet with looped sleeves and ecru lace, with a garnet broach, and new silk slippers."

I turned from them, wondering if the sun would ever rise. The birds were chirping louder out in the oaks. On the front piazza I looked down to see heaps and mounds of importance piled up before the steps in the hovering darkness. The servants with torches and lanterns were hurriedly packing everything into wagons to be driven down to the river. They shouted directions to each other, and every minute or two another wagon would depart for the river where the steamboat waited.

Aunt Alberta soon sent Cousin Jane Anne's trunks to be added

The Treasure of Pawley's Island

to the enormous pile. My cousin's family never traveled without innumerable pieces of luggage, expensive leather luggage with gleaming clasps. Their trunks were filled with change after change of clothing, costume after costume for every possible occasion, many for my cousin and her mother and some for Uncle Sumter. They could afford elegant clothing, for my uncle had been a prosperous banker in Greenville before he retired for health reasons.

Uncle Sumter had ruined his lungs in The War, the War Between the States which had so devastated our beloved South Carolina thirty years earlier. He had received a wound in one lung and had later breathed some burning, fiery stench during a battle, searing both lungs. Aunt Alberta insisted that they spend the spring and summer months with us at the shore, believing the air would strengthen his weak respiration. They wintered in Greenville while Jane Anne was in boarding school in Charleston. My aunt and uncle were older parents, for they had married late in life.

Aunt Alberta was Grandma's younger sister. Grandma was fifteen years older, and I never thought of them as being sisters because they were so different. I guess they did resemble each other in several ways; they were almost the same height, and both were rather tall. Both were blue-eyed and fair-skinned with aristocratic noses. And had Aunt Alberta been silver-haired, perhaps they would have looked more like twins. But I was never able to see Aunt Alberta as a stranger would. She was always Jane Anne's mother to me—a vigorous, rather bossy woman who seldom tolerated my childish actions. Yet I remember times when she was good to me.

At that moment, while I was thinking of her, she descended the stairs, impatiently dictating orders to Aunt Hagey. Then she entered the parlor to talk with Mama and Jane Anne, firmly and with purpose. I knew if she saw me she would issue orders to me as well.

I jumped off the piazza steps and ran down the driveway to the river, passing a couple of wagons returning to the house in the darkness. At the steamboat, by lantern light, the houseboys and yardboys, Teaspoon among them, were stacking bags of rice and barrels of flour on the boat. Then ducks were toted in cages to the rice flat, and finally I saw ten laying hens, in a portable coop with one young, pitiful rooster, carried aboard. Maum Polly said the trip with those hens would make a cock of him, like it always did.

Daddy Buck and Uncle Zeke knew how to pack the *Blue Vista* and the large river flat hitched behind it. Everything was assembled in neat pyramids on board. Soon Grandpa rode down to see the progress and approve of it. He grabbed me affectionately and planted a kiss on

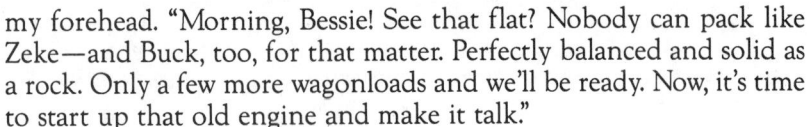

Chapter 2

my forehead. "Morning, Bessie! See that flat? Nobody can pack like Zeke—and Buck, too, for that matter. Perfectly balanced and solid as a rock. Only a few more wagonloads and we'll be ready. Now, it's time to start up that old engine and make it talk."

While Daddy Buck directed the remaining wagonloads, Grandpa and Uncle Zeke checked the gauges, pulled at this and tinkered with that; at last the steamboat rumbled out a full conversation. "Ho-o-o-o-o-n-n-n-k! Ho-o-o-o-o-n-n-n-k! It's time to go-o-o!" announced the whistle.

My heart answered, "Rea-a-a-a-dy!" After that cold, lonely winter at the plantation, I was ready for a change, an adventure.

I saw mystery everywhere I looked in the darkness. Over to the east a faint bit of light showed. As Grandpa drove me back to the house through the alley of huge live oaks, their limbs gnarled into mystical shapes, I said, "Grandpa, see these giants, squatting in two rows, with their arms bowed to the ground. See, the Spanish moss is their tattered clothing. Ever since I was a little girl I have thought they were giants protecting the house. Grandpa," I concluded, "Jane Anne is not my friend anymore."

"What? She's not?"

"I don't think she'll ever be my friend again. I'll have to hunt for shells for our—for *my* collection alone. And I'm going to have to look for gypsies all by myself. We planned to look for gypsies this spring, and now she's not even going to let me walk with her on the strand," I said mournfully, leaning against his shoulder.

Grandpa was silent for a moment. He was the one I always turned to with problems. "Now, Bessie," he said, patting my shoulder, "you are probably imagining that. Why, Jane Anne is even closer than a friend. You girls have ties that nothing can break. A blood tie can never be broken, not even by one little girl growing older. Today she might think she doesn't need you, but wait and see. Anyway, you need to be with girls your own age. I know you've been by yourself too much this winter. How many times did you visit a girl your own age this past winter? Once? Twice? Certainly not enough. I see that now."

I nodded.

Grandpa continued, "We'll make sure you visit Julia Ward. Isn't she your age?"

"Yes, but she may be traveling with her parents this summer. I don't need Jane Anne anyway! I'll find my own mysteries."

"Don't pull away from her, Elizabeth Lois. She's not as grown up as you might think," he insisted.

"She's grown up, all right. She pulled away from *me* this winter. I

The Treasure of Pawley's Island

saw it this morning. She wears a *corset*. She doesn't need me."

"Then that will be her loss."

We climbed down from the wagon, and I trailed after him, up the steps and into the house, then into the library, which was his favorite room. Surrounded by hundreds of old leatherbound volumes and more cracking oil paintings of family members, Grandpa bent over some last-minute paperwork. I was sorry to see him toiling over papers while the morning sun was hardly risen, but his presence comforted me.

I stood before him, looking at his wrinkled forehead. Grandpa must be worried about money, I decided. He and Papa were always worried about money. Taxes, taxes, taxes—how could they pay the taxes? So many mouths to feed—the family, the servants, the plantation workers and their families—and so many taxes.

For all his burdens, Grandpa's brow was almost unlined in his sixtieth year. His hair, although thinner, was not white, and behind his spectacles his green eyes shone like magnolia leaves. He was the true epitome of a gentleman whose desire in life was for politeness—to defer to others with Christian grace and humor. He loved a good laugh but he never stooped to the slightest vulgarity, and he always chose his words with precision. I knew he had stamina, too, even though his health, like Uncle Sumter's, had almost been broken in The War. How I loved him.

"Time to go," called Mama from the base of the stairs. "Bessie! Jane Anne! Grandpa!"

I sped down the stairs and out the front door, then took a flying leap into a buckboard. A line of wagons was filled with family and servants; they had all climbed aboard, clutching bundles, chattering excitedly. Grandpa was the last to leave. He stood on the porch, instructing the servants who were to remain in charge until Papa's return the next week. Then Uncle Zeke, in his ever-present black bowler, drove us down from the big house to the landing. At the steamboat and in royal fashion, oblivious to the confusion around them, Grandpa helped Grandma from the carriage. They turned and looked back up the rise, through the trees, to the plantation house, with its gardens ready to burst into bloom.

"Another spring, dear," said Grandpa solemnly.

"I'm ready," replied Grandma, "but it's very beautiful here in the spring."

"Belle, you know we cannot stay. I want no one else lost to yellow fever. One child is enough," he said, nodding towards Mama. I knew he was speaking of my baby brother, who had succumbed to yellow

Chapter 2

fever ten years before. "We'll have no more deaths, if I can help it," said Grandpa.

From the steamboat Aunt Alberta's strong voice rang out like the caw of a crow. "It's growing late," she shouted. "It's growing late!"

The steamboat's motor was throbbing more contentedly now, and the steam was puff-puffing out of the stack. A sixty-foot rice flat, hitched behind, was low in the water with its weight of trunks, boxes and bags. The trip would certainly be slow.

The geese quacked good-byes to the plantation and the chickens squawked in protest at the indignity of being caged. Grandpa gallantly helped Grandma onto the steamboat. She felt for her purse in the skirt pocket of her lilac wool suit and then looked at her wristwatch at the same moment Grandpa glanced at his pocket watch.

Even after having had only a few hours of sleep, Grandma looked as stately, as regal, as ever. Her purple-feathered and beribboned hat was perched on top of her white hair, with feathers waving. Her shoulders were thrown back. She looked like a queen to me. "I'm giving you the old-fashioned training, Bessie," she told me constantly. "Do not let your spine curve. Now throw those shoulders back. That's it. Breathe deeply of this fresh air. Hold it to the count of seven." And she never failed to add, "Don't stand on one foot. It's not ladylike, dear."

When everyone and everything was aboard, Uncle Zeke and Daddy Buck led the two donkeys, Eyes and Ears, harnessed to the last wagon, onto the river flat; then they blocked the wagon wheels and threw off the lines to waiting hands, who even then were waving farewells. Our two fine horses, already tethered on the flat, neighed and snorted in anticipation. We waved goodbye to those servants on the bank and smiled at each other, knowing the trip was about to begin. Even Jane Anne managed a thin, strained smile as the great paddle began to turn, and a weak sun was showing itself in the hazy, moist air. Grandpa, with Uncle Zeke standing by, edged the *Blue Vista* and the loaded rice flat into the canal leading to the river. A flock of redwing blackbirds fluttered low out of the edge of the rice bank near us.

Before us lay almost a day's journey by slow steamboat from the plantation to Waverly Landing, then farther that afternoon by wagon to Pawley's, glorious Pawley's—the crescent island that meant happiness until October. The first killer frost in the fall would signal our reluctant return to our rice plantation for the winter.

Behind us was home; ahead was joy. Our trip to Pawley's had begun, and on Pawley's I would find my own mysteries.

The Treasure of Pawley's Island

As we approached Butler Island, there was Old Dirty poling and that strange Negro man lying in the dugout.

Chapter 3
On To Pawley's

The first of our ancestors in the New World were English settlers who had obtained a 2,000-acre King's Grant on the Black River, fifteen miles from Pawley's Island as the bird flies and about ten miles north of Georgetown. Within a few years they found out about the summer fever, the dreaded miasma. So many lives had been lost on the river plantation that they became terrified of staying between April and early November. Hence the great exodus to the island every year, that trip so joyful for the young—and happy but tiring for the adults.

Occasionally, before the Great War, the family had gone to a home in one of the pineland villages farther inland, or even up to New England for the spring and summer months; but always they had returned to our home at Pawley's.

There, behind the third row of great dunes, they had built a large frame house with generous rooms. Two whitewashed slave houses were built on the inlet side of the property; and the tiny kitchen, once separate from the main house, was within a few decades attached by a breezeway. Prickly yuccas clustered themselves by the dozen around the front and sides of the house, which had weathered to a soft and gleaming gray.

After The War in the 1860's, our family had continued to bring its help to the island. There was no other way to manage, for the house was always full to the brim with relatives and friends. Yet our servants were more to us than paid helpers; each one was a family friend who had worked for my family for most, if not all, of his or her life. Thirty years before, several of the servants had been slaves owned by Grandpa and Grandma. When slavery ended, almost all of them had left for a while, but many returned to the plantation, to people who knew and, in many cases, loved them. They knew they were needed there, in a

Chapter 3

place they had once called home.

I do not know if in our case their freedom was better than their slavery. The Low Country of South Carolina was so very poor, and often pitiful, during those Reconstruction years. The plantation families needed their help in rebuilding and carrying on the business of living during that difficult time. And although the situation was not the best, I was not usually aware of many problems. Maum Polly mothered me, and Teaspoon was a valued playmate. Uncle Zeke and Daddy Buck protected me and, along with a half-dozen other servants, indulged my every whim. To me, they were family.

A full week ahead of the day we were to arrive, Papa and Frederick, his black boyhood companion, with two other men, had taken the steamboat with some furniture—a couple of small chests and tables—horses, and even a cow, to the island. One of the men returned the *Blue Vista* to the plantation a few days later and helped us get ready for the trip. According to plans, Papa would by now have the house on Pawley's repaired from the effects of the winter nor'easters, those fierce north winds that blow almost all winter. They would also have women from The Neck sweep out the house and clean it thoroughly. The men might even have new canvas tacked to some of the floors. Cords of hardwood and pine kindling would be stacked neatly near the kitchen door, up on bricks, ready for Maum Polly's wood stove and ready for the fireplaces in the main house. All the furniture would have been moved into place. And then Papa and Frederick would have a string of trout cooling in the rushing water of the inlet, under the shadow of the little pier house, waiting for a hot frying pan that would sizzle and pop as each filet of fish, carefully dressed with corn meal, was laid in it.

◆ ◆ ◆ ◆ ◆ ◆ ◆

The *Blue Vista* pulled confidently into the mainstream. I held onto Mama's hand tightly and peered around from my perch on a bench at Cousin Jane Anne. She was sitting beside her mother, pale but proper. The steamboat pushed against the swift current, dragging the heaped-up flat behind us. Beyond that I could see the receding dock and the wooded slope of our plantation home. The early morning vapors clung low in wisps on the Black River as we chug-chugged along, then the breeze grew more brisk as we picked up speed. All my female relatives pinned their hatpins in firmly, and the black women secured their colorful turbans. Mama patted the curls on her forehead, wrapped her gray cashmere shawl around her, and drew me

The Treasure of Pawley's Island

close, for warmth and solace, as only a mother's arms can give.

Mama's face was always alert, and her blue eyes took in details mine never noticed. Her skin was smooth and silky, and her hands never needed lotion. Mama's brown hair was pulled up on top of her head, tight at the back of her neck and a mass of curls at the front, showing off her long neck and delicately pointed chin. Her pink mouth was small and round, ever ready with a gentle smile for me. She smelled of the essence of roses, a heady, wonderful smell. I loved to lean against her with my eyes closed, holding her hand, inhaling the rose scent. I would wear the rose scent someday, but not yet. At sixteen Jane Anne already wore a scent, but it was not the scent of roses.

Mama spoke into my hair. "Bessie my own girl, you are growing up so fast. When I saw Jane Anne this morning, I realized my own girl is growing up. I hardly believe you will be thirteen in a few months. A party. We must have a party for you, with cake, and maybe some melon. At thirteen I was already ordering my mother's house. I sewed, I planned menus, I gave the servants their duties."

She stripped off her gloves and swept my hands up tightly in hers. Then she sighed. "At the very time I look forward to the birth of this infant, I find myself urging you into womanhood. No, no, I must not push you into growing up too soon! You must run up and down the strand, play little girl's games, fish with Grandpa. Yes," she smiled, "fish with Grandpa. He needs you this spring. Some girls may marry at sixteen, but not my Bessie."

She glanced over at Jane Anne, who sat elegantly in her cream-colored suit.

"Jane Anne will surely have many suitors at the shore this spring," she continued. "But as for you, Bessie, I will never, never allow you to marry at sixteen. No, you will wait until at least eighteen, as I did. Your body is still that of a little girl, and it will never make a woman by sixteen." She nodded to herself and kissed my cheek.

"After Cousin chooses her beau, her favorite, I might look over the others," I replied. "I might want one of them. She might miss the best one."

Mama smiled at that. "No, you are still my little girl. You are much too young to think of beaux. And, dear, it will be a long, long time before a man will be willing to take charge of your character."

"I can grow up this spring, Mama. I'll copy Jane Anne. Whatever she does, I will do. I'll sit the way she does. I'll speak the way she does—I think I will do *all* that she does."

"I pray that you do not!" Mama replied quickly. "Since this past winter in Charleston, Jane Anne has become even more petulant—oh,

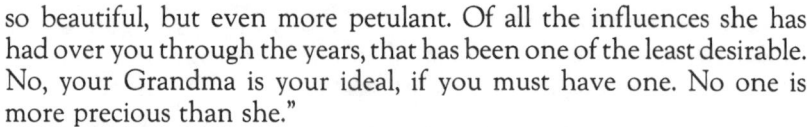

Chapter 3

so beautiful, but even more petulant. Of all the influences she has had over you through the years, that has been one of the least desirable. No, your Grandma is your ideal, if you must have one. No one is more precious than she."

When the early sun jumped higher above the cypress trees, the vapors lifted, disappearing before our eyes. We chug-chugged past the silent ditches and canals of Papa and Grandpa's rice fields, and beyond the fields stood the blue haze of woods on higher ground.

Two weeks had passed since the seed rice had been put in the earth, and in a few days Papa would reluctantly return to the plantation to check on the tender growth of rice. The flood gates and blown-out trunks of the rice fields—those wooden barriers which allowed fresh water in or out of the fields—had been repaired during the cold winter. The breaks in the outside banks and inner check banks had been closely examined and shored up. By mid-March all had been made ready for spring planting.

Before The War—as now on our plantation—rice had always been planted in March or early April at the latest, so as to avoid the migration of the rice birds on their way north. They could destroy a large part of the rice in its sprouted state. After The War, most planters put in rice from the first to the twentieth of June, with easier work and less cost—but not Grandpa. "Spring rice is heavier and is worth the work," he always said. "Any fool can make June rice, but the Lord helps make April rice."

So every year they planted in late March or early April, with Papa now taking charge. How proud they were that rice from Georgetown County was sent all over the world, because the earth grew golden, pearly grains nearly an inch long—rice like no other before or since. As we passed the fields, the rice seed was ready to sprout.

Uncle Zeke stood at the wheel with Grandpa nearby. "Look there, Zeke," said Grandpa, "at that bank. It's going to give way soon with the pressure of this river. We'll have to let Son and Frederick know about it so they can shore it up when they return to the plantation."

He drew our attention to a stretch of our 200 acres which were planted with seed rice. Soon we were beyond our acreage, passing other plantations whose neighboring fields were yet unplanted. Then the current slowed as the Black River widened and curved its way toward the Pee Dee River. The Pee Dee also ran between rice fields and emptied with the Waccamaw, about three miles down, into Winyah Bay at Georgetown, a beautiful little colonial town.

Grandpa has Uncle Zeke cut the engine several times, as he did on every trip down the dark river, for he knew the surging current was

The Treasure of Pawley's Island

strong enough to carry us along. He had often told us how he missed traveling to the shore in the old way, when the noisy silence of the creeks and rivers was broken by the splash of poles as Negroes skimmed flatboats along the top of the dark, swirling water. He remembered when the Negro men sang in deep-voiced cadences as the splashes of the poles accompanied them.

We could feel the loveliness of the water carrying us along the wide bends. And we could hear the noises within the rice fields and swamp—the swish of the wind over the water and grass, bird calling to bird and, beyond in the swamp, creature calling to creature. When we met the Pee Dee River, the engine broke the silence and the *Blue Vista* rounded the bend, heading up the Pee Dee toward Middleton Cut. The short canal would cut through the tongue of ricelands between the Pee Dee and the Waccamaw Rivers.

Up the Pee Dee we went, the engine pushing us against the current. These rivers were dark brown or black, stained from the tannic acid of the cypress trees in the swamps. The earth of the reclaimed swamps was coal-black earth, rich beyond belief. Our riceland had never called for fertilizer, even though it had been planted for well over 100 years. Yes, the earth well nurtured the ricelands and the abundant thick forests, and the marshes and swamps added to the richness of those lands. Grandpa said a man did not have to work to feed his family in the Low Country if he chose not to. He only had to be a good shot from his front porch or be able to drop a line in that dark water and haul up a catch a few minutes later.

We could see fat fish break the water nearby as our bow passed through the murky liquid. Our family would have succulent fish to eat—Maum Polly's crusty, hot fish—everyday at Pawley's Island.

We turned into Middleton Cut, where the banks were close. Uncle Zeke shut off some of the steam, and the engine slowed.

"Look at those fish jump!" exclaimed Uncle Sumter.

"A-ahe-e-e! Ah gotta wet my hook!" called out Daddy Buck, pointing.

"You going fishing in the morning, Claude?" Uncle Sumter shouted to Grandpa in the wheelhouse, where he and Uncle Zeke were busy steering and watching the gauges, feeding in the coal.

"Probably," replied Grandpa, steering the steamboat and flat carefully around a slight bend in the cut.

"You and Zeke?"

"And Bessie."

I perked up at that, listening more closely. I hadn't known I was going along. Than I slipped over and sat on a bench near the door

Chapter 3

to the wheelhouse, scrutinizing their faces as they talked.

Uncle Sumter said, loudly and in a blustering tone, his hands on either side of the door, "I think I'll go along."

"Sumter, you know good and well I'm not going to take you," Grandpa replied with his eyes on the river.

"I told Alberta last night I would get back to saltwater fishing. She was right. She said I need to stay busy and not just sit around," Uncle Sumter declared.

Some color seemed to rise in his sallow face. There were dark circles under his eyes, and six or eight bumps sat under each eye, high on his cheeks. I had never noticed them before. His skin looked dry and flaky, and he had lost weight during the winter. His clothes hung on him now, and even his beautiful bowler hat seemed too big.

"I'll be up and awake," insisted Uncle Sumter. "I'll be ready. I'll be there. What time?"

"That little fishing boat can't hold four, Sumter. It's not that big," responded Grandpa. "Why don't you and Daddy Buck do some casting from the creek pier, or maybe you can try your luck at shore casting."

"No, I think I'll go with you."

"Three in the boat already, Sumter," said Grandpa firmly. "Zeke, it looks clear now. You can put on more steam."

We were almost through the cut.

Uncle Sumter rubbed his forehead. I could see that he was not accustomed to being refused and wanted to protest again. He closed his lips deliberately and looked out at the passing marsh grass. Then he looked around, irritated at my having heard, but said no more. Resuming his seat beside Daddy Buck, he soon clamped his hand on the shoulder of his faithful butler and handyman. Then he whispered a few sentences to him that I could not hear.

Daddy Buck and his wife Aunt Hagey, who was their sempstress and maid, traveled with my great-aunt and uncle wherever they went. Although their loyalty was unbounded, mine would not have been. At that moment Aunt Hagey was fetching a hot drink from a basket for her mistress. Her turban was high and colorful. Aunt Alberta indicated to Aunt Hagey to drink some hot tea also, for the air was cold and brisk.

When we rounded the far edge of the cut leading into the Waccamaw River, my heart swelled as I once again saw the spaciousness of the river, with wide ricelands hugging its sides. The sky-canopy was outstretched and deepening into periwinkle blue. As the breeze crossed the river, bringing a hint of ocean smell with it, every nose on the steamboat twitched in welcome.

The Treasure of Pawley's Island

"Does yuh nose smell de shore?" asked our old, fat cook, Maum Polly. "An' does yuh sniff de bed o' de big fishy? An' cooter? An' udder crawlin' things? De breeze pick da smell offen de shore an' tote it heah f' we folks who wants t' be dere sniffin' de real thing!" She looked in my direction and winked. "An' can yuh smell de trout fryin' an' poppin' in Maum Polly's iron skillet? An' does yuh smell de gingerbraid, dat crunchy yum-yum? With de lemon sauce dat make de red tongue lick de lips? Which one has de hongry?"

From a basket she took out fried chicken, ham slices, and cold cornbread with onion baked in it; these she passed out to the seven members of my family and the six other servants. And how we ate that food! I caught Teaspoon's eye. He was surely enjoying it but was trying to eat slowly, for if he crammed the food into his eager mouth, Maum Polly would pop him.

Well, I thought, if Jane Anne will not play our games this season, I'll fish with Grandpa and help Teaspoon with his fishing, out on the creek pier. And I'll be with Jane Anne as much as she permits. I'll observe her beaux and learn about "repartee." I'll follow them around. And I'll look for gypsies too.

We all talked and ate, ate and talked—happy, happy chatter. The little steamboat was crowded, but it mattered little. The Waccamaw reflected small, rippling half-moons of flashing light from the path of the sun. I walked to the railing with my cornbread. As we approached Butler Island, there, as I have already related, was Old Dirty and that strange Negro man lying in the dugout.

"Dey hunt an' dey fish—po' buckra—*trash*," Daddy Buck had said. Who were they? Why did Daddy Buck act so disgusted? I had never, in all my years, seen him so disgusted with anyone. He was one of the gentlest Negroes I had ever known. Guileless, Grandpa called him. Truly, Uncle Sumter and Aunt Alberta were fortunate that he stayed with them, as they were most demanding people.

Soon Old Dirty, his helper and the black cur—and Butler Island with its iris and scattered cypresses—were all behind us. But the strange sight was still impressed clearly on my mind as we passed Hagley Landing, which sat across from Jericho Creek. There more rice plantations were situated on either side, and the owners were dear old friends and relatives.

After a while, Jane Anne surprised me and came over to perch beside me on the bench. She tucked the loose strands of her blond hair back up under her hat. Her cheeks were bright with spots of color, and she was obviously not enjoying herself.

"If any of those old cinders land on me," she complained, "my suit

Chapter 3

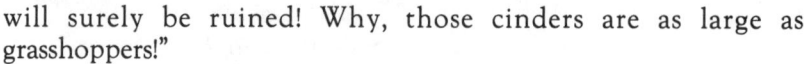

will surely be ruined! Why, those cinders are as large as grasshoppers!"

"I told you so," I said, pleased.

"Oh, hush up," she replied and leaned across me. I could smell her strong perfume. "Are the same families to be at the shore this year, Sis Mary? Is there no one new or interesting coming?"

Mama replied, understanding Jane Anne completely, "One of those handsome Ward boys is home from university in England."

"He is? Which one? Shame on you! How could you think I was speaking of *men*?"

"And the Bouknight brothers will be here in a few weeks," Mama added, "or so I've heard."

"Now, what are their ages?" Jane Anne asked, obviously having forgotten about her suit. "Will they be here in time for the first 'German'?"

"Yes," Mama replied with some humor in her eyes. "Their mother wrote to Mama Belle last week. Oh, you can be sure of a large crowd at the dance. Perhaps as many as thirty."

When am I to go to a German?" I asked, knowing the answer.

Are you sixteen?" said Jane Anne, looking superior. "I have three new gowns, Sis Mary. All made up for me in Charleston. Bessie, brush that cinder off your shoulder. I had a wonderful season in Charleston. Teas, walks in the gardens, dinners, the theatre, concerts—the *horse races!*"

"How were your studies?" Mama inquired.

"French was *magnifique!* Music was *merveilleaux!* We attended concerts and musicals at several theatres, and Mama sent me a new string of pearls and a cameo with seed pearls for my birthday in January. See?" She bent forward again, showing us the rosy cameo at her neck and the glowing pearls snuggling in the folds of her shirtwaist. "Lucinda Middleton has a double string of pearls, but I know she is so envious of my cameo. She studied it for the longest time."

The wind changes directions as the steamboat swung around a wide curve, and smoke poured down on us for a minute. Jane Anne covered her nose with a linen handkerchief edged with inches of Belgian lace.

"Oh! This smoke!" she cried, coughing delicately. "I can never abide smoke. It reminds me of Papa's cough!"

The sky was now a deep, clear blue, arching as high as forever over our heads. The wind blew from the east, through the dense and sometimes swampy woods and over the rice fields or marsh lining the river banks. The cool wind pushed at out starboard side, teasing us along. And the steamboat engine throbbed: "Eatcha' red rice! Eatcha'

The Treasure of Pawley's Island

red rice, won't cha?" it sounded as if it were saying. So we talked and ate more, remembering and laughing over special days at the shore; and longing to see the old worn place again.

Our conversation jumped from memory to memory: Teaspoon yelping as he fell off the pier into the inlet and Daddy Buck's great rescue with the shrimp net; Papa carrying a crying Mama piggy-back down the beach after she stepped on the whisker of a catfish, stiff, dead and half-buried in the sand; Maum Polly passing off poss'm meat for beef in a stew last fall. We remembered jellyfish stings on different parts of our anatomy and discussed the best medical application (bicarbonate of soda); sunburns and the best prevention (do not go out in the sun!); the raging fire in the Haselton's kitchen house and the water bucket line that almost failed to smother it; everyone's whereabouts during the great earthquake of 1886 (the one that almost destroyed Charleston); the big storms and their fierceness; and finally, how we all yearned for the ocean to warm up enough for the joys of bathing.

"Ain't no better bathing dan at de sunrise," declared Maum Polly. Aunt Hagey nodded vigorously.

For all the time we chattered, Grandpa's sharp eyes keenly observed the rice fields as they slid past; he saw the fields of the Haseltons, the Lachicottes and the Allstons. Some of the banks were in good repair, and most of the floodgates and trunks were either repaired or being repaired. Grandpa even pointed out a crew or two of Negroes out working in a canal, throwing the sludgy black mud up high on a bank, singing as they worked at their task for the day. It made him sad, he said, to see fewer acres being worked every year. "Those are valiant men," he said, "valiant men."

As the faithful *Blue Vista* carried us on, pulling its load against the current of the wide and trembling Waccamaw, we saw some pilings that had once stabilized a rice bank but were now being washed into open view, reminding us that not all of the rice fields were still being planted. Nor were they being cared for. Now many excellent rice planters—old family friends and relatives—were turning to other livelihoods. Taxes were high, and they had to feed and clothe their children somehow. Grandpa said life had been hard for many people, especially farmers, all over the United States for about ten years.

Recently Papa and Grandpa, who were physicians as well as rice planters, had taken in more patients, asking for what little money they could get. "I want you to charge if you have to, son," I heard Grandpa tell Papa one day. "You go ahead and get some silver from the able whites. Taxes have to be paid or we'll lose even more of our

Chapter 3

property. But never charge the poor whites and colored people much. They don't have any currency to give us anyway. Let them pay you in foodstuffs—a basket of collards or sweet potatoes, a string of fish. We have mouths in excess around here and every one of them is hungry. But remember, taxes are dear."

When I heard this, I had turned to Grandpa, "I'm going to raise rice when I get big," I told him. "We'll get rich again and have so much money we can tour the Continent and buy Mama a new piano." Grandpa said nothing.

Grandma pointed to the birds flying out of the rice fields or perched on high branches of uncultivated areas: two redwing blackbirds spiralled out of the march where they were nesting, the wife bird looking like a large, heavy-beaked sparrow; they put a vociferous outcry as we passed. The fearless long-billed marsh wren winged past us, looking for a likely location to hunt for spiders, beetles, wasps or flies. The fish crow gave its hoarse, raucous laugh as it patrolled the rice fields on its way to a cypress lagoon to hunt for minnows. A fish eagle, an osprey, flashed its white underside as it headed into the wind from its nest on a dead pine. It circled with shrill cries as we turned into Waverly Cut.

Around the rice banks lined with water iris we followed the Cut to the old wooden landing. We strained to see it and then there was Papa, with starched collar and fresh black coat, newly dusted in our honor, waving his hat and with a big grin showing under his handlebar mustache, so handsome. Our hellos rang out over the nearby rice fields as Daddy Buck threw a rope to Papa, and we tied up.

Soon the wagons were filled with towering piles of belongings, and we were on our way. "Hang on, Lil' Missie!" called Daddy Buck. I was mountain high on rugs, dressers, and bags of rice, an irresistible spot to perch on. Strong mules borrowed from a neighboring plantation pulled us slowly up the hills along two sandy ruts. I could tell we were nearer the shore from that white sand.

The skirts of Waverly Plantation sloped upward from the rice fields; they were lined and dotted with moss-laden live oaks that always kept their green. The trees' strong arms often bent low or even rested on the sandy ground, duplicates of the tired giants at our own plantation on the Black River. Our wagons creaked on through the heavy sand, slowing us considerably. Then through the woods we went, and we were at marsh-side. How the smell affected us! Papa and Grandpa plunged ahead with their horses. Up and out of the first creek, through the marsh, and up and out of the second creek. A little farther to the south we saw the roof and chimneys of the cottage and kitchen, which

The Treasure of Pawley's Island

were almost hidden from view by the bushy trees. The servants' cabin, tucked in some bushes closer to the island road, was more visible.

The spring was just beginning. I knew I had no worries. Yet in that serene and ambrosial splendor of Pawley's Island by the sea, I was to be first awakened from a secure and simple life, to the more serious realities of adulthood. I was to see glimmers of the great controversy between good and evil, between selfishness and selflessness. Yet these awesome concepts are only partially painted in this volume, for they were viewed by childish eyes. Had I been able to look ahead, my heart would have thrilled with the anticipation and yet the dread of events—events unforeseen by a lonely girl on that sunny and beautiful April day.

On to Pawley's! Oh, the exhilaration of being there!

Uncle Zeke murmured approvingly, "Dat lil' missie, he kin cotch um."

Chapter 4
First Fishing, First Adventure

A south-easter was blowing over the dark ocean and onto our wide, low beach as I awoke before dawn, eager to go First Fishing with Grandpa and Uncle Zeke. I dozed in the darkness, tired from our trip and our unpacking, but it was a happy-tired feeling. I listened to the breeze, picturing the way it flicked at shells near the edge of the waves, then sped across moist, packed sand to higher powder-white sand that glowed in our pre-dawn darkness. Sometimes Pawley's sand did that. The steady breeze would lift some of that powder and deposit it among the sea oats that marched up the dunes in front of our cottage. A portion of the breeze filtered through the wind-swept trees which surrounded our house and the twenty-four others on the island, each nestling in close to those protective dunes.

Then the south-easter died. The air was still, and I knew dawn was soon to break. No sound has ever had the same quiet as did our shore house before dawn. Moist stillness lay like a blanket, and only the waves were heard, rhythmically breaking on the other side of the tall dunes, but in their constant rhythm they were not noticed. The rhythm of hiss and crash, hiss and crash was the pulse of the beach, unnoticed as a heartbeat is unnoticed.

The silver-boarded old house sat plumped behind the dunes like a fat gray bird in a full skirt of well-worn feathers. Large porches, or piazzas, surrounded our beach cottage, with two larger piazzas hugging the south and east sides to catch the summer breezes. Dormer windows crouched on the roof above the southern piazza, as though they were three huge eyes surveying the blue cedar, wax myrtle, bay and tamarisk that grew around the house like an abundant nest in the white shelly sand. The ceilings in the house were high, and the windows and doors were numerous, all to allow currents of sea breeze to wafe through the

Chapter 4

rooms in the hot summer months. Most of windows carried shutters that could be closed in stormy weather or in our absence. The house—made of cypress "just like Noah's ark," Grandpa said—had had its timbers hewn on the mainland and numbered with Roman numerals. It had all been transported and raised about 1800, by brickmasons and carpenters who traveled over from the plantation by boat and horse-drawn wagon.

The brickmasons built it up sturdy brick foundations to escape the rise of tides at full moon or the gales that spordaically swept under the cottages from the salt creeks that lace the marsh. My precious swing under the south piazza saw the water from the creeks creep slowly under the house only once a year usually, and that was only to a depth of a few inches. A high tide on a full moon brought the water up as high as it ever came unless we had a Big Storm. Then the water was deep and fierce.

The kitchen, with its huge old fireplace, was attached to the west side by a covered breezeway. Two servant cabins, each with three tiny rooms and a fireplace, sat nearby. These had housed family slaves before The War and now housed our servants. Out near the beach road were the stable, toolshed, chicken house and servant privy. Two other privies, located in strategic spots, had been freshly whitewashed that spring with unslaked lime and water.

We obtained our drinking water from the Allston's flowing artesian well near the middle of the island. Every day Uncle Zeke drove a wagon to their house and brought back two barrels of that strong-tasting water. A number of other families had water brought over every day or to the island from their nearby plantations. We did cook our rice and grits in plantation water, however, for island water gave them a faintly green look and that mealy consistency that Maum Polly detested. But I loved the taste of the artesian water. It had flavor.

I dozed in the stillness and waited for Grandpa's steps on the stairs. I was thirsty. The wooden walls of my attic room were not yet touched with that special pink light of early dawn. Over in the next bed, Cousin Jane Anne slept quietly, her delicate face nearly hidden by warm woolen covers, which were still needed in this cold early spring. Mosquito netting stretched like a turret from my bed to a curved nail on the ceiling of the attic bedroom, but no mosquitos hunted for an entrance to my net teepee. They still slept as snow-like larvae on the waters and uncultured rice fields of the wet lowlands of Waccamaw Neck. When I had unpacked the afternoon before, I knew no gnats or mosquitos would come near, but I had hung the net anyway, as I always did. It transformed my bed into a princess' bed. Jane Anne had

The Treasure of Pawley's Island

sniffed and refused to hang hers—for the first time.

The haze of netting trembled now around my bed; I watched it and fought the desire to go back to sleep. Finally Grandpa's steps sounded. His voice called to me as soft as duck-down. "Wake up, Sailor, wake up. Who is going First Fishing with me? Are you ready to catch some rainbow trout?"

"Please wait for me, Grandpa?" I called out. "I'll dress quickly. Don't leave me!"

I pulled my sailor suit from the chiffarobe peg.

"Dress warmly, Sailor. It's cold out on that water," Grandpa whispered with a chuckle in his throat, and then he crept back down the stairs.

I hastily pulled on a double set of underclothes, the sailor suit, two pairs of merino stockings and my old patent shoes.

My cousin roused at the sound of our voices and my clatter.

"I declare!" she cried shrilly. "Waking me again at this hour! Why, look out the window. It's not even light out there. I can't stand it. You just wait until I speak to Mama about changing rooms!"

I flung my worn cape around my shoulders.

"I'm going First Fishing, and you don't get to go," I retorted, scampering past her and her numerous trunks to the hall, down the stairs, and past the closed bedroom doors of sleeping family members.

Night still covered the island when I reached the donkey and buckboard parked by the kitchen door. Grandpa, with his Irish setters in the back, sat waiting. Tackle and buckets were heaped behind the seat. Uncle Zeke brought out cold buttermilk biscuits and fried trout. Those fish and biscuits had been hot and delicious at supper the night before, when twelve tired people had finally eaten their first meal of the season at Pawley's.

As I climbed up on the buckboard behind Grandpa, he signaled Uncle Zeke and then peered at me in the darkness.

"Elizabeth Lois, what do you have on? You can't wear that new suit! You'll have fish blood and slime all over it before we get back. Zeke, what ever will we do?"

"Miz Sis Mary ain't goin' t' smile at mud on *dat* skirty," said Uncle Zeke, trying to appear solemn.

"Oh, my, what will we do?" Grandpa asked, hiding a smile.

"We kin hold her by de ankles an' dip her in de crick when we gits back," suggested Uncle Zeke. They both thought that was amusing.

"Grandpa!" I said.

"Well, Zeke, if you'll hold this wagon, I'll just have a look through those old clothes Grandma brought with us. She's about to give them to the colored folks over on the Neck, but I'll just look through them

Chapter 4

and see what I can find. We can't let this girl ruin her suit, can we?" said Grandpa, chuckling again.

Delighted with his plan, he disappeared into the stable. In a minute he called for me. Inside, the lantern light glowed on his happy face, revealing a twinkle in his eyes behind those steel-rimmed spectacles. From an old box in one of the cow stalls, he brought forth sundry boy's clothes—an old white collarless shirt, brown breeches that buttoned at the knee, a frayed but serviceable striped flannel blazer, a knitted vest, a pair of ribbed boy's stockings, worn brown boots and a large straw hat suitable for a farm boy.

"My, my, look what I found!"

"Grandpa, you didn't just find these in that box! You brought them for me to wear, didn't you?" His face broke into a grin. I took off my sailor suit in the cold stable and awkwardly put on the unfamiliar boy's clothes, stuffing my two thick layers of underclothes beneath.

Grandpa carefully folded my sailor suit, with its innumerable tucks and darts and pockets and white piping. He put it in an old tin bucket with my shoes and cape and hung it high on the stable wall.

Grandpa looked at me with great satisfaction. "At least you won't be ruining your good suits, and your mama and grandma will not be upset with me for returning you in dirty, muddy clothing and ruined patent shoes. Well, perhaps these clothes *are* too big here and there, but don't you think they will do for our use? After all, you aren't going to wear them to an afternoon tea, are you? And *those two*," he said, nodding in the direction of the house, "will never, never see these." He looked enormously pleased with himself and the clothes.

I tried to smooth the sleeve of the old wrinkled blazer and knew Mama would never accept such an outfit if she knew about it. Then I raised my chin. Well, I said to myself, I *will* wear these clothes and fish to my heart's delight this spring. If my Grandpa wants me to wear them, I'll do just that!

Out in the yard, the cold air filled our lungs and puffs like smoke trailed out of our nostrils. The sun still had not risen, although I could see a little better. But I was warm with all my layers of clothing.

Grandpa looked down at me. "Well, I declare! Will miracles never cease? My granddaughter has turned into a boy!"

Uncle Zeke added, grinning, "Ain't no joke! An' iffen yuh hack off dat long hair, she be de boy sho' nuff!"

Grandpa pursed his lips, struggling to look serious. "Sailor, plait your long hair and tie it with this string. Tuck the braid up in your hat. If we see any other fishermen out there, turn those long eyelashes the other way. Now, don't worry—they probably won't come in close

The Treasure of Pawley's Island

enough to get a good look at you. Anyway, you're going to look like a real boy with that hair up, Elizabeth Lois." He looked thoughtful for a moment. "Elizabeth Lois," he said again. "E.L. We'll call you *E.L.* How does that sound, Zeke?"

"Ain't no joke, E.L. *ib de name*," replied Uncle Zeke. "Jump up."

We climbed into the buckboard. Zeke touched the reins to Eyes the donkey, and on we rolled.

"Grandpa," I said, "it may be a sin to wear boy's clothes, but I don't care what I look like as long as I can go fishing with you and Uncle Zeke. If anyone sees me, well, I'll act like an old boy and they won't know the difference. But please don't tell Mama or Grandma. They'd never understand."

I well knew my Mama's attitude toward clothes, yet she was no different from any other mother of the day. She strove to secure cloth of the finest quality for my clothing. Mama had once told me, "You may not have many clothes, Bessie, but the ones you have will be made of the finest material we can afford. Then they will last and last. Even in this time of little money, you will be dressed like a 'lily of the field'." After seeing only part of Jane Anne's wardrobe, however, I did not consider my sailor suit a lily petal any more.

But now E.L. was going fishing with "his" grandpa. I knew in that minute I could pass for a boy without half trying, and I was going to do it.

Even the two irish setters sensed we were going First Fishing that morning, and perhaps they sense my excitement as well. "Robert E. Lee" and "John C. Calhoun" jumped out of the back of the rolling buckboard, yipped and frisked down the sandy ruts ahead of us as we drove north toward Medway Inlet. They paused to nudge Eyes, who refused to pay attention as she slowly pulled us along. They sniffed for rabbits in the saw grass, and I felt free enough to join them.

From over the trees and dunes we could hear the muffled roar of the breakers. At Medway Inlet we loaded our gear into a small wooden boat. The edge of the red sun was barely peeking above the dark horizon that was the ocean as we scrambled through the mud and hopped in.

"Push her out, Zeke," said Grandpa. Uncle Zeke gave the boat a shove and sprang in himself at the last moment. He paddled us toward "the spot," his paddles barely touching the silk of the water. The air remained still and the water was not moving. It must have been that short span of time between tides, when the water of the salt creeks swirls quietly in marshy pools, resting before resuming its rush in or out between the mud banks.

Chapter 4

"E.L.," said Grandpa, smiling, " we will have no squirming or wiggling around in the fishing boat this morning. And no frowns nor worry—no tears on this ship. You cried every time you lost a fish last year."

Uncle Zeke paddled on in a leisurely fashion toward the special fishing spot. A soft cool breeze began blowing from over the dunes.

"Grandpa, I'm older this year. I'll be wearing a corset soon, like Jane Anne," I responded, indignantly. "I won't wiggle and I won't cry. May we eat soon?"

"Soon enough," he responded. "'Course Zeke might eat it up before you and I get to it," he teased. "You know how he is when he's hungry."

"Ah don't eat enough to feed a gnat. Ah ain't lied, Doc. Ah see you tear int' d' biscuit when we on dis water lak it be yuh last meal befo' hangin'," Zeke joked.

Grandpa replied, "Now, Zeke, why do you run on and on like that? You've got to save those words for the church meeting next week. They're expecting a powerful sermon from you on your first Sabbath back at the shore."

"Ah ain't lied, Doc."

"I catch you lying to me at least one time an hour, and you know it."

They looked at each other and laughed contentedly. At the perfect place, near a sandbar yet in deep water, Uncle Zeke anchored the boat. He turned it around so we could watch the sunrise through the inlet where it opened into the sea. Then, without speaking, he dip-netted until he caught a couple of mullet which were foolish enough to come near the top of the water to look around. He chopped them up and soon baited hooks were dangling from our bamboo poles. All around us the mullet jumped, their shining bodies touched with pink from the sunrise. And here and there a speckled trout leaped. How heavenly it was to be out on the calm waters with the fish vaulting themselves into the brisk air.

Grandpa winked and smiled at me. I remembered Grandma saying, "All it ever takes to set my heart singing is a wink from your Grandpa. He carries tranquility and joy around with him, in the very air he breathes, Bessie, and he is always willing to share it with *you*, his own girl."

After a few minutes of fishing, my cork bobbed twice. I had the first one hooked.

"Grandpa! Help me, Grandpa!"

"Calm down, Sailor," he said. "He's not going to spring off that hook. Let him know you're in charge. Hang on and let *him* set the hook. If he doesn't, then count five and set it yourself."

The Treasure of Pawley's Island

My line cut the water, and the tail and arched body of a great sparkling trout shot clear of the surface about ten feet from us. His mouth is too big, I thought. Uncle Zeke murmured encouragement as I gripped the bamboo pole tightly, but neither he nor Grandpa offered any assistance.

"He'll get away!" I squealed. But I hung on to that pole, believing it would surely break.

"Jus' don' le'm git unduh de boat, lil' Missie E.L. De fish dey look dumb, an' dey ib—but dey ib Gawd's critters too, an' He gib un some bit of smarts t' mek um know what t' do t' git away, clean a-way!"

Although he spoke, Uncle Zeke hardly watched my battle with the big trout. He did turn the boat to my advantage, however. As rows of puffy red clouds hung over the ocean, I finally hauled that speckled trout in hand-over-hand from the salty waters of Medway Inlet. And then when the fish was flapping in the bottom of the boat, Uncle Zeke murmured approvingly, "Dat lil' missie, he kin *cotch* um."

Grandpa showed me how to hold the fish so that the hook would come out of its mouth more easily, and I bravely hung the trout on the cooling line that was tied to the bow.

While we fished and ate the cold cooked trout and biscuits, the air grew warmer. The sun changed from a pink ball near the rim of the ocean to a golden orb moving slowly up the sky. The redwing blackbirds welcomed the morning with their tremulous song, "*Oak-a-lee, oak-a-lee*," and the mist evaporated over the marsh banks and winding creek beds.

"Grandpa," I asked, "why don't you bring Uncle Sumter fishing with us in the morning? I heard him ask on the steamboat if he could come with us."

"No, I don't think so. We've got a boat full of the right people."

"I can sit on a little stool up there in the bow."

"No, Sailor," he said firmly and re-cast his line to a better spot.

"I can't ever remember hearing you say no to anybody, Grandpa."

"I try to accommodate when I can. Most requests are in my power to grant. But that one I will continue to refuse."

"It's just that he pays money to board with us ad I thought you'd have to take him. And he's a relative, too."

He nodded, still looking at the water. He pushed his bowler to the back of his head and then turned to me with a pleasant, knowing look, "Being a relative makes it even more difficult. He and I have a great many years behind us. But you shouldn't worry about it."

"I thought you liked him. When I'm in bed at night, I hear you two laughing downstairs at the table."

Chapter 4

"I do like him. We go back a long way." Grandpa casually pulled in a big trout. No fighting the trout with him. He made it look easy. He slipped the hook from the mouth of the sparkling trout and slid it on the cooling line.

"He's real sick, isn't he?" I declared.

"Sick unto death in a number of ways," he said with a look at Zeke. Zeke didn't move a muscle.

"Then you should do what he wants you to, if he's going to die soon."

"Sailor, Sumter is killing himself. He is pushing *himself* toward that abyss. I cannot help him."

I was shocked at what Grandpa said. "Has he taken poison?" I asked.

"Yes, you might say that, a little poison at a time. But—well, he's going to do what he will."

I could find no words except, "Then you ought to *talk* with him. You could stop him, Grandpa. You are a *doctor*. Bring him fishing with us and talk him out of it."

"He will do what he will do."

"Grandpa, if you let a person die, that's the same as killing him." I was stricken at the thought that my grandpa would not help someone.

"No, Sailor. He's free. I can't force him. I like him; I always have. I liked him when Alberta married him. He's as good a conversationalist as you can find. He's got solid ideas on politics, too, and he can remember a joke better than anybody I know—but I don't want to be in the woods with him since he's been taking that 'poison,' and I don't want to be in a boat with him, surrounded by water deeper than six inches. Zeke and I have seen what he can do in a boat, haven't we, Zeke?"

Uncle Zeke nodded, his black eyes on the surface of the inlet water.

"But Grandpa," I protested, "he's a *relative*."

"That has nothing to do with it. Sailor, I have decided to bring you out fishing with me this spring so that you can learn several important things. Patience and responsibility are the first two, and fishing is a good teacher. Sumter's never been long on patience, and I am not going to have an impatient, sick man with me on a boat. It's too dangerous. *You* need to learn patience before you grow any older. I'm going to see to it that you do."

"But Grandpa—"

"Sailor, you know better than to intrude in adult affairs. I don't know that you are old enough to understand even if I explain. For now you must accept the fact that I know best. Now cast your line over there where the current is moving."

I did as he directed.

The Treasure of Pawley's Island

"Yes, leave your line right over there. And sit still, E.L."

"I'm not very patient. Grandma tells me so. And Jane Anne always said that, too."

"I know that. Fishing will help you learn patience. Turn around and fish."

I turned around to watch my cork bob in the water. "Uncle Sumter never, never speaks impatiently with Aunt Alberta—or Jane Anne."

Uncle Zeke smiled at that.

"He wouldn't dare raise his voice to the women in his family," answered Grandpa, his humor returning. "Certainly not to a woman like *Alberta*. And not to Jane Anne, not this year."

We fished in silence.

"No, he can't come with us," spoke Grandpa, mostly to himself. "Someday, when you're older, I will tell you what was the last straw. Even though Zeke and I still laugh about it now and then, I have good cause to say I'll never take that man out in a boat with us again. We fish for sport, don't we, Zeke? And we need to bring home fish for the table. A dozen and a half people usually eat from our table three times a day. We need the fish." He stared at the horizon for a moment and then shook his head. "Poor Daddy Buck," Grandpa said finally. "He got the worst of it that day, didn't he, Zeke?"

Zeke looked into the water and nodded.

◆ ◆ ◆ ◆ ◆ ◆ ◆

In that hour the sun was glinting yellow on the salt tidewater creeks. We moved the boat back farther from the mouth of the inlet. The air warmed up, so we stripped off our coats, enjoying the sunshine on our shoulders. The three of us had caught eleven trout by then.

"Zeke, it's good to be back on the salt creeks, fishing," Grandpa murmured.

"It beats cuttin' on de fool's bones, Doc—an' de fish an' de birds up yonduh knows we here, don't dey?"

Uncle Zeke's smooth black face was alight with pleasure as he watched a snowy heron's yellow feet step quickly along a nearby shallow creek bed, poking here and there into a deeper pool with a stab of its black beak. We would watch "yellow slippers" hunt all spring and summer as we fished.

Then we were silent, listening to the melody of the water as it swirled around the boat, listening to the snap of a trout as it leaped and plunged back beneath the murky water. We smelled the marshy salt air as it swept over the island and the swash—as Grandpa called the

Chapter 4

marsh.

"Sailor," said Grandpa in his teaching voice, "Why do you think tiny schools of minnows flit and swim together as if they were one creature, like the flocks of rice birds that swoop and fly as one over the rice fields, or the redwings do over the marsh? Look down there, Sailor," he commanded, pointing into the dark water.

Beside the boat, barely to be seen was the second mystery I was to contemplate since we had set out from the shore. There below me was a school of tiny minnows, fifty to a hundred, bobbing and dancing in chorus in the shadowed water. I asked myself "Why won't Grandpa take Uncle Sumter fishing? And why should these minnows dance together with no leader and no mother to guide them?"

"I don't know why minnows dance like that, Grandpa," I replied as the chorus of minnows curtsied beside the boat. The chorus was springing this way and that under the dark ripples.

Neither could I explain the welling of happiness in my heart at that moment. When the sounds of marshlands—the swish of breeze through the grass, the twit-twitter of birds and the sonorous speech of inlet water—combine to speak, human words cannot tell of it. But I knew it all could be expressed in the minnow's waltz.

So I sat statue-still, concentrating my pent-up energies on the little cane pole, on the line leading down to the bobbing cork, willing a fish to bite. The life of the water, with its currents rising and falling below, transmitted itself up the line and through the pole into my hands.

The clouds above turned yellow, then ivory. I looked at Uncle Zeke, that good old man. He was Grandpa's boyhood companion, his most beloved and trusted family servant, yet more, for he was his best friend. Zeke was quite respected among the colored population and proud yet humble. Grandpa had often told me of Uncle Zeke's ability as a keen observer of human nature, yet I could never notice that he watched anyone. "You can't fool Zeke," Grandpa said.

He was skilled in just about everything, which is one reason Grandpa relied on him so, and he was an enormous help in the medical practice. But I was most impressed with his manner. He was forever cheerful, never critical, and he always looked at the best side of anyone or any situation. He preferred not to mention trouble until it was over—except in sermons, of course. Oh, he was fiery there. I had heard a couple. Yet even his bearing marked him as a gentleman. And Grandma had told me, "A refined, cultured Negro undoubtedly is the most elegant person in the world."

You should have seen my Grandpa and Uncle Zeke walk the island together, two kings, one white and the other black, both erect, both strong even with their years. And Uncle Zeke said, unfailingly, every night when they parted, "Now, Doc, we hab put ourself into Sweet Jesus' keepin', an' we should hab no fear. Night, Doc."

Suddenly the quiet moment was broken as all three of us began catching spring whiting—big ones, too—fish after fish. Their silvery sides flashed as they flapped and pitched in the bottom of the boat. We were far too busy catching fish to string them.

"Dey thinks dis bait be 'fish manna,' Doc." Uncle Zeke exclaimed. "Keep on comin', you big mouths!"

Soon ten whiting and a few more trout were flopping all over our feet in the bottom of the boat. I was having the time of my life and taking my own fish off the hook without a murmur. It was even a pleasure to wipe my slimy hands on my britches. I was enjoying the freedom of my clothes.

Then, at the busiest moment, a noise from shore caught our attention; three figures were pushing a boat into the edge of the channel as Eyes he-hawed furiously behind them. They jumped into their boat and paddled toward us.

To me the joy of the moment was gone. I thought of my clothes. Then I wondered, "Who are they?" I turned and ducked my head. I was embarrassed and afraid to be seen.

In a moment I recognized my Uncle Cuthbert's voice, a huge voice that almost made the water shake. He was my great-uncle-by-marriage, and his house was located about a hundred feet to the south of ours. Each summer I played and swung in a hammock on his piazza as my family rocked and talked there.

"Good morning, *good* morning," his voice boomed out. "How many of my fish have you caught, Claude? Are the trout running again this morning? Well, I'm not out here to play, and you're in my fishing hole, so you better move over!" Uncle Cuthbert's voice roared across the water. I ducked even lower, cheeks burning. Uncle Zeke's eyes flickered toward me with unexpected encouragement.

"Morning, Cuthbert," replied Grandpa. "I never have seen you out so early. You must have sat up *all night* to set out this early."

The fish had stopped biting. The best fishing had passed with the sound of Uncle Cuthbert's voice shaking the water, I guess. Grandpa muttered, with a sigh of resignation, "Best run we'll have all spring, Zeke. Well, that's the way it goes."

Again that voice boomed across the inlet. "I tried your old Indian trick of drinking lots of water before bedtime—and I sure woke up early."

Chapter 4

Onward they came, closer, closer.

Uncle Zeke took off his black bowler and scratched his shiny head. His white starched shirt gleamed in the early light. "Little Missie," he whispered to me, "de preacher he'd put de hand on de Holy Book an' swear yuh wus a boy. No joke!"

Did I truly look like a boy in those ill-fitting clothes? Would my uncle recognize me? What would he and the others say and do when they realized I was a girl?

The Treasure of Pawley's Island

Slyly he reached into a bulging pocket, extracted a glob of brown stuff and rubbed it over all of his fingers prior to baiting his hook.

Chapter 5
That Boy Louie

As their boat drew close to ours, Uncle Cuthbert gestured toward a young man sitting in the middle of their boat, near Caesar, who was paddling. The boy squirmed around, looking uncomfortable.

"Claude, do you remember my writing you this fall that a nephew of Clara's was coming up from Beaufort to live with us?" asked Uncle Cuthbert, beaming.

"Why yes," Grandpa answered. "I do remember something about that."

"Well, here he is. Call him *Louie*. Now that his pa is gone, we are his nearest relatives. Louis Hugh Wilson. He arrived late yesterday, just after you pulled in. I'm mighty glad to have some young blood around our dead old house. You should have watched him eat breakfast this morning. The cook ain't seen anything like it."

Then Uncle Cuthbert pointed at me with his cane pole. "I declare, I can't hardly see in this light. Who is *that* young man?"

I looked timidly out from under my big straw hat. I held my breath.

Grandpa gave me a secret wink and introduced me as E.L. He said I was a relative, that I would be visiting for a while—that didn't surprise Uncle Cuthbert, because just about everyone in the area was related in some fashion. Grandpa said that he planned to take me along fishing whenever he and Zeke went out, so they'd see me quite a lot.

"I told his ma I'd teach this *boy* how to fish," he said with that teasing chuckle in his voice. "And this is E.L.'s first real chance to learn. Now what have you heard about what 'Pitchfork Ben' is up to, Cuthbert?"

So Grandpa and Uncle Cuthbert settled into a nice long discussion, talking politics as they always did—Pitchfork Ben Tillman (Uncle Cuthbert's favorite subject), the "Woolhat Boys," state's rights, and

Chapter 5

John C. Calhoun (Grandpa's favorite subject). It was all familiar to me, except for that funny-looking boy over in the other boat. I settled back to fish, now and then sneaking a look at him.

Louie appeared to be about fourteen or possibly fifteen years old. He looked awkward and gangly. His hair was very blond and stuck out straight from under a little straw hat that perched on the back of his head. Both his face and his hands were covered with big freckles, and his front teeth had a slight gap between them. He was not fat, but he looked it in his overcoat. It made my striped blazer look like a perfect fit. At least *my* coat had flat pockets, while his were bulging so that they looked like they would explode.

I thought at once that he must have a great deal of pride, for he seldom looked at me. I wondered if he could see through my disguise, but I was comforted by the fact that if he looked my way, he didn't seem to really notice me.

I turned away and fished, staring at the nearby shore, where mats of dead cord grass stalks had been pushed up on higher ground by the spring tides. Meanwhile I kept my chin tucked into my collar. After a bit I decided Louie must have poor eyesight, and so I paid him as little attention as possible.

But I noticed he *could* catch fish. He was catching fish while none of the rest of us were. He would lean out over the edge of the boat and look deep into the moving water. Then he would stare around at the blue sky and lean back over the water and spit into it, staring down at the bobbing spittle as it swirled around. I tried staring down and could not see into the water past two inches. Louie looked at it through squinty eyes and, when no one was paying attention, casually leaned out and sniffed the water with nostrils flaring. Suddenly, to my astonishment, he tasted two drops of brown water on the pointy tip of his pink tongue. Slyly he reached into a bulging pocket, extracted a glob of brown stuff and rubbed it over all of his fingers prior to baiting his hook. And after catching a fish he repeated the procedure. No one else seemed to notice.

When our boats drifted quite near to each other, I could not resist whispering to him, "Why are you tasting the water? No one can be *that* thirsty. And what is that brown stuff on your hands?"

His blue eyes gleamed. "How much do y' want t' know? What's it worth to yuh?" He stifled a triumphant grin, his freckled face shining.

"Worth? To me? Only a pigeon brain would go through what you do to catch fish!" I whispered back and looked away.

"Then why did y' ask, if y' don't want t' know?"

I thought about it as our elders continued their conversation. Louie

The Treasure of Pawley's Island

tasted two more drops of water and let his bait sink under the dark salt creek. In a few seconds his cork bobbed under and another fish was on his line. Yes, I had to know his secrets.

"Well, it looks like Louie is the only one that knows how to catch 'em this morning," Uncle Cuthbert observed and then returned to the subject of politics. "Now, Claude, you know those 'Woolhat Boys' are going to ruin this old state."

Louie pulled himself up straight, whispering to me, "The greatest fisherman on the entire Atlantic coast taught me how to fish." His freckled face jutted out with pride. "If he needs a fish for dinner, he smells the air and knows where to head with a pole in his hand and *one* bait. One! That's all he takes an' he never comes home empty-handed!"

He paused to bring in a nice-sized whiting and to let the information sink in.

"See," he continued as he jiggled the fish in front of me. "And I know a lot of his most precious secrets. But you'll have to *pay* to learn what they are." His eyes glinted. "So y' want to know what I rub on my hands. Hummm, that's a dandy."

I yearned to know, but I had no money. Silver and gold were scarce. So I shook my head. Just then his cork bobbed under and up came another whiting, only fatter and longer. Ten more minutes passed before we agreed how much it would cost me. We struck a bargain at a dozen cookies or one-quarter of a cake each week, which I had no idea how I could manage.

Louie hissed, "My teacher's comin' in a couple of weeks, give or take a few days. He kin spit a watermelon seed clear across the road from the front porch of his shack. He lives up in Murrell's Inlet. My pa took me up there last year and we went fishin' and huntin' for three whole weeks. What a teacher! If he just didn't smell so bad. Uncle Cuthbert says he's trying to drum up some business here on the island."

"Would he teach me?" I asked.

"He'll teach anybody that'll feed him or pay him. Old Dirty ain't particular."

Old Dirty! The man we had seen in the dugout by Butler's Island.

"If I get to go fishing with him, do you want to go along?" he asked. I nodded. "Well, let me taste those cookies first, and I'll let you know."

As we pulled up anchor, he said, "See you in the morning, E.L. What a name!" Then he murmured, "Just bring the cookies."

Grandpa slowly paddled toward shore, where the setters greeted us with enthusiasm, yips and dancing. Even Eyes gave an appreciative bray in anticipation of breakfast.

Chapter 5

The tide had gone out some, revealing fiddler crabs that scurried away as we beached the boat. As Grandpa and Uncle Zeke pulled the boat into the Spanish bayonets, I wiped the black mud off my old boots on the nearby sawgrass.

Good Old Uncle Zeke and Eyes had dragged the boat from under the house before dawn, all the way to the north end of the island—"where de big-uns lib!" Uncle Zeke knew where to find fish all right. Or anything, for that matter. Grandpa said he had learned to "smell things out" in The War when they went off to "cut on de fool's bones." No matter where or how they learned it, I felt that between them they knew the answer to each and every question in the world

Ha! I said to my self, *Grandpa and Uncle Zeke know more than that Old Dirty any day of the week.*

On the way home, Grandpa congratulated me on my successful disguise. "You sure look like a scrawny little boy," he said. "Why, you even fooled that boy Louie—now that Louie is a character. I've never seen a boy so thirsty he'd taste salt water!" Grandpa shook his head as he spoke, and Uncle Zeke's eyes twinkled. I think they had watched Louie more closely than I realized.

"Anyway," continued Grandpa, "he could fish, and that counts for a lot. He'll be company for you when we fish with Cuthbert—someone near your own age. I guess he's a year or so older. We're going to meet them at South Inlet for the next few mornings to shore fish."

I thought about that as we headed home, past cottages, some occupied and some empty.

"Sailor," Grandpa continued, "you handled that pole like a real fisherman this morning. You made me proud." He laughed. "What a grandson!"

Our wagon rolled on. We passed various cottages tucked far up toward the dunes, like ours, in the wax myrtle trees. Many had arrived from their plantations. Whole families of grandparents, parents, children, uncles, aunts and many servants—along with servant's children—were nestled in here and there. Sometimes as we passed we could see servants hurrying breakfast to the house. Some of them called out helloes to Doc. They were carrying steaming bowls—perhaps grits with blobs of butter floating on top, or sizzling frying pans of ham and fish and covered baskets of favorite oversized hot biscuits which would soon be dripping with butter, honey and special strawberry preserves.

A couple of families who had straggled downstairs to eat saw us passing and stuck their heads out doors and windows to holler to us. "Join us, won't you?" called out a friend of Grandpa's.

The Treasure of Pawley's Island

"Another time!" answered Grandpa.

A fellow hunter and fisherman yelled from his piazza, "Would you like to go hunting later in the morning? Is the whole family on the island yet? We'll be down to see you later on!"

Everyone loved Grandpa. He and Uncle Zeke had saved many a life here in the past decades. We passed the Ward's cottage and, through the open window, we heard old Mr. Ward's deep voice ring out in a morning prayer. At the end, Grandpa joined in with a loud *Amen*! although they probably couldn't hear him. Then came the hubbub of happy voices and the clank of silver. The wonderful odor of brewed coffee drifted out to us, and Uncle Zeke snapped the reins, urging Eyes to hurry home to our pot of coffee.

When we reached our cottage and pulled into the yard, out came the scent of coffee as well as bacon, ham and fried fish and the sweet aroma of oatmeal-nut muffins made with buttermilk and honey. From the kitchen chimney rose the heavy smoke of a woodstoked stove. Maum Polly was cooking away in there.

Then the ducks waddled out to great us with exultant quacking. As I raced into the stable to change clothes before anyone saw me, I tried not to feel too prideful, but I could not wait to see Mama's face, or Maum Polly's as she heated the big frying pan.

◆ ◆ ◆ ◆ ◆ ◆ ◆

We arose early for several mornings to meet Uncle Cuthbert and Louie, who were always accompanied by one or two of Uncle Cuthbert's servants. I became an "old hand" at assuming my disguise before we went to fish rose on the windswept strand or out in the boat. The disguise almost became part of me and, therefore, soon felt quite natural. I was running like a boy and moving around like one, with the bolder movements many boys exhibit. I awoke early by using Grandpa's old Indian trick of drinking lots of water, and I always filled my pockets with gingerbread, slices of cake, cookies and muffins, or even cornbread, for I found Louie to be more hungry than picky. We became friends, although at first I talked little around him. For many days I was afraid I would betray myself as a girl.

One morning Louie and I crossed over the south inlet onto Debourdieu Beach. As on Pawley's, tall rows of sea oat-covered dunes squatted in front of thick brushy woods that were filled with wind-sculptured wax myrtle, sharp yuccas, cedar and the beautiful palmetto. Several miles down the shore of Debourdieu sat "the Castle," the old summer home of the Allston family.

Chapter 5

In 1812, little Aaron Burr Allston had died there in "The Castle." Mama had often told me the story of little Aaron and his beautiful mother, Theodosia Burr Allston, the daughter of Aaron Burr. Her ship disappeared off the Carolina coast when she went north, grieving after her precious son died. The tragedy tugged at my heart.

"Pirates had her walk the plank out there, y' know," said Louie. "They put a gun to her back out there on the ocean, off Debbie-doo Beach. Piteeful. A grievin' mama walkin' th' plank."

"How do you know they had her walk the plank?"

"Oh, people say things, an' I listen."

"You eavesdrop?"

"Sometimes I can't help it. I happen to be around."

"I bet you sneak around listening. Who said it? *Old Dirty?*" I was almost tired of hearing about that man.

"He's th' very one. He don't speak unless he's got somethin' t' say. An' it's always th' truth."

"Eavesdropping puts a mark on the books of heaven," I said peevishly.

"I told ya', I couldn't help it! Anyway, he told my pa a treasure was buried around here." His jaw clenched. I could tell he was irritated with me but I didn't care. "Old Dirty himself found a gold coin around here," he continued. "I saw it, so I know it's true. He bored a hole in it and wears it on a string under his shirt. I guess it was from a *pirate treasure.*" Louie looked to see what effect his works were having on me.

"And it was buried around here, most likely *here on Debbie-doo*, on Uncle Cuthbert's land," he added. "It's part of th' mainland, y' see, an' it couldn't be washed away as easy here as on Pawley's if a storm was t' come. The pirates dropped anchor an' came into this little inlet, I figure, lookin' for a protected harbor, an' they didn't find much 'cause this ain't much of a harbor. But likely this spot was protected enough. Look around, Elbow. Can't y' just see them beachin' their jolly boat an' dragging their treasure bags an' chests up here to these dunes an' searchin' out those woods for a real special place? Y' have t' think like a pirate, y' see?"

"Why did you call me 'Elbow?'" I asked, startled.

"Well, it's better'n your name, *E.L.* What a name! Where did you get that?" he questioned.

"Nothing wrong with my name. Anyway, when are you going to tell me your fishing secrets?" I asked, trying to change the subject.

"I ain't thinkin' of fishin' secrets now! When y' need 'em, I'll tell 'em. No one needs all th' secrets at once when y' gets started. It'd be too much for your brain to handle right now when y'r trying t' learn

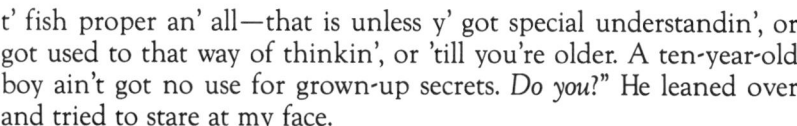
The Treasure of Pawley's Island

t' fish proper an' all—that is unless y' got special understandin', or got used to that way of thinkin', or 'till you're older. A ten-year-old boy ain't got no use for grown-up secrets. *Do you?*" He leaned over and tried to stare at my face.

I turned away, knowing I had begun to blush with his stare.

"No, no, I see right now y' couldn't handle it yet. You got t' be older an' smarter. Now, we'll have t' map all this place and search every inch for th' treasure. An' we're goin' t' do it afore *Old Dirty* comes. He'll be down here t' lead a huntin'-fishin' trip, an' we'll have it found afore then. It's goin' t' take a lot of thought an' figurin'."

Louie paused, waiting for his words to take effect. He was always doing that. He must have thought I needed to think about his declarations.

When he felt he had paused sufficiently, he continued, "Now, where could that treasure be?"

We looked around for a while. I told him I had read *Treasure Island*, by Robert Louis Stevenson, and we talked about the ways of pirates in the book. I suggested we find a telescope. It would help us in mapping the inlet and Debourdieu Beach, if he thought that was the location of the treasure. I could contribute a cedar pencil and some paper from my journal, I said.

"Uncle Cuthbert has a couple of telescopes at the house," Louie replied. "Gettin' a telescope's no problem. He feels sorry for me since Pa died, so I'll just mope around this afternoon. Looks like it's goin' t' rain later. He won't be able to stand it with me mopin' in a closed-up house. Where do *you* think the treasure could be?"

"No pirate would bury it in a dune. Dunes move in the wind and in storms. I believe it will be buried twenty paces from a tree."

"Storms tear down some dunes and push up others," Louie agreed. "We'll have to look for a pirate sign. Pirates left certain markers. I can recognize a pirate marker. And *then* we'll have it!"

We leaped up and down the dunes for a while, making plans. The sand was soft and pure white, squeaking under our boots as we climbed around. From there we could see the chimneys of cottages poking out from treetops on Pawley's. Pier boys, like Teaspoon, were already out checking their nets. Down below on the damp inlet beach of Debourdieu, we noticed that Grandpa, Uncle Cuthbert, Uncle Zeke, and Caesar had caught two large spot-tailed bass, about twenty pounds each, one fish for each family's dinner. They stood around discussing and gazing at the fish. There would be good eating that night.

◆ ◆ ◆ ◆ ◆ ◆ ◆

Chapter 5

One night, hours before dawn, Grandpa and Uncle Zeke strapped a bunch of long sticks to their saddles and led their snorting horses into the blackness, picking and weaving their way through the dunes by lantern light. In the darkness, they headed up the strand toward the north inlet, where they scouted the shoreline for channels left by the out-going tide. Into the deepest channels, by then dry beds, they plunged the sticks and, all along up to the high watermark, they lined out the channels clearly. Then they returned to the house to rest or sleep for a while. A few hours later, just before sunrise, we met Uncle Cuthbert and Louie to fish for the bass that came booming up those channels as the incoming tide headed in to crash on the shore, hopefully driving the big fish toward us in the steady nor-easter.

In that dim, hazy light, I could barely see the strong cord as it stretched from my hand into the foamy water. Grandpa had handed the line to me, already baited with a good-sized chunk of cut mullet. "Always expose the hook tip," he said. He had waded out and cast the hook and weight into a marked channel. The surging water pulled against the line with every wave.

"When you feel him grab the bait, run back up the beach toward the dunes to set the hook," Grandpa had explained, "and hang on until we can come help you. Plant those feet and don't let him drag you out to sea. I'd hate to lose a good man," he joked.

My old boots leaked as I stood in the edge of the cold, cold water, but I regarded my clothes with increasing satisfaction. They had become caked with fish blood and slime, like real boy's clothes. They were quite stiff by now and how they smelled! I was pleased to note that Louie's looked almost as dirty.

When I walked back up the beach to warm up, a bass suddenly took the hook and, with a mighty heave, jerked the line from my cold, reddened hands. Louie, who was fishing close to the water below me, must have seen it happen out of the corner of his eye. He threw himself on the line as it shot past him toward the waves. Then he grabbed it and backed up the beach to set the hook, still holding on to his line as well. The bass ran, heading out to open sea, instinctively knowing his freedom lay in that direction. The line grew more taut, cutting Louie's fingers when he reared back, bracing himself against the pull of the big bass. I looked on helplessly, giving no aid at all. In a moment of slack, Louie wrapped the line around one of the sticks, shouting, "I can't hold him!" Uncle Zeke ran down the beach toward him, but in another moment the bass was loose and a broken cord blew in the wind. Louie and I stared out at the angry surf, beyond

The Treasure of Pawley's Island

which the bass was running free.

Louie's breath came in gasps. He bent over groaning, his fingers red and almost bleeding.

"I lost him," he gasped. "I just lost the biggest fish I ever laid hands on."

"Some yuh catch an' some yuh don't," said Uncle Zeke as he moved to tie more hooks and a weight on the broken string. "He were uh big un. Try one mo' time t' hook uh Samson." Zeke handed me the line and headed back up the beach to where he was trying to catch his own.

Louie edged closer to me, rubbing his poor fingers together. "Why hasn't your Grandpa or your pa taught y' about fishin' an' huntin' any better? You stand around an' let a big, fine bass be blown out to sea, an' all you kin do is hop around like a chicken with his neck wrung off. I see right now you are gonna be a trial an' a tribulation to me."

"Grandpa teaches me!"

"So? No dis-respect, but I can't see that he's taught y' a thing. Now, I could understand y' losin' that bass if y' was a little weak girl, but you're goin' t' have t' pull your weight. Y' got t' smarten up if we're going t' find that *diamond and gold treasure*—an' if I'm gonna teach a peanut like you t' fish half decent!"

Louie was angry. And he was taking it out on me. I resented it, and it made me angry too.

"Well, tell me what to do and I'll do it!" I yelled. "We have a bargain—and it's your fault if I lost that fish! You haven't told me your secrets, 'cause if you had I wouldn't have lost it. And anyway, *you* lost the old fish. *You* let it go there at the end, not me. You're the teacher! You get a high pay—a mighty, mighty high pay—and then you lose my fish!"

I knew I was under scrutiny, and in danger of being discovered. I cast my bait into the chanel, a good clean shot. Louie's eyes narrowed, and he said, "My pa used t' say, 'It takes two mules to pull this wagon—an' boy, you're going to pull your weight!' He meant it, too. Elbow, I ain't decided what you're all about, and how *you* can pull anything."

He moved closer, squinting at me. "Elbow, why do you have that ratty hatstring tied under yer chin tight enough to choke a 'gater in two minutes? And I never yet seen th' color of yer hair under that droopy straw hat. What color is it? Maybe y'r *bald*. Haw! An' I never even seen yer face real good. But maybe that's just as well. I don't think it's much of a face under that hat. Uh, what I mean is, I don't think

61

Chapter 5

it's growed up much. Elbow, it looks like I'm goin' t' have t' back up an' start even more from the beginnin' of scratch with you."

Now *that* made me angry. "I got *brown* hair and I *like* wearing this hat! And you won't ever see me without it, so you might as well get used to it. And I *have* got a good face. If you ever looked you would know, but you don't really look at a person. I think you have got bad eyes!"

Louie was taken aback at my fiery reply. He gulped and said, "Why, I kin see yellow paint splatters on that man's clothes down there fishing near the inlet. Kin you see that? If you like a hat like that—well, each to his own. I'd never get within a hunerd feet of a mud dob like *that*! Now, don't you hold that line thata way, or you'll never even feel a nibble. Wrap it around your finger like this, and hold these two fingers like this, so y' kin feel th' slightest tug. Yuh gotta pay attention t' details if we're gonna find treasure. I'm gonna put you in serious trainin'."

On and on he talked, with his irritation soon behind him, teaching me and teaching me. "A Wilson is worth his pay," he declared proudly. I learned that morning to sling my weighted fishing line out into the channel with dexterity *every* time, placing the weight within ten or fifteen feet of a chosen spot. By the time we stopped fishing, I was holding my line like a expert. And although Louie sounded as though he were complaining, I know he quite enjoyed the idea of teaching a younger boy how to hold his fingers properly around a fishing line, how to distinguish a bite from the tug of a wave, how to set a hook in the fish's jaw, how to remove a throughly swallowed hook from a fish's belly. He soon forgot to be gruff and was patient and even rather kind and gentle. It was not two hours before I felt confident and could shore fish with ease while thinking of other things. And this is one of the real pleasures of fishing. I beached several small spot-tailed bass that day, but not one was the size of the one that got away.

Louie stalked up and down the sand, tattered hunting coat flapping in the cold wind, like a little bantam cock, full of confidence and bravado. I fished and copied him, determined he would never find me wanting as a boy, and also determined he would never see the braids that were pinned firmly inside my hat.

Yet, I asked myself, how long would it be possible to masquerade as a boy while we looked for the treasure? What would Louie do if and when he learned? My heart jumped with fear at the thought.

The Treasure of Pawley's Island

The hawk paid me no heed as he scrutinized the vista below with telescopic eyes.

Chapter 6
Almost Caught

When we returned from fishing, Grandpa and Uncle Zeke always let me off the buckboard after Louie had climbed down and walked up his driveway and before we reached our driveway. They were careful to let me out before we reached our property, so that I could sneak through the bushes to the stable and change clothes. If I saw or heard anyone around the stable, I waited for a chance to scurry under the house, where I had hidden an old dress. I could change clothes in either place and tiptoe into the house.

But I always had to watch for Teaspoon. He had almost caught sight of me several times during those first days, until I learned the paths he followed to and from his duty of contributing fish, shrimp and crabs to keep the kitchen larder full.

Teaspoon took his tasks very, very seriously. Before breakfast he usually scampered out to the creek pier, his territory, to check the chickenwire crab traps. He removed the crabs and, if need be, rebaited the traps with smelly fish heads, even though chicken necks were his choice lure for crab traps. If certain fish—spots, whiting, trout—were running in the salt creeks, he would be out on the pier setting droplines; these stretched down from a stout cord spanning the salt creek from one grassy bank to the opposite bank. Or he might be using his dinghy to paddle across, checking his trotlines and throwing fish into a bucket, or stringing them on a cooling line.

But if he had caught a half-bushel of crabs, he could be up near the kitchen, where Maum Polly would throw his crabs and shrimp into apple vinegar-water to boil and then set the maids to picking out the crabs and peeling and deveining the shrimp. If it were after dinner, around three o'clock, the maids might be sitting under the trees behind the kitchen—resting, gossiping and working the day's catch. If the day were quite warm, later in the spring, then they would sit on the

Chapter 6

creek pier in the shade, but only if the breeze was blowing.

On one particular morning, I was sneaking toward the stable with my usual caution. I knew it was too early for the maids to be dressing the crabs and shrimp, and I knew Teaspoon was not allowed to help with that task. "He dun et up his part ob dem critters lo-o-o-o-n-n-n-g time a-go," Maum Polly would say. I also knew he was not far out in the marsh, fishing in a larger boat. "My pa he be drowned," he always explained, "an' ah run my business fum de dinghy an' de sho'!"

I knew he could also be out roaming the property at that time of day. His favorite pasttime was "collectin' an' tradin'." Nothing was too insignificant for him to pass by. An old button lying on the sand would be thrown into his gripsack and eventually sewed onto the front of his bowler, amid feathers and bright string. Tangled fishing line, a muddy, discarded pair of muddy swash boots, a broken kitchen knife, an old shirt full of holes—these were real treasures to Teaspoon. He could hardly pass a clump of weeds without scrutinizing it. Sometimes it took him an hour to deliver a note or gift to a neighboring house, because he had to "trade" with the servants and scour that property for collectibles.

The hour was too early for him to be on neighboring property, but I knew he might be roaming ours. I must be careful. As I looked around for him, I wondered if he had discovered the bucket filled with my girl's clothes in the stable, or if he had ever glimpsed me trudging through the marsh with Louie. Yet I dared not ask him, for eventually Teaspoon spoke of everything he knew to any person who would listen, secret or not.

I peeped around the trees and bushes. Up ahead at the stable, Uncle Zeke had unhitched Eyes and was leading him into a stall. I saw Grandpa carrying our string of fish to the kitchen door. I crept back to check the pier. Sure enough, there was Teaspoon, checking lines and nets.

When I looked back, Uncle Zeke was disappearing around the corner of the kitchen, going to wash up in a tin bucket out back. No one else was in sight. I crept closer to the stable door. When I entered, I heard someone in one of the stalls, humming and singing as he mucked it out. Then Daddy Buck broke into song with his vigorous baritone, emphasizing each word as his pitchfork threw out straw and manure. I paused. Since he was in a stall at the other end, I felt safe enough quietly entering the stall at my end, next to the cowstall, where my bucketful of clothes hung.

Daddy Buck sang on. Just as I reached up for the bucket, I heard a sound.

The Treasure of Pawley's Island

"Huh!" someone said behind me.

"E-e-e-e-e!" I screamed.

I wheeled around. There was Teaspoon!

He stood with a hand clutching each setter's collar. The dogs eyed me curiously, while Teaspoon looked at me defiantly.

"*Robbuh buckra*! Yo' stand *dere*! I sic dese dawgs on yo' iffen yo' move uh hair! Daddy Buck! Daddy Buck! Dis here buckra stealin' de things otta de stable! *Cum jack rabbit*! Bring yo' pitch fork! He *lettle*, but he *mean*!"

Daddy Buck came running, "Teaspoon, who dis?"

"Use de pitch fork!" Teaspoon yelled excitedly. "He gwine run!"

I felt like bolting out of the stable, but my escape was blocked.

Daddy Buck came up close, pushed back his bowler and peered at me. He leaned way over and looked intently under my floppy straw hat. When he grinned, I saw he has lost another tooth during the winter.

"Hee! Hee!" he laughed softly.

"Don't git close," Teaspoon warned. "He *mean*, he *mean*!"

"Git back, runty—*dis buckra* knock y' flat! Hee, hee!"

Just then we heard the faint sound of a bell tinkling.

"De bell! Ah got uh fish!" Teaspoon had rigged a bell to one of his trotlines to call him back when a fish was hooked.

"Go, runty. Doc he kin take care ob *dis heah buckra*!" said Daddy Buck.

Teaspoon reluctantly released the dogs and ran off to catch his fish. When he was gone, Daddy Buck beamed and took off my hat. The dogs sniffed me in casual greeting.

"Yeh! Hee, hee! Ah knows yo'! Yo ib leettle missie. Why yo dressed lak dat? Yo look lak buckra, sho' nuff!"

"I put on these clothes to go fishing with Grandpa, so I wouldn't ruin my good clothes and make Mama upset. See?" I showed him my girl's clothes folded neatly in the bucket.

"Please, don't tell anyone! Don't tell Teaspoon!" I pleaded. "Grandpa and Uncle Zeke know my secret, but no one else does. And I can't bear to go back to wearing that old suit now that I've worn this. You won't tell, will you?"

Daddy Buck started chuckling again. He nodded and nodded. He loved secrets.

"Missie, don't wor-ry," he said grinning. "Ole Daddy Buck won't tell no-body, not even Auntie Hagey. No-body! Ketch de crik empty now! Dat Teaspoon, he got up-set, but don't *wor-ry*. Ah tell him Doc he took care of de buckra. An' dat be truth!"

He left to stop Teaspoon from returning and to tell Grandpa while I hurriedly changed clothes and ran to the house.

Chapter 6

I spoke to the setters as I climbed the breezeway steps. "You won't tell, will you, Robert E.? You'd never tell Mama, would you, John C.? And you'd never tell Jane Anne, would you? She'd *never* get over it. And you won't tell that boy Louie, either, will you?"

Except for this scare, I had had a wonderful time fishing and roaming the marsh. I woke up early each morning, eager to start the day. Jane Anne grew accustomed to me rummaging around for a few minutes before dawn. She ignored me then and usually for the remainder of the day. I didn't much care. I was having too good a time. Mama and Grandma were pleased at my happiness and let me go with their blessings, but as far as I knew, they had no idea I was masquerading as a boy.

♦ ♦ ♦ ♦ ♦ ♦ ♦

Louie and I appreciated being left to our own devices on many fishing days. On sunny mornings we roamed the breeze-swept marsh flats by the hour with cedar pencil and a square of paper in hand. We took secretive joy in mapping the area as we made our own treasure map. He and I developed tactics for rapid movement through the marsh. Without resting our full weight on it, we learned to run over the pluff mud. We carried three short pine planks along with us—one for each of us to stand on, while the last board was to be passed to the front as we moved along through the soft mud or high cord grass which slowed our progress toward the firmer mud where glasswort, needle rush and sea myrtle grew. Occasionally Louie would have to attend to private business (to leak, as he called it). Then I nonchalantly turned away. "You must be able t' hold a gallon, Elbow" he declared.

His floppy coat with its many pockets carried a growing assortment of treasure-hunting necessities—cedar pencils and paper, two pocket knives, Uncle Cuthbert's small telescope, a bag of lemon drops, *Treasure Island* for ready reference, a ball of heavy fishing cord, five feet of stout rope, a false mustache made of Louie's hair, a cloth bag for collecting snakes and lizards (horned ones in particular), a small glass jar, and the blade of a slender spade, plus a variety of fishhooks, corks and lead weights. Each item occupied a corner of a certain pocket, and the rope was pinned in the sleeves, running from one sleeve over the shoulder to the other with an end dangling out of each.

"I can grab it fast," insisted Louie, "but I couldn't if I had to carry it coiled up. See?" he said and whipped it out fast as lightning.

Louie found it necessary for me to carry certain important items—cookies, slices of pound cake well-wrapped in oiled paper, slabs of

The Treasure of Pawley's Island

gingerbread, balls of string, a tin spoon and cup, a pocket knife which Grandpa gave me on request. Many is the time we paused to search our pockets for an item and ended in a pause for Louie to fill his stomach with Maum Polly's baking. Our daily cartography had noticeable breaks. "It's a good thing Maum Polly bakes everyday," I thought.

As the days and then weeks passed, Old Dirty's secrets came out of Louie one by one and very, very slowly—like pulling teeth from one of the Bald Eagles that flew lazy circles over the marsh. Like the eagle, Louie would circle around a subject, hint, hint, hint—and then drop to the secret suddenly, just as the eagle plunges from the sky at the perfect moment when its prey is unsuspecting. By mid-May I had heard much of Old Dirty's "wisdom" and was curious to see the man up close. For weeks now we had been loping through the marsh, and Old Dirty had still not shown up. "Delayed by a good hunting trip," proclaimed Louie. "He'll be here. You just wait and see."

As we moved through the mud and grass, we chewed over Old Dirty's wisdom, as well as other puzzling questions: Where do the swamp alligators have their babies? In nests? Are any conch shells left-handed? Is it disposition or hardships that make people patient? Why do the boards in old beach cottages never rot? Why do Negroes have such smooth, pink palms? Why does the sun burn more easily in the spring than in the summer? What are the signs of a big storm coming? We spent hours discussing these questions as the pleasant days and weeks drifted by.

Freckles were beginning to pop out over my nose and cheeks. The appearance of those faint little spots made me fearful that Mama would not let me continue fishing with Grandpa. Jane Anne had no freckles. Her complexion was baby-doll perfect, rosewater and glycerin perfect. She walked the strand only when the sunlight was weak, wearing a wide brimmed hat and carrying a white parasol.

I need not have worried, however. Grandpa hugged me and told me he had struck a bargain with Mama: I was to be allowed to fish as often as I wished, for he had assured her it would improve my health.

"And how can she dispute a physician, Sailor? Look at you!" exclaimed Grandpa. "Your diet agrees with you, and you're almost as fit as you were when you were an infant. Then, too, your mama needs the rest and quiet now, before that next squawling infant arrives in July. It does her no harm to have you out of the house."

Mama and Jane Anne were, therefore, no wiser to my masquerade after a month or more than after the first morning. I was getting into the full swim of "being a boy." As I marched day after day through the swash, I never again worried about the freckles that crept across

Chapter 6

my nose, even if Jane Anne had none.

Overhead, the hawks and crows would often harrass one another, arch enemies that they were, but Louie and I grew used to hearing them and barely noticed. We discovered "Unknown Valley," a wide and sandy mud flat hidden in the south marsh. It was firm at low tide, with secret trails leading outward from it; at high tide it had only a few inches to a foot of water covering it. There we spent many hours, day after day, returning again and again. It became our secret retreat, holding a personal collection of skewered walking sticks which were draped with a couple of extra buckets, a crabnet, and an emergency jar of fresh water.

In Unknown Valley we watched the purple-legged fiddler crabs, washed with lavender, gray and burnt red, scrambling around on the sandy mud, each waving his one large claw and scurrying to find an escape hole as we passed through his crab territory. We herded them like giants herding tiny cattle, "Yi! Yi! Yippie-yi-yi! Go you crabs!" We watched the myriad winking creeks that were fed by sweeping tides as they cut sharp patterns in the surrounding mud flats. The tides surged in and out of the inlets, rhythmically filling and emptying the salt creeks and producing a tremendous amount of food for sea creatures, birds and man.

When the tide went out, we clambered over the barnacle-covered oyster beds that edged the mud flats and watched periwinkles inch their saucy pointed shells up grass stalks, scraping food from the surface with their rough tongues. Marsh snails, too, inched their paths across the mud flats, leaving winding trails in memory of their travels. Baby shrimp that had been spawned offshore were pushed up into the salt creeks where they found food in the estuary—the rich marshland.

The marsh hen, or Clapper Rail, was our constant companion as we moved through the swash grass. Never did the marsh hen fail to set off a clacking that was taken up by other birds, and the marsh rang with those wild calls—groans, shrieks and clacks—as it disturbed and alerted the entire area to our passage. The bird was busy searching for the crabs, fiddlers, insects and minnows that must have given it that fishy flavor the Negroes tried to get rid of when they prepared it for cooking.

Another frequent visitor to the marsh was the Po'Jo' (as the Negroes called him), or Great Blue Heron, so noble and slender. It stood motionless, searching for watery delights until a mullet appeared in range of its dagger-like beak. Then, after swallowing his prey, Po'Jo'

The Treasure of Pawley's Island

would flap his great wings, squawk raucously, fold his thin legs back together and rise into the air, heading for a platform nest in the top of a tall pine on the Neck. In contrast to the deliberate movements of Po'Jo', the Snowy Heron or Snowy Egret seemed forever moving on its black legs and yellow feet, its "golden slippers." This white bird was quick and graceful, poking here and there into marshy pools with its black bill, looking for fish, crabs, fiddlers or shrimp. If we ventured too close to Po'Jo' or golden slippers, the birds would move to another salt creek to resume their never-ending hunt for food.

As we trudged through the prickly needle rush on our way deep into the marsh, fat gray-brown marsh rabbits often scurried ahead, shyly wanting to hide. Up above, a vigilant marsh hawk rode on rising warm air currents, criss-crossing the marsh, disrupting the placid herons below as he scouted for his meal of rabbit or marsh rodent.

◆ ◆ ◆ ◆ ◆ ◆ ◆

One morning a hawk sleuthed the mud flats above us, and while it steeply banked on pointed wings over the curve of grassy islands, I left Louie and dared to venture out alone—for the first time—onto the edge of a mud flat. Behind me Louie was plumbing the depth of an oyster-filled salt creek, at a bend in the creek where the current slowed enough for the oysters to take hold. It lay in our intended path. I knew he was trying to figure out a way around those oysters. He had always been the leader, with me following close behind.

The hawk paid me no heed as he scrutinized the vista below with telescopic eyes. I regarded his graceful flight and longed to have that same vision. Then to my surprise, I discovered my feet were mired in the oozing mud, which was clutching and moving upward past my ankles. The gelatinous stuff slowly crept higher and higher; because of the suction of it, I could not pull out my limbs, as much as I tried. I used my walking stick and the pine board to push against the mud, to no avail. Although flailing this way and that and twisting and turning, I was stuck fast.

I hated to do it but I cried out, "Louie! Louie! Come pull me out!"

But the mud would not give me up. Soon it was halfway up my legs and still moving, and even then Louie paid me no attention. This mud is swallowing me alive, I thought, just as if I were a morsel of food, and my legs are not strong enough to pull out my feet. I am too weak.

By then I was quite alarmed, squirming around, even digging into the mud with my fingers. The pluff mud felt bottomless. In my mind's

Chapter 6

eye it reached down, down into the earth for a hundred feet. My imagination was unbridled, for I *knew* people had foolishly wandered there and become helplessly trapped. Could there be, beneath me, the bones of a gigantic animal from Noah's flood? Perhaps some little trapped creatures preserved in the mud? Sharp and dangerous shells that would slash my legs? Boots—or even human bones? The mud oozed upward—or rather my feet went further downward. And my mind reeled. I was in the grip of emotions that held me as fast as the pluff mud. (I would have been even more fearful if I had known that Louie was close to discovering I was a girl.)

"Louie!" I called out, throwing down my stick and plank, "Don't you care if I die in this mud?"

At that he looked my way, unsurprised at what he saw. "I been expecting that," he said as he looked at my encased legs.

I whispered, almost in spite of myself, "Kind Father in Heaven, help me out of this." Then in a flash I threw myself forward, flat on the pluff mud. My limbs went not an inch further in. How I knew to do that I do not know, other than believing that God answered my prayer and spoke into my mind, for falling flat down in mud is naturally abhorrent to any girl.

"Now *why* did y' do that?" Louie asked.

"It saved my life."

"Awww, y' ain't much stuck."

"I am. And you haven't moved an inch to help me!"

"Ya ain't stuck! Here!" He dug his fingers into the appropriate pocket and threw his shovel blade at me. His shoulders shrugged as if to say, well, y' got y'self into this mess, now git y'self out!

So I shoveled and shoveled with the blade, making that sticky mud fly, while Louie continued to poke into the low places near the edge of the salt creek with his walking stick.

"I'm gonna git me a mess of softshells," he said, all the time watching me out of the corner of his eye.

No help from him. It was the first time I consciously remember having to fight a welling desire for the sympathy and comfort which most of us want in times of distress. I decided then and there never to be stingy with sympathy. How many times had Grandma urged me to be a "young woman of purity, courage and sympathy"? (And Papa never failed to add "with self-control, too.")

As I dug at that mud, I remember how Grandpa often spoke of Southern people: "Southern men and women have manners and spirit," he told me, "but their best trait is Christian gentleness and sympathy. You, Sailor, can cultivate gentleness and sympathy just as

The Treasure of Pawley's Island

a farmer learns to cultivate his land." No, after this I would never, never withhold my sympathy. That was the second thing I learned.

What was the first? It was the realization that I was being watched over from above. So on hands and knees I crawled over the soft mud with my stick and plank until I reached into the marsh grass, and there I held on.

Suddenly Louie was beside me. I saw in his eyes that he had been concerned for me all the time—that he had chosen that way of toughening me up. My heart was still pounding but I felt tougher.

"You're as black as Uncle Zeke, Elbow, and he's got the blackest skin I ever seen. Now he's a mighty fine man—but *you* ain't up to *that* grade yet. An' don't y' ever wash those clothes? They was filthy before y' got into th' mud! I been trying not t' say anything about those nasty clothes, but now I got t' speak: Go on over there and wash y'self in that salt creek—and don't kill any of th' fish when th' stench washes out! You could antfixiate th' minnows. Go on! We gotta git this here map finished, or Old Dirty will be here before we know it an' I won't have time, 'cause I'll be off fishin' or huntin'. Now look, I won't tell you what it is but I'm noticin' somethin' mighty odd on this here map that we drawed out."

I circled around the pluff mud, that demon stuff, plunged knee-deep into the cold, cold salt creek and splashed at the front of my clothes. I was freezing but the stuff was washing out. Pluff mud sticks like glue, and it needed more than the few swipes I was able to give.

"An' y' face is black under that hat, Elbow. Only thing I can see is y' eyes. Y' even got a glug of mud on that scraggly thing y' call a hat."

I worked on my face some more and felt the hunk of mud on the hat. "Is it off now?"

"Wa-a-a-al, how kin y' wash a hat with it still on y' head? And that coat and shirt—git 'um off! Y' musta drug y'self along like a worm. Hurry up!"

I knew I could not take them off.

"You go on ahead," I said. "I'll catch up."

"Can't y' see those trousers? They're so stiff they'll stand up like kitchen stovepipes!"

"If I don't care, why should you?"

"Aw-w-w, stop whinin'! When we go huntin' in th' fall, y' gonna have t' slog in an' outta water an swamps an' mud an' stuff, an' y' gotta get used to a little bit of cold water. Draw y'self up tall, an' tell y'self, 'I ain't cold! I ain't cold!' Then yank off them clothes an' scrub!"

"I *ain't* yanking—I'm going home!"

"Now, if you ain't th' stupidest—Aw, git outta here! Why doesn't

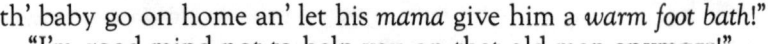
Chapter 6

th' baby go on home an' let his *mama* give him a *warm foot bath*!"

"I'm good mind not to help you on that old map anymore!"

"Well, y' ain't been much help!"

"I have too! What do you see on it?" I asked, shivering.

"Somethin' is th' matter with yuh. I ain't figured out what—but *somethin'* is! Aw-w-w, go on home!"he bellowed. "If y' ain't sick, I'll show y' tomorrow!"

I lifted my trembling chin and marched toward home. When I finally reached there I changed clothes and scrubbed those muddy things a half-hour in a creek, then hung them over some limbs to dry.

Louie had almost caught me. I could tell by the look in his eyes he suspected something. He just hadn't put it all together yet.

The Treasure of Pawley's Island

I'll be glad to tell your mother what you've done!

Chapter 7
At the Lookout

During the spring, the oleander bushes near the beach cottage and kitchen house awakened and put on tiny new leaves. Papa returned from the plantation to spend a few days with us. After dinner, he and Grandpa sat rocking on the piazza. Papa told Grandpa that the locks had been opened in the rice banks, allowing the river water to flow in and kill the weeds that had sprung up in the rich soil along with the rice shoots. The rice could grow under water, but not the weeds. All the weak banks were now secured. Papa had taken crew after crew of plantation workers out to shore up the unsound places, and he assured Grandpa that he had given special attention to that weakened bank on the river. The rice was growing, and a good crop was promised. All was well on the plantation.

Because of the intermittent coolness of the weather, they felt that the dread yellow fever and malaria—the miasma—would probably not begin to stalk the inland plantations until late in the spring. I will admit to feeling fear for Papa's life whenever he returned to the plantation. He reminded me that as a young man he had fought a battle with a mild case of the miasma and hoped that bout would prevent him from having to fight it again.

Papa and Grandpa, so alike, rocked and spoke of old friends who had been lost to the diseases of the area. And they spoke of some who had lost the battle for their way of life, too. Some old friends were going to work for the Atlantic Coast Lumber Corporation in Georgetown, or for the turpentine works in nearby counties; others had been forced to sell off some pine, virgin timber of enormous height, on the edges of their plantations. They spoke of the indignities suffered by a friend who had to sell off her gracious home, the family home of a hundred years, because she could not pay her taxes. "I'd help her if I could, Son," said Grandpa. "You know I would."

Chapter 7

Then they spoke of our baby, due to arrive in July, and of Mama's health. While he was at the shore, Papa often walked hand in hand with Mama on the damp sand. They walked in the dimness of twilight, for Mama did not usually go abroad in daylight hours. Papa was planning to leave us in a week. He would kiss us all and go back to the plantation again. I would miss him. But he and Mama would send letters to one another every day by the mailboat that came up from Georgetown, stopping at Waverly Mills on its way to Bucksport and Conway one way and bringing more supplies, mail, ice and passengers down the river the next day. Mail and news came to us from both ends of the river when we—Grandpa, Uncle Zeke and I—rode the buckboard over to chat, pick up letters and send off our own mail. And once in a while we brought home a block of ice, a real treat.

After dinner we visited friends and were visited by them too—the Simonses, Wards, Tuckers, Nebits, LaBruces, Allstons, Lachicottes, Woods, Westons and Frasers—old and dear family and friends, for we were all related in some way. Occasionally the Flaggs came down from Magnolia Beach to visit after church, and what a high time that was! I played with Julia Ward occasionally in the afternoons at her cottage or mine. If I had nothing else to do, I fished on the pier with Teaspoon, or read and studied half-heartedly. I made notes on Louie's fishing techniques in my journal and described our adventures. Soon, with Grandma's encouragement, I began writing more and more.

Quite often we entertained at supper. Then I either ate at the mahogany table with the grown-ups or in the kitchen house at my tiny table with Maum Polly.

The beach cottage ran smoothly under Grandma and Mama's direction. They never had a cross word. Such love existed between them, such perfect trust, that they never had a cross word. They were both immensely charitable and deeply religious. And how they loved handwork!

In fact, all the women in our house loved handwork—except me. They carried it with them wherever they went, from room to room and house to house. Even Jane Anne professed to love it, although somehow I doubted it. Of them all, I guess, Aunt Alberta and Grandma loved it best. Their needles flashed and their tongues wagged as they strove for perfection in the quality of embroidered and appliqued monograms, flowers, leaves, et cetera. They used large embroidery frames as they embroidered fire screens, pillow shams, table covers and tidies for furniture and sofa pillows, lambrequins for windows and doorways. Each used her own small frame to embroider silk pieces together for quilts and aprons, belts and sashes. They also cross-stitched

The Treasure of Pawley's Island

and knitted, crocheted and tatted, not to mention the needlepoint and petit point that poured from their frames. Aunt Alberta and Grandma complimented each other in graceful terms, oooohing and aaaahing as their handwork progressed. Yet even I could tell that Aunt Alberta's work was matchless.

Grandma and Mama had been teaching me the "all too necessary" needle arts since I was nine years of age. Grandma said at that age my eyes were "sufficiently mature for the intricate work," so they had taught me to crochet. And before our stay of six months at Pawley's Island had ended that year, I painfully completed enough white string "squares" for a doll blanket. In subsequent years, I knitted and tatted. In 1892, I worked in needlepoint. However, during this spring of 1893, I was firmly placed between Grandma and Aunt Alberta and taught the rudiments of cross-stitching my name in red thread on an old piece of white linen.

The linen square was to take days and weeks of half-hearted devotion as I sat longing to be back fishing or jumping on the dunes with Louie, brandishing an old Confederate sword instead of a silver needle and thimble. The once-pure white linen was soon grimy and frayed; the back looked like a battlefield of wildly-crossed red threads. I was told to practice patience with every stitch, and also temper control; the latter was my undoing on too many occasions that spring, as you will see. I redid those stitches over and over, often with wild irritation. It did *not* teach me patience—or temper control.

Early one sunny afternoon before supper, I grew tired of fighting red stitches, threw the linen square under a table and climbed the boardwalk to the Lookout. I wished later that I had not.

The Lookout was at the end of the boardwalk, on top of the third row of dunes from the house, overlooking the ocean. It was capped by a jaunty roof, ringed with benches, and surrounded by waving sea oats. The island and marsh were in back and the wide, twinkling sea was in front. It was a charming place, Aunt Alberta's "station." In the spring and summer months, she sought the shade of the Lookout for protection from the Carolina sun, for her complexion's sake. From it she could view the entire strand and it allowed her to keep check on the activities of those going to and from the house. It was the ideal place for her "station," and it was one of my favorite places, too.

I had been playing there beside the Lookout in the sea oats for a few minutes when up the boardwalk came Aunt Alberta and Jane Anne. The wind blew their capes out over their leg-o'-mutton sleeves like seagull wings. Aunt Alberta's dress was of white linen, as were all the island ladies' dresses at this time of year. White linen that swished

Chapter 7

as they walked, and wide-brimmed straw hats. On Aunt Alberta's sleeves were embroidered blue lilies-of-the valley and on Jane Anne's were yellow irises.

Seeing them walk toward me, I jumped behind the stairs leading up to the Lookout and scrambled up under the floor to a little hollowed-out place I had had for years. Impetuously I thought that perhaps I could tease Jane Anne, jumping out in a few minutes and scaring her, or reaching up to tickle her through the boards with a long piece of sea oat grass. With a sigh, Jane Anne climbed the stairs, sat, and stretched out her long slender legs before her on the bench. As I waited for my chance, I looked around and felt for a piece of grass. There, hidden from their view, I found an old sandy towel, a spent shotgun shell, and a small, round, neatly-made hole in the damp sand. Perhaps turtle or snake eggs lay at the bottom. Perhaps, with digging, I could find out if it was the home of a crab.

Looking up through the cracks, I felt that surely Aunt Alberta and Jane Anne could see me, what with their penetrating eyes and my humming and digging. I even thought our eyes met, but Aunt Alberta continued searching the boards and murmuring to Jane Anne, who would answer briefly. They decided that Daddy Buck must white-wash the Lookout shortly so that it would look decent for their company. They decided the steps needed repair. They decided the roof needed repair.

Then I heard Aunt Alberta speak to Jane Anne of Grandpa, calling him by name. It concerned Uncle Sumter and his desire to resume fishing.

"Claude has hurt your father's feelings *again*, Janey, and I won't stand for that to happen another time! He's feeling worse and worse every week. And I want him out of the house! I'm tired of him being underfoot—following me around all the time. He needs the fresh air."

"Mama, I think he has lost at least fifteen pounds since I saw him in the fall. He doesn't look strong enough to hold a fishing pole," declared Jane Anne.

"He wants to keep busy. He *is* strong enough," Aunt Alberta retorted indignantly.

"Why, Papa hasn't been fishing in years. He looks like walking death. And why on earth would he want to fish now? He and that silver flask stroll up the strand, visit friends, and that's about all—besides following you around. As for fishing, it's probably your idea, not his."

"Now, don't you say that. I can't think it will do him any harm. Perhaps he won't need to use the flask as often when he's busy fishing."

"Humph, nothing will keep that away. You are determined, aren't

The Treasure of Pawley's Island

you, Mama?"

"I am sure Claude could take your father fishing *if* he wanted to."

"Why can't Papa and Daddy Buck put a boat in the water?"

"Your papa said Daddy Buck almost drowned him a few years ago," answered my aunt.

"Be that as it may, which dress should I wear when Mr. Bouknight comes to call this afternoon? The yellow linen?" It sounded to me as if Jane Anne were trying to change the subject.

"Poor Sumter—what can I do?" fretted Aunt Alberta.

At that moment Grandma walked up the boardwalk and began climbing up to the Lookout. After pleasantries, Aunt Alberta casually mentioned how much Uncle Sumter wanted to go fishing with Grandpa. Grandma listened. Aunt Alberta's voice grew louder as she presented her case. Grandma demurred, saying it was up to Grandpa to make that decision. Then Aunt Alberta's words turned into a tirade. I wondered why she sounded so desperate. Their voices rose and fell with the same inflection but not the same gentleness, the wind plucking at their words.

"Annabelle," declared Aunt Alberta, "although Sumter had no interest in saltwater fishing for a number of years—forgetting what happened a few years ago, that was nothing—he wants to try again this season. I feel it would be good for him to get away from the house. I want you to speak to Claude and arrange it."

I was aware that Grandma had learned, long years before, to disregard Aunt Alberta's wordiness and bombast, to secure peace in her family. They usually had a good relationship, for Grandma tried to keep the conversation on topics which did not incite Aunt Alberta. The melody of Grandma's words and the tact with which she spoke sounded like the cooing of a dove. Not so her sister's voice on that day.

"Arrange it! You must arrange it for Sumter!" cawed Aunt Alberta.

"Alberta, Alberta," answered Grandma soothingly, trying to calm her, "now you know I never interfere in men's business. If Claude asks my opinion, I am only too happy to give it. But in matters such as 'fishing'—well, that is certainly an area in which I am uncultivated, so I cannot presume to approach him with any suggestions."

I peeked up through the cracks of the floor but could not see their faces. By the tone of her voice, I knew Aunt Alberta's face was flushed. She was not accustomed to being thwarted by Grandma, who usually bowed to her wishes.

"Sister," Aunt Alberta returned shrilly, "you know I have never, never interfered in 'men's business'—unless absolutely necessary, of course—but this is a matter of more than *hospitality*. I believe we are

Chapter 7

being insulted by Claude, a family member! Claude should arrange it. He should, and you know he should."

Grandma tried to speak, but Aunt Alberta did not seem to notice.

"As for interfering," continued Aunt Alberta with a squawk, "I can think of a number of times when I would have interfered, had I been in your shoes. Lives would have been quite different had *I* been in charge. Remember how Sumter sent his money out of the country during The War—if Claude had done that, wouldn't he have money now? And think of your servant problems—we certainly don't have any of those. Think of certain family problems—"

"Alberta," interrupted Grandma finally, "you are delving into private matters that do not concern you. I do not push myself into your affairs, no matter what problems I see there. You overstep yourself today."

I was startled. Never before had I heard cross words like these pass between them.

Aunt Alberta continued her harangue. "And you have not treated me as your dear sister in many years," she proclaimed. "You have not allowed me to offer any suggestions, any advice. Why, it's as though we are just casual friends. You haven't really talked with me for years!"

"Alberta, I have never been able to stop you from offering advice," said Grandma—reasonably I thought.

"You never *took* my advice! *Not one time* in these last years. You *must* make the arrangements for Sumter. I will not stand for him to be hurt!" she said finally.

"And I say again, I *do not* presume to tell my husband what to do." Grandma turned to go.

"We may have been reared that way, Sister," said Aunt Alberta, "But I certainly have not let that stand in the way of a single instance when *I* believed *I* was right. Certainly not when our feelings were being hurt. My Sumter will fish this year, no matter what you say. You tell Claude to leave Zeke home and take Sumter. I will *not* be opposed this way! Tell Claude! Tell Claude!"

Crouching down below the Lookout, I was horrified. Up above, Grandma answered quietly, although I did not see how she was able to. "You must know by now that Claude will never, never leave Zeke home from a fishing trip," she said, "or any other trip for that matter. They have been together too many years for that."

I myself knew they had been through much together. Their boyhood, The War, the years of labor on the plantation, the treatment of patients side by side.

"No," Grandma continued, "I'll never ever ask that. Tell Sumter to

The Treasure of Pawley's Island

speak to Claude himself. Zeke brought Claude back to me after The War, and I'll never forget that."

She turned and started down the stairs to the boardwalk. Aunt Alberta made a few noises, trying to control herself and stalked to the ocean side of the Lookout.

When I saw Grandma's shoulders shaking as she walked down the boardwalk, I knew that I should never, never have overheard that conversation. I could not understand the meaning of Aunt Alberta's words that day, but in later days, I think I understood. I started to cry myself, seeing my dear Grandma crying and feeling like an eavesdropper. But, I asked myself, when had been my moment to leave?

Suddenly Aunt Alberta swung around and called out to Grandma as she neared the house, "This is a poor, poor way to conduct hospitality here, Sister! Perhaps we should go up to Pineland!"

Grandma looked back for a moment, and then went into the house.

"Mama, no! I don't want to go up to that old place," declared Jane Anne.

"We'll have to see," said Aunt Alberta.

Down below, I watched them with tears in my eyes. I felt cold and upset. Besides, the wind was whipping sand up into my hair and eyes, and I itched all over.

I crawled to the edge of the overhanging floor of the Lookout. When Aunt Alberta walked back to the far edge and faced the white-capped ocean, I lit out down the dune, up and around another one toward the privy on the north side of the house. My skirt was flying and only the elastic band under my chin kept my sunhat on. At the last possible second Jane Anne spied me and gave a screech.

"E-e-e-e-e! Mama, there goes Bessie!"

"*What?*"

"She was under the Lookout, Mama! Hiding under there! Look, you can see her footprints!"

"Down there? What was she doing?"

"*Listening*, Mama, listening to you talk about *Papa*."

"*She was?*" That child is always up to something. I'll take care of *her*," she said as she plowed her way down through the sea oats after me.

Their voices carried after me in the south-easter. I knew I should stop to face her, to explain as best I could, but I did not. Instead I ran even faster. Into the privy I sped and latched the door with trembling hands. In a minute I heard Aunt Alberta's determined approach. The old privy had been moved from place to place on the property, and now its ancient boards hardly held together. She nearly jerked the door from the frail building.

Chapter 7

"Open up this door, child," she cawed breathlessly. "I know you're in there! You come out or I'll call Daddy Buck to tear it down!"

I covered my face with my hands. What had I done?

"Open it! Open the door!"

"*I'll never open it!*"

She gave a tremendous wrench and the door's rusty hinges gave way. Suddenly I was face to face with my puffing, red-face aunt.

"Jane Anne would never hide and listen to grown-ups talk! What do you mean hiding there and listening?" She gave me a shake.

Jane Anne arrived to stand behind her mother, hands on her hips, silently smirking at me.

"Answer me! Speak up!"

"I'm sick! I want my Mama!"

"I'll be glad to tell your Mama what you've done!"

"You are a *pig fish*! Leave me alone!"

"Well!...I have never, never been spoken to in such an insulting manner before!"

"You are a *big fat* pig fish! And your teeth tear people up! And Jane Anne is a *shark*! I never want to see you again! I wish you would go home!"

I gathered my strength and continued wildly, yelling into their shocked faces, "You leave me alone! You order Uncle Sumter around and it's no wonder he runs out to the piazza to smoke! And you order anyone else around who will listen! I feel sorry for poor Daddy Buck and Aunt Hagey to be working for *you*!" I gasped for breath. "And you made my Grandma cry!"

"What?" Aunt Alberta seemed genuinely surprised. "Made her cry?"

I sobbed into my hands.

"Why, I never thought that—" she was still for a minute. I wiped my face on the skirt of my sailor suit. That old suit. I was sick and tired of looking at it.

"Come out," she said. "You can't stay in there."

"I can, you old—you old pig fish," I answered, still crying.

That seemed to revive her attack.

"Jane Anne, go fetch this girl's mother! Run! Run!"

What was I to do? I sobbed in anguish.

The Treasure of Pawley's Island

Yuh need another switchin' wid de peach stick!

Chapter 8
Heartsick

When I awoke in my bed at the top of the house, night had fallen. The house was still. Over in the other bed, Cousin Jane Anne was snoring with gentle clicks. Then I remembered: Mama had retrieved me from the privy and led me to the piazza to where Papa was rocking. They were dismayed at my lack of control, my sobbing, my red and swollen eyes and nose, and especially at the frank report which Aunt Alberta and Jane Anne gave of my "shocking words and behavior."

"And give the child a handkerchief—so she won't use her skirt," ordered Aunt Alberta. "Jane Anne always has a handkerchief with her. See?" she said, jerking a lacy cloth from her daughter's pocket and wagging it at us while propelling Jane Anne from the piazza into the house.

Mama slipped her handkerchief from her pocket and wiped my nose and eyes. I continued to sob as my parents tried to reason with me. Their eyes met and then Mama finally shook her head. Her tender gray eyes looked me over. Damp sand still clung to my skirt and hair. My hands were grubby. My stockings had fallen down. I plopped myself down into a cushioned rocking chair and leaned over on a small covered table, tucked my head between the potted plants and boo-hooed.

They sat down to rock, talking quietly about the warmer weather, about the plantation, about me. When I heard my name, I cried louder.

"Elizabeth Lois," Mama said. "Elizabeth Lois, how could you call Aunt Alberta a fat pig?"

"No!" I cried out. "I called her a fat pig fish! And she is one, too!"

"Bessie!" Surely I was mistaken in thinking that Mama was covering a laugh.

"She is! She is! You should have heard her speak to Grandma—and

Chapter 8

she said mean things about Grandpa to Jane Anne. I heard her! And you should have seen Grandma's shoulders shake when she was crying! I never have seen Grandma cry, never, never. She is a *fat pig fish* to do that to my Grandma!"

I pushed my head farther in among the potted plants so they couldn't see my face. They were silent, thinking about my words. I sniveled a moment or two and then ran to Mama, threw myself into her arms, and really cried. How sorry I felt for my grandma. And then, as I heard myself cry, I began to feel sorrier and sorrier for me.

"What shall we do with her?" Mama asked Papa.

"Bessie, will you stop that and talk with us for a few minutes? Then you can go on up to your room for a while," said Papa, sounding discouraged.

"Mean old Aunt Alberta!" I wailed.

"Bessie," said my papa loudly, "you must stop that."

"Mean! Mean! I can't stand it!" I cried out, louder than ever, loud enough for my entire family and the servants to hear. Out of the corner of my eye, I saw the maids peeking around the corner of the house, eyes wide. I quieted a little at that.

"If you were caught under the Lookout and didn't mean to eavesdrop, I certainly understand—and that would make me feel so much better," said Mama. "But we cannot allow you to lose control like this. All of your elders are to be obeyed and respected, and Aunt Alberta—who has been entirely generous to you in past years—seemed terribly distressed that you called her a fat pig—or so we thought."

She patted and stroked me and pulled me against her, seeking to calm me as she spoke, and her tenderness broke my heart.

"We will have *no* name-calling, Bessie. She's your relative, and—well, we need them here. How can we offend Grandma's sister?"

"They pay money, lots of money," I sobbed.

"Will she ever stop crying?" asked Papa.

Mama must have shaken her head again, so Papa carried me, crying still, into the house, past the parlor where "those two" sat, and up to my room. He laid me on the bed. I covered my face with Mama's handkerchief.

I was spent as a white-tailed deer is spent after a heart-pounding, exhausting chase in the woods of Waccamaw Neck.

◆ ◆ ◆ ◆ ◆ ◆ ◆

I must have slept for a while. When I awakened, I remembered what

The Treasure of Pawley's Island

had happened and saw Papa was beside me, dozing in a chair. I remembered that he had spanked me soundly a few minutes after he brought me to my room. I remembered how much better that made me feel.

I looked around for Jane Anne but saw that Papa and I were alone, and the sun was setting. Rosy light was coming from the marsh-side window. I thought about Louie. How glad I was that Louie knew nothing about my shame. He would have said, "Eavesdropping, huh? Now, what were you telling *me* about eavesdropping?"

I watched Papa sleep for a few minutes. Then I called his name.

He started and awoke.

"Bessie?"

"Yes, Papa," I answered in a tiny voice. My head was pounding and I felt sick.

He lit a candle on the dresser. With tenderhearted words he whispered comfort. Tears spilled down my cheeks at his sympathy.

"No, please, Bessie. No more crying. I'm going to have to go if you cry anymore. I'm tired of all those tears. I've always been so thankful that you weren't a crying child."

"No, don't leave. I'll stop." I pressed the wet handkerchief against my nose.

"You were always such a placid little girl. You only cried when you saw an animal hurt." He poured water into the basin and dipped a cloth for my face. It felt so good.

"I hardly ever cried when I was a boy either. I didn't even cry when your Grandpa and Zeke rode off to The War," he said. "I was six years old. Your Grandpa held me in his arms and told me to be a true Duvall all my life. That I was to help take care of Grandma. She was going to have another baby—just like your mama is going to. He told me not to worry her—just like we've told you not to worry *your* mama. And he told me to obey her."

He poured a drink of water for us both and sat down beside me.

"And Grandpa left?"

"He was gone for nearly four years, he and Zeke."

"I couldn't stand for you to be gone that long. And did you obey her?"

Papa twisted his mouth under that fine mustache.

"No," he said, "only when I chose to. I was a wild boy. I had been given just about everything I ever wanted. I had the freedom of the plantations, servants, everything. I worried her. I know now how much. And I was even wilder at ten years when your Grandpa came back sick and weak from being in a Yankee prison. Zeke brought him home

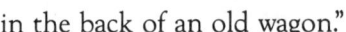
Chapter 8

in the back of an old wagon."

I pictured Grandpa sick and weak, nearly dying, in the back of a wagon. Oh, it was terrible.

"You see, your Grandma could not restrain me, and I had no self-control. She had too much to deal with during those days—two children, the plantations, Negroes—or what was left of them—and the houses. When your Grandpa came home, he was nearly dead, just a few breaths away, and I spoiled and undisciplined without a man to rein in that wildness, that spirit we Duvalls have—you have that spirit too. Oh, you're a bit shy now and then, but you've got that spirit, Bessie."

He touched my wet cheek and held my hand.

"Well, anyway, your grandpa lay up in his bed, too weak to raise his hand for months. He listened to my insolence to your Grandma and to our colored people. He didn't know that I was doing even worse out of his hearing. But Zeke knew. Then, when Pa was strong enough to hold a belt, he took me down to the trunk room. I'll never forget that room. He beat me and said my heart was as hard as stone. And it was. I couldn't blame him for doing it."

"Did it hurt?" I asked.

"I guess it did. I don't remember much about that. I do remember that he said he was ashamed."

"Mama said you were ashamed of *me*," I whined and turned away, looking at Jane Anne's bed.

"And rightly so. I haven't seen such poor behavior since *I* was a boy," he answered.

"Did you stop being mean after your strapping?"

He thought for a moment. "I guess I did for a few days."

"And you were never bad again?"

Papa laughed at that. "Oh, I was still spoiled, wild and mean. I was just careful not to let my parents know it. I was mean until I had been at The Citadel for a couple of years."

He sat there shaking his head.

"Not you, Papa!"

"Yes, *me, your* papa. I struggle even today with an unkind spirit and a selfish heart. At times I would like to tell Aunt Alberta just what I think. But I can't, and I won't."

"Because it's not right," I declared.

"That's it. Because it's not right," he repeated.

I asked, "What made you stop being mean at the Citadel?"

"When I was there I learned about integrity. I guess I was old enough to notice it by then," he said. "Your Grandpa and Grandma had scraped money together to send me to school there after The War. I

The Treasure of Pawley's Island

didn't want to go. I wanted to stay back at the plantation, to ride and hunt, to do what I wanted. I don't know how they paid my way there. I took so much for granted back then. Zeke would ride a mule down to Charleston, with money from my Pa hidden under his shirt. He'd be standing outside the barracks, waiting to give me a tin of cake and cookies from mama. I remember standing there one day at the side of the parade field when Zeke rode that mule off toward home, and I was crying like you did today. Only I wasn't angry, and I hadn't talked ugly to an adult."

"I'd have climbed up on that mule and ridden home behind Zeke."

He laughed and stood up. Papa walked to the window to look out. The sun had set by that time. He raised the window and a breeze blew across the room.

"I wanted to go home, but I told myself 'I will see this through. They must want me to stay here for many reasons.' I decided I'd stay no matter what, no matter where else I wanted to be. I'd be a man of integrity like Zeke, like Papa."

He looked to see if I understood. I was watching the mosquito netting above my bed as it moved softly in the breeze from the window. The wind was whistling outside. A nor-easter was coming in.

"Bessie, you tried to punish Aunt Alberta for hurting Grandma's feelings, didn't you?" I nodded. "You can be just like Aunt Alberta if you want to. Now she does have some wonderful qualities—she's generous and sometimes she's funny. She makes us all laugh. Doesn't she?"

"Yes, she does—but I'll ever be like her! Never! And I won't be like Jane Anne, either!"

"Oh, you're just like Jane Anne."

My heart was as dark as the room, and my feelings were terribly hurt. I sat up in bed, saying, "Papa—"

"If you aren't, then go ask Aunt Alberta's forgiveness."

"But she hurt Grandma!"

"*She* will have to deal with Grandma about that, not you."

"I can't! I can't! *You* couldn't change all at once, and I can't either! I'm sick! I feel terrible! I have a headache!"

"When you go to Aunt Alberta, ask to be forgiven, and give *no* excuses, not one."

"She was the cause of everything, not me!"

He was silent for a while. Then he looked at me very sternly and moved the candle closer so he could see my eyes.

"Never shift the blame. Now I expect you to go and apologize to her either tonight or in the morning. I'll stay here for awhile. Are you

Chapter 8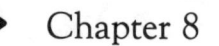

hungry?" I shook my head.

Papa held my hand as I lay back, hoping sleep would come. He told me that all people make mistakes, and the best we can do is seek the Good Lord's help. He only wished he had done that more often, he said. He talked about The Citadel and enjoyed reminiscing.

"Those were hard days, but they made me learn the value of persistence. Why, I almost ended up a man before I left, and nearly a gentleman—but not quite." He sat there smiling.

Before I fell asleep, I heard him say, "When it comes right down to it, Bessie, all you've got is your character, and I want you to be a lady."

And I heard him say with a chuckle, as he tiptoed out, "She does look a little like a pig fish."

The wind whistled mournfully around the eaves, and finally I slept.

• • • • • • •

When I awakened I could hear voices. My head was still pounding. I drank some more water. The voices belonged to Jane Anne and her mother, standing down at the stairs on the second floor. Jane Anne was just about to come up to bed.

I made up my mind to go on down there and say my apology to Aunt Alberta. I wanted to get it over. I climbed out of bed and crept down. Jane Anne was just coming up the stairs.

She looked at me with a start, as did her mother. The lamplight from the hallway showed Aunt Alberta's expression to be surprised and then grim. She stopped where she was, waiting.

I looked again at Jane Anne as we passed. "Humph," she said. That was beginning to be one of her favorite words to me.

I looked back at Aunt Alberta and raised my trembling chin. As I stood before her, I tried to make myself tall.

"Aunt Alberta, will you please forgive me for acting so bad today. I'm sorry I eavesdropped, and I'm sorry I yelled bad words at you." I looked back over my shoulder and saw that Jane Anne was listening.

She threw up her head and said "Humph!" again.

Aunt Alberta raised one arched eyebrow. Her eyes were rather hard, but then I saw them soften as she looked at my face. I stared up at her, hoping she would speak. She continued to look at me; I guess she was deciding what to say.

Finally, she cleared her throat and said, "Jane Anne, you get up those stairs and go straight to bed."

Jane Anne's indignant feet clattered on the rest of the stairs. I could hear her "Humph!" her way into the attic room and slam the door—but not too hard, or it would make her mother irritated at *her*.

"Will you forgive me, Aunt Alberta?" I asked again, in a pitifully tiny voice.

"I think so, child. I can't understand why you talked that way to me. I would have washed Jane Anne's mouth out with camomile soap if she had done it."

"I got a spanking," I said, and looked down at my stockinged feet.

"Good. You needed it. Now, I have some hair ribbons for you that I bought in Spartanburg last Christmas. Let's have a look to see which ones you like best."

In we marched to the ribbons. They looked like a rainbow. She gave me a special piece of chocolate mint candy, too. We sat on the bed and ate a piece, talking about the ribbons.

She smiled at me and began brushing my hair with her silver brush. Over beside the chiffarobe sat a huge blue bottle of Uncle Sumter's cough medicine. The room was cozy and warm. Bright silk quilts lay on the end of the bed. Pieces of her beautiful handwork were all about the room, throwing gorgeous color here and there. Every inch of the room was filled with irresistible things. I longed to put my hands on some of them.

Aunt Alberta saw me looking around and said in her crow-like voice, "Perhaps you would like to come visit me here in the next day or two. You can look at some of these curios. We'll have another piece of chocolate."

I thanked her for the ribbon and chocolate and said I would like to come back very much. I ran upstairs, undressed for bed and threw myself on it in a stupor. Too much had happened that day. I was sick, in body and heart.

◆ ◆ ◆ ◆ ◆ ◆ ◆

I must have slept fitfully most of the night, awakening at intervals and feeling ill from the ordeal of the afternoon and evening. I dreaded seeing anyone. When morning came, I was still ill and stayed in bed. I told Jane Anne that as she dressed. She said "Sick, humph!" as she went out the door.

I remembered the privy and felt sick. I thought of Louie. We were to have mapped an important part of the marsh today. When food was sent up, I refused to eat. Mama climbed the stairs to see me, saying how glad it had made her for me to apologize like such a lady. I told her I was sick and would be in bed all day. Then I turned my head to the wall. Later I ate a couple of bites.

Chapter 8

When she left, I leaped up and threw my linen cross-stitch square out of the bedroom window. It whipped this way and that in the nor-easter. Finally, it lit in a low tamarisk tree, well hidden from view. I was confident it would never be found.

Downstairs, I could hear Jane Anne giving orders to the servants. She was preparing to "hold court" in the early afternoon, and she wanted the rooms prepared "just so."

From my window I could see Louie's house across the trees. I looked out on his creek pier. There he was, sitting alone, fishing. I was tempted to change into my fishing clothes and sneak over to join him, but I did not. I turned to my books and my journal but could think of nothing to write. Then I heard Grandma's tread on the stairs. Teaspoon had found the rumpled linen square in the tamarisk tree. I hung my head and my shoulders slumped.

◆ ◆ ◆ ◆ ◆ ◆ ◆

Papa left early the next morning after he had come up to kiss me goodbye. It was Saturday and, as usual on Saturday, Grandpa and Uncle Zeke had driven the buckboard off the island, carrying Grandpa's medical bag and supplies. After they treated Negroes over on the Neck, they would be home by sundown at the latest.

I longed to see Grandpa and tell him how awful I felt, how guilty and ill. I knew he would understand. When sundown came, I fell into a fitful sleep that lasted off and on until morning. I seem to remember the entire family discussing me in the parlor that night; my name floated up the narrow stairway along with snatches of adult conversation.

When Jane Anne entered the bedroom, I had turned my head away. She made no effort at conversation. I felt terribly lonely.

Two days passed. I remained in my room, sleeping and occasionally reading, eating little. When Mama brought my food, she urged me to try cross-stitching, saying it would make me feel better to be busy. When she left, I threw the linen square under the bed.

"Come on down, Sailor," called up Grandpa.

"I'm sick, Grandpa. I've got a headache."

The longer I postponed going downstairs, the more I dreaded it. The headache became constant—from inactivity, Grandpa said, and I knew it was true. I walked to the window several times a day and watched Louie fishing from his pier or sitting on his piazza. I longed to go fishing, too, but then I could not find the energy.

Even Jane Anne became concerned. She left a tiny vial of perfume

The Treasure of Pawley's Island

beside my bed with a note to hurry and get well.

One night, long after all the others had gone to bed, another conversation climbed the stairway and reached my ears. Grandpa and Uncle Sumter were standing in the hallway at the bottom of the stairwell, talking.

"Now that Bessie's sick," said Uncle Sumter in a low tone, "you have room in the boat, and you need my help catching fish for all these hungry folks. Oh, I know you use the money I pay you to buy food and supplies, but over these last few years, all I have done besides that is shoot an occasional deer, bring home a turkey. I'll be glad to come along tomorrow," he wheezed.

"Are you having money problems, Sumter?"

"No, no money problems. I'm paying as usual. Do you need more? I'll be glad to pay more," he offered, adding, "I'm going to fish with you and Zeke tomorrow."

"Remember what happened a few years ago?" I heard Grandpa say. "You never wanted to see another fishing pole."

"But that wasn't my fault." Uncle Sumter's voice sounded whiny, like a child.

"It never is your fault, is it, Sumter?"

"I'll hunt then. I'm going to talk to Cuthbert about it."

"You have no real interest in hunting or fishing, Sumter. You're just being stubborn."

"I'll do what pleases me."

"You need to cut down on the flask."

If Uncle Sumter replied, I did not hear his answer.

◆ ◆ ◆ ◆ ◆ ◆ ◆

At mid-week Grandpa took me down to the kitchen house and sat me at the table in front of a big cup of green water. It was the first time I had left my room. He gave Maum Polly strict orders: "Don't let her leave until she drinks two cups of this pot likker. This morning and every morning until I give the word, make her drink a cup—or two—and some of that rhubarb you canned last year, or several spoons full of molasses and sulpur—here's the sulphur—and try to cure her headache, too."

Then he turned fierce eyes on me. "You will drink this, Sailor. I want my own granddaughter back so that she can go fishing with me." His burning look was enough to make the color rise in my cheeks, but I knew none was there. Then he patted my head and left, with a look that said to Maum Polly, "She's all yours now."

Chapter 8

I stared down at the dreadful liquid. The salted, strong-smelling water was left over from a pot of boiled greens, and little bits of green floated lazily around in the cup. As I smelled the pot likker and the smoky fumes from the woodstove, I made up my mind not to drink the stuff. No, I would not touch that poison.

Water for washing dishes bubbled on the big black stove. Maum Polly was making the morning gingerbread and starting dinner, all at one time, and her voluminous apron showed smudges of graham flour. She paused from beating sugar and butter to glance at the pots, then grunted, bent over and with delicacy put a whole peeled onion into the edge of the hot oven. Pleased with it, she resumed her beating, only to ask, "Where dat Hagey? Where dat Tassie?"

I looked down at my sailor suit. Jane Anne never wore sailor suits anymore. Well, I thought, I will get rid of this one. I will wrap it around a rock and sink it in the inlet, under the pier, or I will cut it with scissors and braid an Indian rope with it. Then I thought of Louie, out fishing without me. Was he finding the treasure without me too? No, Louie—not without me!

"Why does yuh make yuh grandpappy so worried?" Maum Polly said. "Yuh happy, then yuh low down, then yuh up an' happy." Her hands swung up and down like pink fans. "Yuh was wild fo' weeks befo' we pack t' come heah. An' den yuh neber settin' in de house sewin' lak de lady. Out fishin'! Look at those speckles on yuh cheeks!" She pointed. "Yuh runs 'round lak uh chicken with he haid wrung off!"

My head hung even lower, but I shot back, "And you fuss at me everytime you see me. I'm going to tell Mama on you!"

Her eyes flashed and she loomed over me in the crowded room. Behind her I could see the shelves full of condiments and canning jars, their contents painting a patchwork against the gray boards. Barrels of rice, flour and cornmeal sat in the corner, and pots and pans swayed above the stove like birds coming to roost. Maum Polly was a tyrant in her kitchen, but she was famous as a cook.

"Yuh tells her iffen yuh like! Yuh need another switchin' wid de peach stick! Dat's de best switch, an' it'ull learn yuh t' be uh *lady*!"

Her fussing was already making me feel better. Yes, I probably had needed another switching, one like Papa had when he was a boy.

"Now, drink t' de bottom! An' *git* yuh hand offen yuh forehaid, an' push up yuh chin!" She demonstrated dramatically.

Then, leaving the bowl of gingerbread batter, she gazed into an immense pot of dried, speckled butterbeans that had been soaking all night. After rinsing them, she added water and set the pot on the stove to cook for dinner. Ummm-um! Speckled butterbeans were my

The Treasure of Pawley's Island

favorite, and she knew it.

"See de bean?" she asked. "Iffen yuh drink, ah'll pick out de baby beans fo yuh. Now drink! Quick like, drink-k-k!"

I knew I would never taste a bean unless I drank that pot likker. My sad, weak eyes were reflected in the stinking green liquid. Poison.

"Put yuh foots in dis hot water," she ordered, setting a bucket of steaming water before me. "Now, ah cool it off some an' it take away de haidache. De blood run t' de foots t' cool um off an' de haid stop de ache!" I pulled off my wool stockings and obeyed her.

The hot water felt wonderful.

"Quick! Drink!" I grabbed the cup and drank half.

Maum Polly looked pleased as she plucked the roasted onion from the oven, smeared it on a bandana and wrapped it around my forehead, with my long hair hanging down in the back.

"Keep de bandana tied down to de haid, an' wid yuh foots in de water," she said firmly, "no mo' haidache! De hot water an' de onion mek de haidache run. Now, tell yuh Maum why de sad eye, leetle missie?"

"I'm poorly. I've been sick."

"Awww, ain't yuh got de family dat loves yuh? Ain't yuh got talky an' smiley wid Missie Jane Anne? Two leetle gels dat sits side-by-side fo' years?"

She worked with the batter some more, tasted it and licked her lips.

"She hardly speaks to me any more. She might speak one word or one sentence to me all day. She's too busy making *repartee* with her friends!"

"Ain't Bessie got no friends?"

"Yes, I have friends," I said, thinking of Louie.

"Hummmm," she grunted. "An' yuh ain't upset at fussin' wid' Auntie Alberta, is yuh?"

I looked at her knowing face. "No," I said slowly, "I guess not. She gave me some ribbons."

Maum Polly talked as she worked in the kitchen. She never paused. She pushed another stick of hardwood into the firebox of the iron stove and nudged at it until it was perfectly placed; then she poured the gingerbread batter into a well-greased pan and set it to bake in the oven at the other end.

"Quick! Drink-k-k!" she called out. I did, finishing the cup.

"When ah wuz uh gel, ah get so low, so low. Now, mah first husband, he were chilesom," she said, and I knew she was ready to tell me a story. "From de time we jump ober de broom, when he were sick he say he rather be sick dan tek de tonic. An' he die, he *die*," she murmured,

Chapter 8

shaking her head solemnly and sneaking a glance at me.

Then she raised her hands from stirring a pot on the stove, "He die sho nuff, an' he were bury wid his feet to de east lak any man. Iffen he tek de tonic," she pointed to my cup, "he be heah now! An' praise Gawd, Gawd keep *me* heah! 'Cause yuh Granny an' yuh po' Mammy needs me, praise Gawd! An' ah needs dem! Now, eat dis rhubarb an' taste it *good*. Eat dat slow an' it snap yuh up! Remember, it's not what happens t' yuh, it's how yuh look at it. Tek uh bite."

I did and it was delicious. I chewed it slowly, slowly, so that she would tell the rest of the story.

"I didn't know you had a husband before Uncle Zeke, Maum Polly," I said.

"Ah marry mah first man in slave time befo' de War. He were black as coal, black lak Zeke, an' he lib on one of Doc's rice plantations. He were Tupper. He were smart man an' not too tall. He were carpenter who build an' repair de locks fo' rice fields. It were a big job—now, where ib dat Hagey? Auntie Alberta keep dat woman busy, an' she know ah need huh in dis kitchen! Kin she cook, o-o-o-h-h-h, kin she cook!"

That was a high compliment from Maum Polly.

"Until ah were twelve, ah hep de ol' colored womens mind de babies an' chilrens at de slave nursery. Den when ah were older, ah work in rice fields an' in de Big House garden. Den ah marry Tupper when ah fine age, not too young."

In the midst of stirring this and that, she beamed at me as I ate the rhubarb. Encouraged, I held out my plate for more.

She dipped out a bit more.

Then she continued, "an' we had chilrens. Back when ah were wid Tupper, we kep' chickens an' vegetables. An' we et fish, rabbit, squirrel, deer, wild turkey, 'possum an' 'coon. Den in de War ah went to de Big House an' Maum Edda teached me—an' could she set de table? You think *mah* cookin' good?"

She looked at me questioningly. I nodded vigorously.

"Den yuh shoulda seen Maum Edda set de table! Maum Edda ambrosia settin' in de crystal goblet mek yuh cry, it were so good. When she got too old, she stand me by de table an' she set in de chair, tellin' me ebery pinch t' put in de pot. An' when she too old t' set in de chair, dey carry her in on a pallet, 'cause she not too old to rule. An' *ah* ain't too old eber!"

She shook her spoon at me, indicating for me to finish eating the rhubarb.

"Where dat Hagey? All dis cooking wid no help gwine kill Maum

The Treasure of Pawley's Island

Polly. After de War, we lef' an' settle on Sandy Island wid de udder folk. Dose niggers don't half work. Tupper start gettin' sick an' nobody know where de roots wuz. An' ah drug Tupper back, an' yuh granny hug me an' gib me de Big House t' run. But it were too late fo' Tupper. Ah gib him leetle bite of 'coon an' 'possum, cause de woods still packed full. 'Possum meat kep' Tupper breathin' longer."

I remembered how Maum Polly loved 'possum meat. Waccamaw Neck was yet full of white-tailed deer, wild turkeys, 'coon, 'possum, bear and wildcat. Just before a killer frost blackened the red leaves of the persimmon trees that were scattered throughout the woods, I would lie awake, listening to the waves crash on the beach and, on the other side, hearing the long melodious notes of hounds as they chased a red-eyed 'possum in the darkness of the woods. Then would come yelps of triumph and ecstasy from the dogs as they treed the terrified creature.

The next morning that skinned 'possum might be swinging from a kitchen rafter with Maum Polly pleased as punch, cooking and singing. She would let it hang there for forty-eight hours at least, to age it. Then 'possum meat and onion smells would crawl out of the pot on the back eye of the stove and drift out the window to pull at our noses.

"Now, be de lady yuh is," she ordered me, "an' not no po' buckra! Ah seen y' Grandpappy 'bout dead an' y' Granny 'bout dead time aftuh time, an' she neber said one word. She be de lady. Now, *you* act lak dat."

My rhubarb was gone, and I felt surprisingly better.

"I'll go back to bed now," I said.

"No, leetle missie. No mo' throwin' yuhself on de bed. No mo' haidache. Go set by yuh sweet Mamma, who ain't seen her baby fo' days. Git yuhself dere an' kiss her sweet cheek."

She patted me, then gave me a push clear out of the door.

I straightened up and marched across the breezeway toward the house. But all of a sudden, out of the corner of my eye, I noticed someone standing at the edge of the tamarisk trees, near the kitchen. A boy was there in the shadow of the trees, motionless. It was Louie! He had seen me walk across. Why was he there? Oh no!

The blood poured out.

Chapter 9
The Oath

Would Louie recognize me in a dress, with my hair down and that old bandana around my forehead? He was staring at me. I could either run into the house—or speak to him and take a chance that he would recognize me. I hesitated.

"Excuse me," he called out most politely, "can you tell me if Elbow—E.L.—is any better? His grandpa told me he was sick."

I turned my head toward him nervously. "He's still kind of sick," I called back in a high-pitched voice. "But he's better today." I could feel the hot blood rise in my cheeks.

Louie moved closer to the breezeway. "He is? Do you know when he'll be back to fishin'? Tell him I'm sorry he's sick, and I'll be seeing him."

For a moment I couldn't reply. I was struck by Louie's refined pronunciation of words. He didn't even sound like the same boy. Then I realized he had that facility of slipping so easily from one dialect into another that he didn't even realize what he was doing.

I took a deep breath and said, my voice trembling, "I'll tell him. Who are you?"

"I fish with him. I live over there," he said, pointing toward Uncle Cuthbert's house. He turned to go, but he suddenly swung back around. "What's the matter with him? Did he catch too many fish? Haw!" Moving up even closer, he looked at the house, searching the windows. For Elbow, I guess.

"No, he's not real sick," I answered, wanting to get away but at the same time enjoying the predicament. "Mostly he's taking tonics." I moved back, well into the shadow under the roof.

"Tonics—he needs them. Puny fella. Well, if he's not real sick, may I see him? I have a message for him."

"No! He's too sick for that. What's the message?" I continued in my

Chapter 9

high-pitched voice.

"Please tell him Old Dirty is on the island. *Old Dirty.* And tell him I need to see him. And tell him to get well quick. And tell him I'm going to leave a yarb under that brick—that one over there—at eight o'clock sharp *tonight.*" Louie saw my puzzled look under the bandana. "Don't you know what a yarb is? *Yarb.* It's medicine made from plants. And the one I got is a sure cure—but he's got to take it in a cup of warm water. And tell him to leave that book, *Treasure Island,* under that brick for me to pick up when I leave the yarb. Maybe you can put it there if he's too sick to do it. Please tell him I spotted something on the map. Tell him about the brick. I need to *practice,*" he said, moving yet closer and staring at me, hard.

"Practice?" I asked, moving back again.

"You know, running in here like an Indian and picking up the book quick as a flash, and leaving the yarb and not being seen. You never know when you'll be needing that skill."

Finally, he turned to leave.

"Too bad you wasn't a boy," he said as he loped out the driveway.

◆ ◆ ◆ ◆ ◆ ◆ ◆

The gray afternoon sky sent down a steady, cold spring rain that lasted until late in the day. I marked several pages in *Treasure Island* for Louis to study, carefully wrapped it in greased paper to keep out the water, put it in an old pillow slip and placed the brick firmly on top of it, all at about sundown. The dogs sniffed at it a couple of times and lay back down.

As I sat in the parlor with my family that evening—the first time in several days—I thought they were pleased to see me much improved. Even Jane Anne was cordial to me, sitting beside me and showing me her handiwork and talking about one of her beaux in a quiet voice. I learned all about him, even to how he wore fine shirts sewn together with silk thread. At eight sharp we were listening to Grandpa read, doing mending and needlepoint—and cross stitch—by the illumination lamp. The glass globe magnified the light, sending luminescence onto our handwork.

To all appearances, I was hard at work on my cross-stitching. When the clock chimed eight times, Grandpa's setters gave a couple of sharp barks outside near the kitchen, then a low growl, then nothing. They were silent. Immediately I thought of Louie and wondered why the dogs had not continued barking if they had noticed him in the darkness.

The Treasure of Pawley's Island

At about eight-thirty I tiptoed out, making an excuse to go to the kitchen house. I found a little cloth pouch with the yarb in it, lying where Louie had said it would be, under the brick. A note in it said, "Best wishes for a fast recovery. We have got much work to do. Take this yarb tonight. Stir it in one cup of water. Take it three times tonight and you will be completely healed in the morning like a miracle. Your friend, Louie."

The powder was bitter, and it took quite a lot of character to swallow that yellow stuff stirred in water. But I knew it would work.

I was fine the next morning. My headache was gone, although I was tired from making myself wake up during the night to drink the stuff.

Grandpa found me before dawn on the kitchen steps, dressed as a boy, eager to go fishing. He smiled with delight and showed me the bucket of cold fried fish we were going to eat out on the strand. "You feel strong enough to go out there, don't you?" he asked, smiling.

"Yes, Grandpa," I answered, smiling up at him. I looked forward to seeing Louie and getting back to work on the map. He then declared, "I'm surprised you recovered so quickly. Sometimes Maum Polly is a better doctor than I am."

Things were back to normal, finally, and I couldn't wait to see Louie. I hoped he would tell me more about Old Dirty—and I was determined to find out what he had discovered on our treasure map.

But while Uncle Zeke was loading the buckboard, raindrops began to fall.

"I'm not taking you out in this weather," proclaimed Grandpa, looking up at the sky. "Zeke, unload the buckboard and then walk over to tell Cuthbert we won't be fishing this morning. Sailor, you run back into the house before it really starts to pour."

Oh, disappointment.

Later in the morning a gale wind sprang from the nor-east, bringing a resurgence of biting rain and winter coldness which we longed to see the last of, and which prevented me from being with Louie. I knew he was over in his house, staring out his window, just as I found myself staring out mine, wanting to be out in the marsh, just as I was wanting to be there.

So once again the ladies in our house reluctantly donned merino stockings, warm shawls, and woolen coats. They had the servants light the fireplaces to warm up the cold damp rooms. The rain lasted almost a week.

Finally, when the rain stopped drenching the island, the bitter coldness continued. When at last the temperature rose, we were driven

103

Chapter 9

out into the brisk wind to seek the jovial conversation of Pawley's Island friends and relatives who were out doing the same, walking on the strand and searching for companionship after being house-locked for so many days. Grandpa said it was too cold for us to go back fishing. "Sailor, it's always colder out on that water than it is on the land," he told me.

I looked for Louie on the beach but he was not there. Jane Anne, in desperate loneliness, consented to walk with me in search of conchs, unusual seaweed, or any pretty shells that the stormy ocean might have thrown up onto the sand during the night. In a brief moment of friendship, we declared to each other that the leaden-sky days appeared to be "here to stay." Then she "found" the companionship of two young men who were racing their horses on the hard sand beside the water. I left her talking to them and carried our armload of seaweed and shells back to the cottage. After that, the young men were constantly around.

After several more days, the overcast sky suddenly parted to show a brilliant blue. In a rush, the days lengthened as springtime came to the Low Country. Over on the Neck, the crimson and white flowering quince awakened and greeted spring by opening their tight little buds. On the plantations, azaleas of lilac, rose, orchid, coral, red and white trumpeted spring's arrival. Drooping clusters of purple, winding wisteria, white and delicate blossoms of the fragrant bay tree and the green-centered dogwood blossoms were lacy against a backdrop of green grass and tender green leaves. Yet the coastal water was still too cold for pleasant bathing. It was this coolness that had helped delay spring on Pawley's.

On the very afternoon that the sun broke through, Louie and I sat resting against one of Debourdieu's tall dunes which overlooked the inlet, eating cold buttermilk biscuits and chunks of fried whiting while we studied the map. Above us the sun grew hotter and hotter. I was amazed that Louie wore his aged coat in the heat of that sun, and finally I said so.

"And I ain't goin' t' take it off in the weeks t' come either! How else will I carry all our gear?"

"I can help."

"Na-a-ah. You ain't strong enough. You been sick."

"I'm well now. If you won't let me carry part of it, why don't you strap it to your back in a cloth bag?"

"Ain't handy," he said firmly. "You dress how you like, an' I'll dress how I like."

"Louie," I asked, "why didn't Grandpa's dogs keep on barking that

The Treasure of Pawley's Island

night when you came over to pick up the book from under the brick and put down the yarb?"

"I tossed them some meat," he replied. "Like as not, if y' give a man or a dog what he wants, he'll stop barkin'."

From our vantage point, we could see the waves rolling into the inlet, pushing water into the salt creeks and lapping at the shore. We had spent the early morning hours surf fishing. Fat whiting, Maum Polly's choice—besides flounder—had been biting. But now the sun was growing hot, and I wanted a cool drink.

"Who was that girl at your house?" Louie suddenly asked.

"Uh, you mean my cousin?" I replied.

"Yeah, your cousin. Is she nice?" he asked, looking casually at his fried fish.

"I guess so."

"She didn't talk much. She looked scared of me. Well, anyway, we've eaten an' rested. Now we have work t' do," he declared. "See them down there workin' in th' sun?"

Down below, Grandpa and Uncle Zeke were seining for tiny shrimp and spring mullet to be used as live bait. Grandpa seined slowly at the deep-water end of the net, pulling it cautiously under the cool water in an arc around Uncle Zeke and toward the shore. They were in water above their waists. One long pull of the net was enough to bring up a wriggling mound of wee mullet, flounder and shrimp—all tiny, delectable bait. It was hard work, and they moved slowly, not wanting to step into unexpected holes or on unexpected crustaceans.

I knew Grandpa and Uncle Zeke had been awake most of the night at the Lachicotte cottage, where Grandpa had brought another new baby into the world. Ever-faithful Uncle Zeke had been ready to help if needed, and he then waited patiently for Grandpa in the buckboard as the long night hours passed, so that he could drive a weary doctor home. Now they were tired and I could see it in every movement.

"Now look here," said Louie as he chewed enthusiastically on a biscuit, "I'm gonna seal y' t' secrecy about this here map. An' no tellin' your Grandpa or Uncle Zeke. No tellin' brothers, sisters, cousins, or *anybody*—even on their death beds, 'cause they might recover if I was t' give 'em Old Dirty's yarbs. An' no talkin' in y' sleep. We're goin' t' swear an *oath*! Now, our oath is this—we'll mingle our blood on this here stick, an' then break it in half. You git *yer* half t' carry around with y' forever, in a pocket or somethin', an' *I'll* have mine. An' they'll always fit together like a two-piece puzzle, an' we'll notch both of 'em for each treasure we find. Now, git out y' knife."

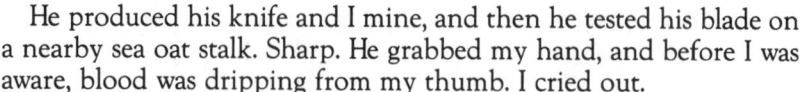

Chapter 9

He produced his knife and I mine, and then he tested his blade on a nearby sea oat stalk. Sharp. He grabbed my hand, and before I was aware, blood was dripping from my thumb. I cried out.

"Now!" he said triumphantly. "You cut my thumb an' then we'll mingle th' blood an' say th' words." He shoved my knife into my hand. "You're gonna hafta sharpen that knife someday, but if y' hurry, y' kin use it today."

I was speechless. Me cut his hand? And with a dull knife?

"All right," he said, "y' kin use my knife. Here," he declared, thrusting the knife toward me.

I couldn't move. When he saw I could not cut his thumb, he shook his head and gave me a lecture which went on for several minutes with hardly a breath.

"Elbow," he said, "y' got a million-kazillion problems—one of which is you are a coward. A *man* cannot be a *coward*, because he can't make it through life that way. The next problem is y' ain't got no muscle on y' puny arms, or y'd go ahead an' cut my thumb no matter if th' knife *is* dull. Bet y' can't lift ten pounds! Th' only good thing about y' is y' got more brain than a shrimp, an' y' bring plenty along of cookies an' cake an' muffins an' cornbread. Where y' get all that stuff I don't know. Now don't be discouraged. Y' got good eyesight, if y'd only use it. And y' keep y'self pretty clean now. One of y' worst problems is y' *won't ever talk*! You're about th' silentest person I ever seen. Sometimes when I'm with y', I talk just t' fill up an hour of silence. An' how come y' always turn y' head when I speak t' yuh? It ain't natural! Sometimes when I see y' trampin' along with y' puny body an' no courage, it almost makes me laugh. It oughta make me cry, but I'm not a cryin' sorta person. Now take that knife an' *slash my thumb*. We gotta get on with th' oath! Y' losin' blood, an' y' ain't got much on yer skeleton t' lose."

I stared at him in silence.

Finally I said, "I'm afraid I'll *cut off* your old thumb."

"*Get to it!*"

"I've never cut anybody with a knife before."

"Well, y' grandpa hacked off many a arm in Th' War. Ain't y' gonna foller in his footsteps? An' if y' don't open y' puny eyes, y' might cut my *throat!*" he yelled.

"All right!" I yelled back. "I'll do it! Just stop pestering me!"

He stared hard at me. "You ain't scared, are yuh?"

I was silent. "Well?" he asked.

"Yes, I am."

Louie sighed. "Yer honest. That's th' best I kin say fer yuh. Git t'

The Treasure of Pawley's Island

cuttin'!"

By that time the two red setters had figured out that something interesting was happening up on the dune and had bounded up to see. There they stood, tired from chasing gulls, panting and quivering from exertion, dripping saliva and breathing into our faces while they sniffed at me and watched my blood drip, drip in the white sand. "Get, you old dogs!" I yelled at them and stamped my foot.

I worked up my courage by pretending Louie's thumb was a stick of wood and gave him a good cut that made him jump. The blood poured out. "Huh," he said. "When yuh do it, yuh do it."

He smeared blood from his thumb and mine all around the little piece of driftwood and then pressed our thumbs together. It was a serious ceremony.

"Now, here's th' oath," he said. "I swear before God up above I'll never, never tell anything Louie tells me not to tell about his map or treasure, cause he's th' leader an' if he says not t' tell, I won't tell. An' if he fergets to tell me not t' tell, I won't tell anyway, 'cause I have made an oath."

"Louie," I said, "I won't tell, but I know it's a very, very serious thing to swear before God. Grandpa says—"

"Ferget what y' Grandpa says! I *know* how serious it is. Oaths are written down in a *big* book in Heaven. Now look, Elbow, this treasure is goin' t' be split in half between two—just two—people, an' I ain't takin' that lightly."

So I swore the oath. But we had to smear blood on the stick twice because the first time it broke clean—Louie wanted some jagged edges that would fit like a puzzle. We blew on the sticks to dry the blood and wrapped them in a couple of bits of greased paper, then we went down to the inlet so we could hold our thumbs in the salt water—"to heal them."

Grandpa always said salt was a miracle curative for cuts. It had saved many a man in The War, he said. "A cut will never hurt again if you pour salt into it immediately," he told me. "It will heal twice as fast, and it also stops the bleeding. Of course," he admitted, "it does hurt some when the salt is poured in."

Salt would also heal colds, according to Grandpa. "A cold will only last a day or so if you swim in the ocean, dive under and get salt water into your nose—providing you don't keep eating cookies."

As we bathed our cuts in the shallow water, Louie said, "Look me in th' eyes, Elbow, even if it's a strain fer yuh. I been figurin' whether or not t' mention this. I been worried all those days it was rainin'—now, remember y' oath—look here on th' map an' out there on th' marsh.

Chapter 9

That mud flat out there is shaped like an *arrow*, or an *arrow head*. An' it's pointin' this way, just this way. Ain't that the peculiarest thing y' ever saw? Th' way I figure it, th' pirates carved up a mud flat an' left it pointin' back t' th' treasure by that sign—a clue that wouldn't be noticed easy. 'Cause just who is goin' t' notice a *mud flat*? I mean, *I* almost didn't!"

"But how in the world can a mud flat be carved up?" I asked. "With those long pirate swords—or maybe with shovels?" Louie nodded. "Well, that is strange."

But then I told him that to me an arrow-shaped flat was no more peculiar that the T-shaped one out from the inlet pier behind our house, or the S-shaped one up near the north inlet, and then I told him that a wagon yoke was sticking out of one of those dunes over there—had he seen it?" That seemed far, far stranger to me.

Louie yelled and broke out of the shallow water at a gallop, his cut finger forgotten, and headed between the dunes where I pointed. Sure enough, there was the wagon yoke, gray tips exposed from the side of the tall dune. Louie was confounded.

"Now what is an old wagon doing buried under a dune? Why ain't y' ever mentioned this afore?" he bellowed.

"I only spotted it about a half hour ago, when we were eating," I answered.

"Now why ain't somebody dug this up afore now? Hey, maybe th' rain exposed it this week," he said.

He stood there staring at it. "Where's th' blade? I got t' see about this," He started to dig at the yoke with the blade from his pocket. I began pulling sand away with my hands. We dug and dug.

Louie could really make the sand fly. He was digging like a ghost crab, throwing sand up high in the air like one of those little white crabs that makes a hole on the strand and throws sand out behind him as he digs. Back, back we dug, far into the dune, uncovering the small wagon as we went. Finally we had just about dug the damp sand away from the front half of the wagon.

"I'm going to stop," I gasped after a while longer. I pitched myself down on the sand.

Louie's face was so red that it was almost purple. Sweat was pouring down his face and neck. He flung off his heavy coat in triumph.

"At last, at last, at last! We found something at last!" he crowed, falling flat on the dune, gasping and twitching. He was caught between excitement and exhaustion.

"If there's nothing under there but the wagon, what does it mean? How in the world did it come to be covered up?" Louie asked.

The Treasure of Pawley's Island

We contemplated the old wagon. It was rotting under the sand. Some of the old boards were broken. It looked like an old wagon, just an old wagon covered with sand.

We dug a while longer and then stopped. Nothing appeared in the sand but more of the wagon.

"Surely we can find some reason it was buried here," I said.

"I'm goin' t' think about it, an' I'll find that reason," replied Louie.

He stood there staring at it. Then we heard Uncle Zeke calling to us. It was time to go fishing with the minnows and live shrimp.

"Ain't that th' way it always is? Y' find somethin' an' then y' hafta quit. We're comin'!" he yelled to them. "Now listen," he said to me as we stared through the dunes, "we got work t' do, real work. We got t' figure this thing out. An' now is when your oath starts t' work, so don't you speak a word about this to nobody, especially to that *girl* at your house."

"I won't," I answered. "I'll never break my oath."

"If you tell her, she can't keep it a secret. I ain't known many girls, but every girl I ever knew couldn't keep a secret."

"Well, I've known a lot of girls, and most of them could keep a secret, most of the time."

We walked through the dunes. High tide was in, and the arrowhead mud flat stood out more clearly now that it was surrounded by inlet water.

"Yep!" exclaimed Louie. "Just as I thought. The arrow points right to the wagon. An' sittin' somewhere back in there on Debbie-doo, before our very eyes might be th' treasure."

"If Old Dirty were here," I replied, "he'd say that mud flat is pointing at the wagon, and the wagon yoke is pointing *back* into the myrtle bushes of Debourdieu."

Louie stopped stock still and looked at me. He looked from the mud flat back toward the dune. Then he nodded to me.

"Tomorrow," said Louie, "we're comin' back tomorrow. No matter what, we're coming back."

We shook our heads. We couldn't believe it. The arrowhead mud flat and the dune-covered wagon surely pointed toward the treasure.

Straight over the bushes it sailed, straight and true.

Chapter 10
Old Dirty

At first grandpa could not understand why Louie and I wanted to explore part of Debourdieu, the part across the inlet from Pawley's, the wooded section behind the tall dunes. Louie told him straight out that we would be seriously hunting for pirate treasure, and Grandpa reacted just as Louie wanted: His youthful green eyes crinkled into a smile, he laughed and said we could go exploring. While he and Uncle Zeke fished, we were to be allowed hours of exploring, within calling distance of the tall dunes.

We stood on top of the wagon yoke dune and contemplated our strategy for exploring. Beyond us lay thick wax myrtles that grew out of white sand. The myrtle thicket seemed like an endless stretch. Sea breezes had sculptured the myrtle bushes until they resembled firm hillsides covered by leafy grass. The compactness of those bushes invited us to run up their sloped sides and over into unknown terrain. It was impossible but compelling. The bushes were so thick that we could see no immediate passage through them.

The mysterious buried wagon urged us onward. Wildly, Louie suggested we hack our way through with heavy knives and hatchets. "We kin do it!" he declared. "Three full days and we kin have a straight tunnel through that stuff."

"Three days!" I said. "Why not throw a rock tied to a line over it? Then we can look for a way through somewhere around here."

"Straight over th' myrtle? An' then run around somewheres an' find that rock? Why, I kin do that. You'd never throw it straight—it'll have to be in line with that mudflat back there an' this wagon—but I kin do it."

"It's the very thing," I declared, pleased at having thought of it.

"It's th' very thing," he echoed. "*I'll* have ta do it."

"Well, good. I don't want to. And if I threw it and messed up, you'd

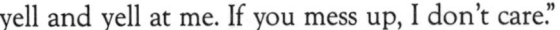
Chapter 10

yell and yell at me. If you mess up, I don't care."

"If I mess up, we're goin' t' hack our way through, so git yer hackin' arm ready. Now, have we got a line long enough?"

We checked our exploring gear, which was packed in two large tin buckets with handles. We had a hundred or more feet of stout string, a small book with blank pages, cedar pencils, a generous supply of gingerbread with lemon sauce, some citronella to wipe around our eyes to ward off the gnats, our sharpened knives, a bottle of fresh water, a compass, an old rusty sword that Louie had vowed to sharpen and shine until it blinded me, two rusty hatchets, and some lemon-drop candy.

We searched the inlet beach for a rock and found a flat slab of sandstone about five inches across. Louie tied the cord on with "sailor's knots." He stood on tiptoe, peering over the bushes.

"All I kin see over those bushes is more bushes an' then trees, all kinds of trees."

He handed me the end of the cord. "Git a good grip on that cord," he said, "'cause it might jerk outta yer hands."

I tied it around my wrist. He looked over his shoulder at the mud flat and heaved that rock. Straight over the bushes it sailed, straight and true.

"See, I been practicin'," he said. "You take that as an example of what a man is supposed t' be able t' do. I practice throwin' rocks every day. About an hour, I guess. Usually off the creek pier and into th' marsh. Sometimes at th' birds an' sometimes at th' crabs. Now you take that as an example as t' whatcha oughta be doin'."

"What do we do next?"

"Hand me that cord." He tied it to the handle of the sword and stuck the sword deep in the top of the dune. Behind us lay the strange, desert-like band of dunes, undulating as if they were white waves. Here and there sat patches of yuccas. The white sand gleamed with a silky sheen, piled in peaks in that white and green corridor. The sandy floor was sprinkled with conchs, angel wings and scallops, half-buried shells of the deep.

We turned, picked up our buckets and looked for a break in the wax myrtle bushes. About a 150 feet to the right we saw a hole in the bushes as if small animals had used it to crawl through. On our hands and knees, dragging the buckets, we wriggled through.

On the other side of the myrtle thicket grew cassinas, palmettos and small scraggly live oaks, yuccas and more myrtle in thick profusion. The contrast of leaf and color moved before our eyes in the unhurried breeze. We dodged the rapier leaves of the yuccas and made our way

The Treasure of Pawley's Island

to the rock and cord hanging over the thick myrtle bushes.

Louie dug into his coat pocket for his compass and took a reading. It was almost exactly south by southwest, so we plunged ahead a few feet at a time through the brush, with Louie in front trying to follow the compass. Soon the cord behind us was obscured. We passed between saw palmettos, myrtle and scrub oak. Louie pointed out animal tracks in the damp white sand—bird, rabbit, ghost crab and even a deer. Some of the tracks he could not identify.

"I don't see nothin' yet. Do you?" he asked, his head shifting back and forth. He was determined not to miss a clue.

"Bushes and sand. That's all."

We moved on, skirting more bushes draped with trailing plants. We walked to the edge of a luxurious growth of saw palmettos. Their pointed leaves looked bluish-green in the hazy light.

"I'm having a hard time following the compass, Elbow. Twenty feet either way will make a difference."

I said, "I think we ought to go back."

"Go back? Why?"

"I think we ought to go back and tie more cord from the end of that cord in a line through here. Then we'll know just what that mudflat and wagon are pointing at."

"You're right," he nodded.

But it was time to go. Thunder rumbled in the distance, and we heard Uncle Zeke calling us to the boat. We hardly felt we had started with our explorations.

Our next trip was planned for the following morning, but once again gray skies sent showers, then cascades of rain, for several days. It was a typical spring. I knew Louie was in his house feeling even more impatient than I. Several mornings Grandpa and Uncle Zeke sallied forth declaring, "Fish love to bite during rain," but they would not take me.

For those of us who remained behind, those rainy days were filled with family conversation sprinkled with jokes and much laughter, and some bickering between Jane Anne and myself. She had no patience with me, no matter how hard I tried to please her. The family gathered in the parlor and talk, talk, talked—until we were all tired of the closeness of so many people together under one roof where there was precious little privacy.

We finally retreated to our rooms and various corners to read special novels saved for rainy times. Those were days of sameness, with the rain tic-ticking at the rippled glass windows and my female relatives rustling around in their long white dresses as they moved from room

Chapter 10

to room, all the while urging me to make high efforts on the cross-stitch linen and read, read, read. Other hours were passed in playing checkers with Grandma or adding piece after piece to an enormous wood-bottomed jigsaw puzzle laid out on a round oak table in the parlor. Jane Anne's beaus stomped up the piazza steps, wet and bedraggled but ready for repartee. Every eligible young man on the beach came to call on her. I often sat in the other end of the room acting as chaperone, on Aunt Alberta's orders.

Late one afternoon of that rainy week, there was a hurried knock on the side door at the breezeway. Another beau, I sighed, as Uncle Sumter rose to answer it. For a short time he stood mumbling through a crack in the door, and then he returned. "That foul-smelling man and his helper have come to lead a hunt for the wildcat that's killing livestock over on Debourdieu," he announced. "Cuthbert told him to ask if the two of them could sleep in our stable. I told him they could. And his dogs, too. He's got more than half a dozen."

Grandpa looked up. "So you and Cuthbert called Old Dirty down here?"

"Yes. We did."

"Well, he's a good hunter—I've got no complaints about that. Old Dirty has a genuine game sense that's almost mystical in some ways. He can find game all right, and he'll probably flush that cat out."

"He will," said Uncle Sumter, nodding. "And I'm going to be there when he does."

"Are you going to use your new gun, dear?" Aunt Alberta asked.

Uncle Sumter nodded again.

"Well, I won't tell you not to go, Sumter," said Grandpa. "But be careful. Dirty will find that cat, but he always turns the responsibility for safety over to the hunters. He's probably right—you're all grown men and he can't baby you in the woods. I've never seen that black man Dirty has with him. He must have found him in the past year."

"If Dirty has him, Claude, he's got to be good," wheezed Uncle Sumter.

"Yes, you're probably right. Well, you can have your hunting. Give me some clean tackle and a good fishing spot, a tight boat, a few companions and a pleasant sky—I'll take fishing everytime."

Old Dirty had earned his name by never shaving or trimming his scraggly beard, rarely bathing and never changing his clothes. Once or twice every year his cronies at Murrell's Inlet would throw him, clothes and all, into a salt creek when his stench became unbearable. He wore about a quart of alligator teeth strung around his neck on a

The Treasure of Pawley's Island

leather string and went barefoot winter and summer. Grandpa said his feet were as tough as wood. They looked horny and gray-black, with long yellow nails jutting off the ends of those things that barely passed for toes. From under his wrinkled hat hung saggy strands of greasy, matted, yellow-brown hair, and creases seamed his brown face behind his beard. His watery eyes were gray and alert, but they looked sad to me. Grandpa knew him to be an educated man, but no one could tell me how he had come to this point in life.

He could stick like glue to the back of a fast horse, but he rarely rode, preferring to lead his horse. And no one was better with hunting dogs. He talked low to that yelping, swarming pack of hounds, making indescribable sounds as he slouched along.

Old Dirty was a silent man, almost shy in his demeanor, except when he was discussing secrets of the forest in his low, growling voice. He never smoked but chewed tobacco, spitting ferociously into a tin can he carried with him. He had certain authoritarian and even superior elements in his character, Grandpa told me, but I certainly did not realize it that first day when I came around the corner of the kitchen and saw him sitting on the kitchen steps with a black dog at his feet. He must have taken advantage of the short break in the rain, as had I, for when I crept through the dripping bushes to spy on him, I could clearly see him eating his food from the blade of a sharp and dangerous hunting knife.

Old Dirty's helper, also sitting there eating, was a dark, dark Negro man of indeterminate age. Hardtime Swinton was his name. I stared at the pair of them, for I was unaccustomed to viewing such singular and incongruous men, especially since we had few unusual visitors on our remote island.

Hardtime Swinton was a small, stooping man who rolled his piercing eyes back and forth and flashed a suspiciously broad grin, showing huge white teeth and bluish gums. His drawl lisped out in a loud, high-pitched whine as he caught sight of me hiding in the bushes. "Leetle gel," he declared, "de cook in dis kitchen she could mek boil' sand taste like de angel food!"

Immediately Maum Polly poked her turbanned head out the door.

"Yuh done had all y' gits! Now git down dos risers!" She was pleased with his compliment, but her normally placid face now showed some signs of repulsion. "Yuh too close to mah do', an' de wind blow de smell right in!"

Maum Polly set a steaming pot of coffee on the top step and briskly retreated, slamming the door ever so slightly as a sign of her attitude toward those uncouth men.

Chapter 10

"Dat ol' mama she kin cook, but she thinks she kin mek me jump. We see ... we see ...," Hardtime whined out. He poured coffee into two cups. Maum Polly might not like the two men, but she was proud of her skill as a cook and would prove it even to them.

Old Dirty did not speak. He gave the black cur at his feet a quick hand signal that brought the dog to his feet. Then he laid a piece of cornbread on the flat of the dog's long nose. The dog held it steady for a couple of seconds, then flipped the cornbread up slightly and snapped it in his teeth, as neat as could be. Old Dirty rubbed the cur's ears and murmured undecipherable sounds, looking past me as if I were not standing a few yards away.

Then Tassie came swishing around the corner, climbed the steps and brushed her way between the two coffee drinkers.

"Hey gel! Where goin'?" Hardtime called in his irritating voice. Tassie cut her bright eyes toward him for a moment, raised her chin and swept into the fragrant kitchen. At that hour of the day she carried tableware from the kitchen to the dining table in the house, in preparation for the dinner meal. Hardtime grunted in appreciation of her beauty. Tassie's treble voice floated out through the moist air. Hardtime grunted again and chuckled to hear her insulting comments about him.

Suddenly, as I peeked through the bushes, Louie walked around the corner of the kitchen. I moved back into the bushes so that he couldn't see me. He stopped in front of Old Dirty, looking at his face expectantly. Old Dirty's expression changed slightly.

Louie finally spoke when he realized that Old Dirty was not going to speak. "Dirty, you goin' t' shoot that wildcat?"

Old Dirty spat and looked up, "Eha, you here, boy?"

"I'm livin' next door with my uncle, Mister Cuthbert Haselton."

"He your uncle? An' where's your paw?"

"He died."

"That so? Sorry, boy."

"You goin' after that wildcat?"

"Unnnn, we're goin'."

"You goin' too?" asked Hardtime.

"I'll be there! Easy shootin' for you, Dirty," said Louie admiringly.

"Ain't no cat easy," drawled Old Dirty, slowly. "They're like rattlers— you can't tame a cat."

"You kin get him, Dirty," insisted Louie.

"He's cruel even as a kitten. Strikes out, goes for the throat every time," mumbled Old Dirty.

"Dat sheep ob Mr. Haselton's—" said Hardtime.

The Treasure of Pawley's Island

"What sheep?" asked Louie quickly.

"That cat killed a sheep last night, nearly full-grown," explained Old Dirty, slowly. "On your uncle's property. Drug him over that five-foot fence to a thicket like it was nothing. Ain't never goin' to take nothing for granted round a wildcat." His voice sounded like low, rumbling thunder.

"Y' gun ready, boy?" asked Hardtime Swinton.

"I'm goin' t' work on it now," Louie said eagerly. "When's th' hunt?"

"Few days," said Hardtime. "We goin' over t' tek a look. See what dat cat up to."

"Kin I go along?" asked Louie.

"No, boy, you get dat gun ready," Hardtime replied. He smiled, showing all his teeth and his blue gums.

"Kin I help you git ready?"

"We're ready now." Old Dirty looked away, and Louie knew he was dismissed. He went on back around the kitchen and then home.

The drizzle began again. I waited for a minute and ran back through the bushes and around to the piazza, into the house. I had seen enough to tell me those men would be interesting to watch.

I was cold and shivering with water drenching my skin, running off in rivulets, and soaking my hair.

Chapter 11
Discovered

As a pale green light crept over the dark island the next morning, we saw the world dripping wet from the days and days of rain. Water steadily dropped from every leaf and blade of grass, from every weed, from every bush into already saturated sand or into wide puddles that covered the sandy trail leading to South Point. The cool air was heavy with moisture as well; a deep fog was settling upon us that could hardly be penetrated by the sun.

"And you two want to explore Debourdieu on a morning like this?" Grandpa asked, as we rode along in the buckboard toward South Point.

Louie and I were eager, after many days of rain, to get started. We knew in our hearts that a treasure lay somewhere over there.

"Well, what will you do if it rains?" before we could answer he rambled on, "that hunt is going on over on the Neck. Sumter, Cuthbert and Daddy Buck woke up before dawn and rode to the highway to join about twenty other men, plus Old Dirty and his helper. The cat has already carried off a calf this week," he said.

"And a sheep," added Louie.

"Ah, that too? Well, he's a hungry one."

"I talked to Old Dirty yesterday," said Louie.

"You did? What did he say?" asked Grandpa.

"He said wildcats are mean," answered Louie.

"And you can't tame them," I added before I thought.

Louie started and gave me a look.

Before he could say anything Grandpa continued, "Now you two stay near the dunes. If you hear noise in the woods, you walk down to the inlet, and we'll see you and come over and pick you up. Do you understand, Louie? Don't walk so far back in those woods that you can't get out in a minute or so. Sailor? Are you listening?"

"Yes, sir, I understand. Not too far in."

Chapter 11

"Now, Zeke, where do you think those hunters will be?"

"On up neah de sheep, 'bout five mile."

"I told Sumter that he better take a couple of oil slickers. Do you have yours, Sailor?" I nodded and pointed to my slicker lying in the floor of the buckboard.

"Good. Now, what about you, Louie?" he asked.

"I ain't got one, sir. I'll be all right. I've been wet plenty of times in the woods with my—uh, hunting and all."

"Well, you'll be fine then. We won't be far away. Why aren't you out there with Cuthbert on the hunt?" questioned Grandpa as we watched Eyes the donkey plodding along through wide puddles. The water didn't seem to bother him.

After a moment Louie answered quietly, "Uncle Cuthbert wouldn't let me go along. Said I was too young to go wildcat hunting. I ain't young." I could read on Louie's face how much he wanted to be a part of the hunt.

Grandpa thought about it for a minute. "If you had been my boy, I probably would have let you go. But Cuthbert must have had his reasons."

Louie said, "He never had a boy, sir, just daughters. He don't know what a boy kin do. I even been alligator hunting with old Dirty. A wildcat ain't nothing."

I had heard snatches of talk about that wildcat for weeks. It had been killing a few cattle and pigs that roamed in the woods on the plantations between Pawley's Island, Debourdieu and Murrell's Inlet. Finally Uncle Cuthbert, Mr. Ward and Uncle Sumter (even though he owned no plantation and had lost no livestock) had called for Old Dirty to come down and lead the hunt with his dogs. No one wanted to lose his own dogs to a wildcat. Some of the local farmers and their croppers were joining the hunt, as well as several planters and their servants. Most of them would hunt on horseback.

As our buckboard rolled on through fog and puddles toward the inlet, Grandpa, in his gently way, tried to keep us from going exploring. He didn't want to forbid us. He knew what that would do to Louie—and to me.

"Don't you want to fish with us?" he asked. "Lots of fish out there, aren't there, Zeke? Rain *always* stirs up the fish." We shook our heads, and he tried another approach. "I really need your help this morning," he told us. "We're mighty low on fresh fish at the house. No? And all you want to do is look through that wet myrtle at the edge of the dunes?"

"And some of those trees behind the myrtle, Grandpa," I said.

The Treasure of Pawley's Island

He thought for a moment. "Well, you stay in that area, and if you get too wet or tired, you walk down to the water and call, we'll paddle over to the edge of the inlet and pick you up. Now, you'll call, won't you?" We promised that we would.

The fog and mist were heavy, and I was surprised that Grandpa would let me go on such a poor morning. I guessed that he felt sorry for Louie and knew he would need company. And he knew how unhappy and lonely I had been.

I thought of Uncle Sumter and wondered if he was the "fine hunter" that Aunt Alberta had bragged about—the "fine deer hunter," the "fine quail hunter," or even the "fine wild turkey hunter."

Grandpa had hunted with him a number of times through the years and reported him to be "an all right shot, sure enough." I wondered how a man could be a good shot but a poor fisherman. Grandpa seemed uneasy about the hunt. I wondered why.

When full daylight came, the mist was still heavy over the island and inlet. We rowed slowly across as the mist rose in sheets around us. The boat was crammed full of the four of us, our two big tin buckets stuffed with exploring gear, and plenty of fishing gear. Grandpa and Uncle Zeke were going to drop us off on Debourdieu and row back out to fish on the inlet side of the breakers and maybe into a salt creek. After promising Grandpa that we would climb a dune every hour or two and wave to him that we were all right, we hopped out on Debourdieu. We were anxious to get started. When the sun was almost overhead, at about noon, we would return to the same spot to be picked up.

We waved good-bye and trudged through the band of dunes to where the wagon was still poking awkwardly out of the sand.

Louie climbed to the top. "Yep. Still pointin' in there. Sometimes I think I've been dreaming that a wagon is truly buried there in the sand."

We loped down the dune, found our way through the bushy tunnel and traced our way back to the rock and cord hanging over the myrtle thicket. Thunder rumbled far in the distance, but the sun came out over our heads and surprised us. That's as it is in the spring along the coast—sunshine overhead and thunder—and sometimes rain—not too far away.

"Raining out to sea. Hear it rumblin'?" said Louie, and he searched through his bucket for more string to tie on. He had brought along another hundred feet.

"Sound carries far over the water," I replied, trying to sound knowledgeable.

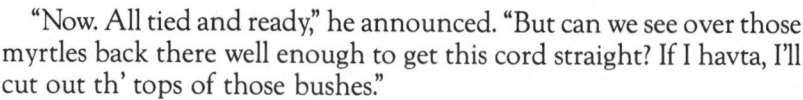

Chapter 11

"Now. All tied and ready," he announced. "But can we see over those myrtles back there well enough to get this cord straight? If I havta, I'll cut out th' tops of those bushes."

"Don't you think you could see *me* above the myrtles if I go stand on the dune and direct you?" I asked.

"I think so. You're mighty short, but I think so."

I directed him from the dunetop and soon we had the mud flat, the wagon yoke, and the cord all lined up, each pointing directly down the same line.

"Look," said Louie as it thundered again, "our direction was off about thirty feet, an' that's a lot when y' looking for a treasure chest." The sun went behind a cloud. Louie noticed it and said, "We better hurry, 'cause I'm thinkin' that it's goin' t' rain. Well, maybe not."

We tore up a old red handkerchief and tied it at intervals all along the hundred feet of new cord. Then we were ready to take the cord through the palmettos.

Thunder rumbled, much closer this time. I went back and directed Louie through the palmettos from my position at the top of the dune. When we couldn't see each other any more, I ran back around to find Louie tying the cord from palmetto to palmetto, keeping it in a straight line. We were tying on more pieces of red handkerchief when the wind picked up in a rush. We could see it waving through the palmettos as it moved quickly toward us.

"That rain is gonna be here in a minute," Louie announced. I was tying knot after knot as best I could when a gust of wind almost lifted my droopy straw hat off my head. Louie and I looked at each other but kept tying. Once again we had hardly gotten started.

"We're gonna get soaked!" exclaimed Louie.

"I don't want to get wet, Louie," I cried. Then I realized I had left my oil slick in the boat. "Run!" I shouted. "Let's call Grandpa and hurry home before it really breaks!" I started running back through the palmettos and under the myrtle with my bucket. Louie hesitated, then followed, and in a minute we climbed the tall wagon dune to look for Grandpa and Uncle Zeke, thinking that from there we could see them still fishing in the inlet.

"Where are they? Look way over there in the salt creek!" Louie yelled over the wind. "They'll never hear us, even from the edge of th' inlet. They don't realize that rain is really comin'."

The rain started peppering down, a drop here and a drop there. It wasn't even raining out where Grandpa and Uncle Zeke were. They kept on fishing, and in a minute they disappeared behind the bend of the salt creek.

The Treasure of Pawley's Island

"They ain't comin' t' get us—an' anyway, if they did, we'd still get soaked before we could get back t' th' house."

It began raining a bit harder.

"I got an idea," Louie said as he ran down the dune. He began stripping off his coat and hat. "We'll take off all our clothes an' put them in our buckets an' turn the buckets upside down! An' when th' rain stops, we'll turn the buckets back up an' put our clothes on *d-r-y!*"

He jumped around, jerking off his boots and coat.

"Why are you standin' there like a dunce?" he yelled up at me, but I couldn't speak. I didn't know what to say.

"Get busy or you'll be soaked," he ordered. His boots and coat were off, and he was starting to unbutton his shirt.

"Louie, I can't," I spoke feebly into the wind and peppering rain.

"What's th' matter with you?" He jerked his shirt off.

The rain was falling in bigger drops. I had to tell him.

"Louie, "I'm really a *girl*—and I can't put my clothes in that bucket!"

Louie stopped unbuttoning his britches and stood thunderstruck, his mouth hanging open.

"Jumpin' Judas!" His astonishment hung in the moist, windy air, suspended. He said, "You? A *girl*?"

"I'm that girl you met at my house," I called back to him.

I took off my hat, and my long braids fell down around my shoulders. He stared at the proof.

"I'll be a catfish's whisker...," he murmured. "Well...well, get down the other side of that dune with y' bucket an' put y' clothes in it! I'll be on this side. I'm not gonna git *my* clothes wet!"

The rain started coming down harder. I slid down the opposite side of the dune and started to undress. Soon I had all my clothes stuffed into the bucket. I turned it over and sat huddled on it as the wind blew torrents of cold rain and lightning flashed once or twice overhead. I was freezing, and I thought it would be a miracle if we didn't catch a fever or get struck by lightning.

The wind howled around us, but through the wind, rain and thunder, Louie's worried voice reached me. "Elbow, are you still there? Are you all right?" I shouted yes to both questions. The wind slackened a little, and I heard him say, "A girl, Elbow is a girl. I kin hardly believe it. A girl. With long, long brown hair...."

The rain poured on, and we were stung by wind-driven sand. I wanted to cry. Then, after a while, I heard Louie's voice again. "If I'da known this storm would be this bad, I'da—well, I don't know what I'da done, but I'da got you to some cover somehow. But it's not goin' t' kill us now, 'cause if that lightning was goin' t' kill us, it would have

Chapter 11

struck us afore now. So don't you worry over there, Elbow, we ain't gonna be struck."

To the south the sky was clearing, but the rain over us had not eased up yet. I was cold and shivering, with water drenching my skin, running off in rivulets, and soaking my hair.

"Louie," I called, "look to the south!"

"I kin see it!" he called back. "Ten minutes and this rain'll be gone out t' sea. So hang on for ten minutes, Elbow!" The rain continued to pour. He called again, "Why'd y' do it? I can't figure out why y'd want t' wear boy's clothes an' act like a boy. And t' top it off, *why* didn't y' *tell* me?"

I yelled back, explaining about my blue sailor suit which would have been ruined when I went fishing, and how Grandpa had brought me the boy's clothes, and how I thought if Louie knew I was a girl he wouldn't have wanted to take me along on our trips through the marsh—or even fishing. And all the while I yelled to him, I was thinking that he certainly wouldn't want to take me along now that he had found out. And I couldn't blame him.

The lightning struck on both sides of us, on the ocean and the Neck. Then the rain slackened and suddenly only a sprinkle was falling on us, as the storm moved out to the northeast in a black wedge over the ocean.

"I'm getting dressed!" I yelled to Louie. I began to jerk my clothes on.

"Y' almost ready?" he called back in a minute.

"Yes!"

When Louie rounded the dune, he peered at me. "Are y' goin't' get sick or somethin' from that drenchin'? Y' lips are purple an' y' look kinda weak." His wet face looked pinched and drained to me.

"*No!*" I answered indignantly. "I'm *not* cold, and I'm *not* going to be sick! You wouldn't have said that an hour ago, you *boy*! And you have no cause to say it now. Since you found out who I am, I'll bet you think I can't keep up. Well, I *can*! You'll see. And Grandpa will be walking over those dunes in a minute unless we let him know we're all right." I jammed my hat down over my dripping braids and grabbed up my bucket, nearly hitting Louie with it. I only wished I *had* hit him.

We ran to the top of the dune nearest the inlet and waved to Grandpa and Zeke. Sure enough, they were rowing toward the shore. "We're fine!" we called, waving them away. They saw us, turned around and headed back out to deeper water.

We made our way back to the cord that was hanging where we had left it. Louie was unusually silent as we pushed through.

Then he spoke, "A girl, Elbow is a girl. No wonder I thought you

The Treasure of Pawley's Island

were puny—but you acted just like a boy. I thought you were just a weak, puny boy. I'll tell you right now, I thought somethin' was wrong with you. I just couldn't put my decision on what it was."

We reached the point where we had stopped exploring.

"Is that cord tied tight?" he asked. "Now you go stretch it out about twenty feet that way. An' I'll stand here an' see if it's in th' right line. I guess you're no different from before," he added, "Y' just got braids hangin' down. An' I can put up with y' now if I could put up with y' then."

The clouds and mist flew away, passing out to sea with the storm. The sun came out within a moment and quickly warmed up the moist air. A breeze blew, and we could hear hounds baying way over on the Neck.

"It's th' hunters," said Louie. "They've moved on out since the storm is over." We paused under a palmetto tree to eat some gingerbread. "Now, ain't it good we didn't let these git soaked?"

"Have you seen anything you can count as a clue?" I asked as we ate.

"Not a one—unless we can count this palmetto. Look, there's another one right in line."

Not only was that palmetto in line, but about twenty feet away another one was in line as well, and we thought that was something. We tied the line from palmetto to palmetto, knowing that the line would not only point to the treasure but would also be our guide back from the woods to the inlet.

"How could pirates move such big old trees?" I asked.

"Palmettos ain't got no long roots, just a little bitty ball of roots. They take in water through their leaves. Look there, see how they form drinking cups where they join th' tree?"

"So a few pirates could have dug up a little tree and dragged it over into line as a marker?" I questioned. "And then it grew bigger?"

"An' it wouldn't take but a couple of them and a horse maybe. Or maybe not even a horse. Pirates didn't have horses," he remembered.

I said, "I'm going to add these trees to the treasure map, all right?"

"Add 'em," Louie pronounced. "They're th' only signs we got."

Beyond the three palmettos grew more myrtle bushes and a few scrub pines. Louie was determined to hack a path through them, so we set to work; soon we had a number of myrtle branches hacked down. After a while, an opening was clear, and we stretched the cord through. The sand under our feet turned into a gray mixture, then into a black, leafy soil as we strung the cord into a wooded place filled by small, bushy live oaks. Past those, towering overhead, were two huge live oaks. We tied the cord to a holly underneath the oaks,

Chapter 11

making sure of its trueness to our line.

The sky was clear. Sunlight poured down on us as Louie and I faced each other, listening. The bay of the hounds and the yapping of Old Dirty's ratty dogs seemed closer, much closer. Soon we would learn why.

The Treasure of Pawley's Island

But soon we saw the brown log slowly move toward the egret.

Chapter 12
The Pond

Under the towering live oaks where we next walked, light filtered down through leaves and branches just as light flickers into a half-shuttered room. The oaks were draped all the way to their rounded pinnacles with long, swaying Spanish moss. Up above, jaunty forelocks of fresh resurrection ferns marched along their horizontal limbs. A lone bluebottle fly, a dragonfly of vibrant color, droned past us as we looked around the untouched woods. Tiny white blossoms on delicate holly trees hummed with interested insects. Striped spiders ran helter-skelter before our boots, over and under layers of musty oak leaves and pinestraw. On the forest floor, a few scrub pines covered with trailing scuppernong vines braved the shadows. The leaf-carpeted floor beneath them was uncluttered with vines or bushes. Into the stillness came the distant call of a woodpecker. Then, up above the oaks, two ospreys shrilly cried together as they drifted in the warm air currents, back and forth against the yellow-white sun. The air above was warm, even fetid, after the rain, but the ancient forest below was cooled by the giant oaks, by cypress, myrtle, pine and palmetto. The trees whispered on the breeze, their branches flicking sunlight on the dead leaves below. It was a world apart.

Louie looked at the scene, "Do y' want t' go on?"

"I'm going on even if you want to turn back."

He looked over at me. "I'm pushing on, but I can't get used t' th' idea of y' not bein' a boy. I half feel y' tellin' a tale." I started to speak but he held up his hand. "No," he said, "don't tell me any more about it. I'd rather not think about it at all."

"I'll be happy if we can go on as we were before," I said.

He shook his head. "It's done now—but we're in this, and we ain't gonna turn back—oh, no! Now that you're a girl, I'm even gonna have to watch my *grammar*! Why do you have to be a girl? Well, I can't

Chapter 12

worry about it for th' time bein', 'cause somewhere nearby that treasure is hid. I'll truly honor our oath now, even though something tells me not to. Anyway, my family never goes back on an oath. My grandpa was a *captain* in Th' War, an' we stand by our word."

With that he had made up his mind. He marched up to the first massive tree-trunk.

"Th' line is pointin' dead center at *this* oak."

There were two giant oak trees, the first 100 feet in front of the second, and both about twenty-five feet in circumference at their bases, or perhaps more. They were tremendous, even larger than the giants on our plantation. We leaned our heads back and looked up into their ponderous limbs. It was breathtaking to be under and surrounded by such massive. imposing oaks.

"These trees are up on high ground," I said. "This is flat country, but, look—it's built up, higher than any other ground around here." We walked around and around, inspecting and kicking at leaves.

"An' th' high ground is what saved these old fellas from th' storms. Do y' think this is one of those old Indian mounds?" asked Louie. "One of my friends down near Beaufort has an island with an old Indian mound on it. It's some higher than this, and not so flat ... an' it has little trees growin' on th' top. But when he dug down under a layer of black dirt, he found it had oyster and clam shells in a great big heap all under it."

"Grandpa told me there are a couple of oyster mounds up near Magnolia Beach. But no pirate would bury his treasure in one of those anyway, would he?" I asked.

"Na-a-a, and how could these big fellows anchor themselves in oyster shells? This has got to be dirt under our feet."

In the distance came the reports of several gunshots. Louie drew up short at the noise.

"Old Dirty can always turn up game," he said. "I should be there with him, instead of here. I ain't hardly seen him since he got on th' island. Last year I had a high time learnin' Old Dirty's secrets while we stayed up at th' Inlet—an' now they don't even hardly let me see him. My pa would have had me right there beside him an' Old Dirty, goin' after that cat." He was silent for a moment. "I miss my pa," he said finally.

He turned away with his head hung down, and I could tell he was grieving for times past, and for his pa. I knew if my papa had been dead for less than a year, I would have been filled with a mighty lot of grieving. But at that moment I could think of nothing to say to him.

I know now that a person has to work through his own grief, and

The Treasure of Pawley's Island

it takes time. And words are cheap around grieving. Anyway, I couldn't think of a thing to say.

I also know now that a grieving person doesn't want to be left alone for long. That day I instinctively drew closer to Louie and, although we were silent, I could tell he was glad someone was there.

In the distance, the hunting dogs howled. We listened. After a minute Louie shook himself and sighed, "I ain't never worried about somethin' I couldn't do nothin' about, an' I ain't gonna start now. We gotta find some good, straight sticks—heavy ones, in case of snakes. Forget those huntin' dogs. We got work t' do."

We poked around under the two trees, wishing we did have sticks and glad we came across no snakes. On the other side of the first tree trunk, Louie bent over and found an old hollow turtle shell, stuffed into a crack in the base of the huge tree. It looked mighty curious, because someone had to have put it in there.

"Anything inside?" I asked. He shook the shell. It was empty except for dead leaves and bugs. Louie examined it closely and then stuck it into his bucket.

He sort of kicked at the rotten place in the tree. It was filled with mouldy leaves.

"We'll have to study this shell," he said. "Why anybody'd stuff a turtle shell into a tree, I don't know. It might mean somethin'—an' it might mean nothin'."

"It could be an Indian sign," I said.

We walked around the other oak but found no clues. Then we made our way from under the trees, down the slope and around scrub pines, bushes and saw palmetto to a freshwater pond surrounded by willow, blue iris and cattails.

The curious pond, so still and dark under the clear sky, was about a hundred yards across and partially covered by water lilies. On the opposite bank an egret stood motionless on one leg, near a log which was half-submerged at the very edge of the pond. Bordering our side were small troughs and ditches. They were salted on top with floating jessamine flowers that the storm's rain and wind had knocked from vines that crawled up the nearby pines. Those jessamine vines, plus scuppernong vines, had draped themselves on small trees and overhanging bushes like creatures that had come out to sun themselves. They crawled over the wild and dense smother of jungle-like thickets that surrounded the cattails, iris and bushes lining the pond.

The warm, brown-black water was forbidding and still. A breeze blew ripples on the pond's surface, where tiny insects leaped up and down or flew over it. Occasionally a fish jumped between the flowering

Chapter 12

lily pads.

It should have been beautiful.

But behind and to the right of us stood the mystery of shadows and light, and in front of us lay a pond that looked to be the favorite haunt of strange animals, birds and reptiles. I was ready to turn back.

"I believe this old pool would scare away an entire army of pirates," I declared. "That treasure has got to be behind us," I added, pointing back where we had come. "Up there, I think it's up there under those oaks. I don't think pirates would carry a treasure this far from water and then drop it in water again. Let's go back," I said urgently. "Come on! Those aren't ordinary oaks, Louie! The arrow, then the wagon, the palmettos in a line and the two oaks—I'd dig in the *exact center*, between the two oaks."

"You mean about where that old dead tree is?"

"Yes, right there! It's got to be right there!" I insisted, wanting to leave that pond.

"No, no, I think they dropped it into this here pond," Louie exclaimed. "See, this shell is from a *ocean-goin'* turtle, a sea turtle—I kin tell the difference between a snapper shell and a sea turtle shell at a distance of a hundred feet. An' those pirates stuffed it in there to be a *sign*! It's probably straight down th' bank from those trees, right through this little path th' deer take to reach th' water. It don't matter to gold and diamonds if they're under water. An' th' chest won't be far from th' bank, either, so's th' pirates could dive down an' hook a rope to it and pull it out finger-snap quick."

He scrambled back up through the cattails and felled a couple of tamarisk saplings with his hatchet, then skimmed off their branches.

"Now we got t' feel in th' edge of th' water. You move on down with this stick," he directed me. "Go on down that path th' deer take. The ground'll be firm there. Move on through those cattails growin' in th' mud. See th' deer tracks?"

Sure enough, the deer path was firm. I poked my stick into the water and felt a soft, muddy bottom.

"Nothing along here."

"Move on out to that spit of mud. Go on!"

"I'm not stepping in that mud! It's soft as cotton. I might disappear." I remembered miring down pluff mud. "You come on down, if you think it's safe."

"I'll stay back here 'cause I'm too heavy. Step on that cattail grass and those stalks—if anything happens, I can pull you out, but you're too weak to pull me out. Now head on out that way," he pointed.

The Treasure of Pawley's Island

I walked apprehensively toward the brown water through cattail grass and black mud. Behind me Louie spoke encouragingly as he rambled through the bushes, and in the background we heard the howls of dogs giving chase. They sounded closer. I plunged through the mud and toward the pond without miring into it too badly. At the edge of the pond I made a little cushion of weeds to stand on and began to probe the dark waters with the pole, expecting at any moment to see a cottonmouth moccasin look up at me from the swirling water where I had disturbed its home.

Suddenly from behind me came a thud and the sound of scraping. "Well, glory," Louie said, "it's a little dugout canoe!"

He had discovered an old cypress canoe about eight feet long—shallower and much lighter than those great cypress canoes the Indians once used although, like them, it had been hewn from a single tree. Louie had discovered it pushed up among some myrtle, sparkleberry and sweet bay bushes, its lower half in mud. Soon we had it cleaned out and in the water.

"Jump in," he said. "Let's pole it out."

In we went. Louie gave instructions as we poled along, the bow of the canoe slowly pushing aside the large green lily pads. Within a few minutes we had learned to turn the canoe whichever way we wished. It was fun. I inspected the canoe and remembered Grandpa's description of cypress. "Hewing cypress is like chiseling stone," he had said, and this canoe showed no signs of decay. Gnats and deerflies rose up to meet us as we poled around to the spit of mud and cattails that stuck out into the circular pond.

"Have you felt the treasure with your pole yet?" joked Louie.

"No, the only thing I've felt is old black mud that goes on down forever—and some roots, I guess."

From across the pond came the sudden rustling of a creature stirring in the brown carpet of leaves that covered the woods floor. A flock of crows rose out of the pine trees, cawing shrilly. Then came the sudden, penetrating call of a wild turkey, that wily and plentiful bird of the South Carolina wilds. It came high-pitched and vibrant—puck-puck-puck-pucka! The noise echoed through the forest and over the water, startling us both. I looked around, but I could see nothing unusual.

Back in the woods the hounds were making a considerable cry; now and then a stunning burst came from the pack, a whole orchestra of dogs crying in full chorus. Arooo! Arooooo! Their enjoyment of the chase sounded in the music of their baying. To me they sounded as though they were tracing and re-tracing their own scent, yet a few

Chapter 12

moments later I was certain they were headed straight toward us.

"Listen to that, Louie. Grandpa said if the dogs came toward us we should go back to the inlet."

"I feel it! I feel it!" he exclaimed. "If that's not a big trunk full of treasure then I'm a fool, 'cause there's a root down there shaped like a trunk!"

At the instant that Louie said "trunk," a large wild turkey, a long-bearded old patriarch, burst out of the trees on the other side of the pond. It made a powerful fuss, its heavy wings beating the air furiously. In a blue of feathers, with head and feet extended, it flew about forty feet above the water to a high branch in one of the old pines behind us. Then a mockingbird, one of nature's best watchmen, cut the air with its warning call.

"Somethin' has scared that turkey sure enough," hissed Louie. "*And* scared that mockin' bird. Sit low!" We crouched and peered over the side of the shallow dugout. The great egret across from us lifted its graceful ahead in contemplation of all the commotion. In the forest, the dogs cried out.

Then a long moment passed with nothing stirring.

But soon we saw the brown log slowly move toward the egret; with a snap, and a squawk from the poor bird, the *alligator's* toothy jaws snatched its prey. Shaking its head from side to side, the alligator—looking to be about twelve feet in length—devoured the bird.

"Louie! Did you see that?" I whispered frantically. "He'll be coming for us after he finishes swallowing that bird—let's go!" I started to push with my pole.

"Sit down!" Louie whispered back. "What are y' goin' t' do? Call him over here? An' look over to th' left, near those blue irises. I see four more 'gators!"

He pointed to where three more "logs" lay still, sunning their hides on the muddy shore. Still another companion was floating close to them in the water, nose pointing our way. Then suddenly one of the three on the bank, a six-footer, plunged into the water.

"Goodness!" I exclaimed. "Let's not wait for him to reach us. Push this thing back to shore!"

"Sit down, Elbow. He's not chewin' on y' leg yet."

"But look at him move through that water," I protested.

"Sit down! Sit low!"

I did as he told me with a trembling heart, for to me alligators were silently repugnant, waiting patiently until that moment of intense cruelty. I knew they had killed cows and bucks over on the Neck and on our plantation, and they could easily kill a man. They were not to be trusted, even in a drowsy state—"just like some people," Uncle Zeke had said.

The six-foot alligator surfaced completely and drifted slowly toward the twelve-footer which had just finished its feathery meal.

"Y' don't have to worry," Louie whispered, "those 'gators won't bother us in this dugout—unless you call them to look us over. Now *sit still*, Elbow. Listen to those hounds. Uncle Cuthbert said Old Dirty and Hardtime only took the under-sized and ratty dogs, but those runts will stand and fight and then come back to do it another day. Listen to 'em—they got something in 'em that better dogs ain't got!"

We crouched even lower and listened as the sounds of the chase slowly approached us through woods. I kept my eyes on both alligators, even while listening to the dogs. Then we heard a series of branches crashing in the dried bracken and leaves.

Something was moving frantically toward the pond and us. Soon it was quite near. Surely it was in one of the trees across from us, but we could see nothing. Where was it and what was it?

We could hear him tearing through the quagmire and briars above it.

Chapter 13
Hear The Tones of His Cry?

"There he is," whispered Louie. "It's th' wildcat!"

Suddenly my eyes caught the flash of a creature skimming a high branch, flinging itself to the next tree and scrambling with fluid grace up to a high forked branch in one of the great oak trees across the water. There it settled.

"Still, be still," said Louie urgently. He squeezed my arm so tight I almost squealed, but I hardly dared to breathe. The seconds passed like minutes and the minutes even more slowly.

In the woods beyond the cat, the pack sounded as if it had lost the scent and doubled back away from the trail. Still the baying of one staunch dog penetrated the thickets and continued, closer and closer. How could he smell the cat's scent in the treetops? Was he lost from the pack, I wondered, in the thick cover of that vine-entangled place? We could hear him tearing through the quagmire and the briars above it. He gave off inspiring notes. *Yelp, yelp, a-a-a-r-o-o-o-o-o-o!*

"Hear the tones of his cry?" whispered Louie. "He knows—yes, he knows what that cat has done. Don't ask me how, but he knows. But that cat is smart—he tried to lose that hound an' he's just about succeeded."

Up above the pond, the wildcat rested and listened.

"A hound don't like briars and saw palmettos," Louie explained. "They tear up his coat and lash his nose and eyes. A dog's got to have a real reason to press on through that. He must have tangled with that cat back there in the woods. Ooooh, I need a gun." His whisper was almost inaudible.

"Where are the hunters?" I asked.

"They've split up. No tellin' where they are." Then, with the lone dog's cry in the background, Louie raised his hand from the gunnel and pointed. From out of nowhere a figure on horseback appeared,

Chapter 13

slowly picking its way around the edge of the pond, dodging briars, pines and bay trees entwined with vines, heading for the two great oaks where we had explored. It was Uncle Sumter on a mare.

The mare was skittish and nervous, with her ears up. Did she smell the cat, and the alligators, and perhaps some diamondback rattlers? I wanted to signal Uncle Sumter, but Louie shook his head.

"No, that'll give the cat a chance to run," he barely whispered. "That dog'll be here in a minute, and he'll show your uncle where it is."

I looked up in the oak tree and saw the silhouette of the wildcat, perched behind leaves and moss, its tail lazily switching as it watched Uncle Sumter moving carefully toward that very tree, unaware of the peril above.

"He'll jump on him!" I whispered.

"Na-a-a—the cat would only do that if he couldn't run," Louie whispered back.

I remembered then what Old Dirty had said about wildcats: "They cannot be tamed, and they always go for the throat."

Uncle Sumter stopped and dismounted under the oak; he coughed, removed his hat and took the opportunity to pull his silver flask from a pocket of his hunting jacket. He drank long and slow.

In the near distance we could hear the cur persistently ripping his way through the woods, steadily and eagerly, calling to the rest of the pack to follow.

"Is that the dog that Old Dirty keeps near him? That black cur dog?" I whispered, listening to the eerie call. Louie nodded. "What's his name?" I asked.

"Sam. His name is Sam."

In a minute the other dogs heeded Sam's beckoning cry and came on, circling to avoid the briars. The woods rang with their baying, and now we could hear the clapping and whooping of Old Dirty and Hardtime Swinton as they urged the dogs on. Those whoops were perhaps more fear-inspiring than the dogs' raucous baying, and so a further shadow of fear passed over me.

I crouched and trembled, knowing instinctively that something would feel pain and die in the next few minutes.

The brave little dog named Sam came on.

Between drinks from his flask, Uncle Sumter's eyes surveyed the trees, the pond and the thickets, yet he did not see us. His horse snorted and moved nervously. He removed his gun from the saddle and checked the chambers.

"A Winchester thirty-thirty," Louie whispered. "Watch, he'll *pin* that cat. It won't be a minute." Uncle Sumter was nervous now, but he

The Treasure of Pawley's Island

looked ready to shoot, if he could find something to shoot at.

At the sound of twigs cracking behind him, Uncle Sumter nervously whirled. Seeing movement behind a nearby myrtle bush, he unsteadily fired two rounds. And then we heard a scream of pain—human pain.

"Don' shoot no mo'! Don' shoot no mo'!" someone moaned.

Then Daddy Buck stumbled out from behind the myrtle and iris, still clutching a stick he had used for beating the thickets.

"No, Buck!" cried Uncle Sumter.

Almost at the same instant a black dog bounded out into the opening under the oak. He howled up at the wildcat above. The cat had eased slowly down the limb over Uncle Sumter's head and there he stopped.

Daddy Buck stumbled toward Uncle Sumter, and I could see he was bleeding profusely from his right shoulder and thigh. He called out once more, then reeled and fell into the edge of the pond where he lay thrashing and moaning. Uncle Sumter seemed frozen to the spot.

As the wildcat tensed and prepared to leap, the twelve-foot alligator turned toward Daddy Buck, floating. Blood was spreading in the black water, shading it with dark red.

Then the pack burst from the woods, seconding the alarm raised by the black cur, Sam. They were leaping, bounding, howling, for they heard the wildcat's snarl of alarm. Their mouths foamed; the hair bristled on their backs; venomous hatred was in their eyes.

Suddenly three shots rang out. The wildcat tumbled, his heavy body crashing through the lower branches until he fell with wild gyrations at Uncle Sumter's feet.

Instantly the pack closed into a tight semi-circle around him. The cat was wounded but not fatally. He reared up on his hind legs, his forepaws raised like a fighter. The dogs shrieked as the cat snarled, dancing, rearing and crying in a frenzy.

While I fought the darkness that seemed to be closing around me, Louie lurched to his knees and began to pole the canoe. I had to clutch the dugout to keep from falling into the pond.

The bull alligator was swimming with slow and deliberate strength toward Daddy Buck, who now seemed to be in a half-faint, face up in the water, and so still. The alligators on the bank launched themselves into the pond with vigorous splashes, sounding like gunshots. They stayed on the surface, their eyes and nostrils visible and pointed our way.

I shook off my terror and clearly saw all the action on the bank and in the pond, and there was a mighty lot of it, too. I gathered my forces and poled with Louie, sending us faster over the dark water.

Chapter 13

But soon we could not touch bottom with our poles and had to paddle with them instead, so that we moved with agonizing slowness.

On shore the gallant Sam, with heroic defiance in his eyes, faced the cat. They glared at each other, fur bristling, fangs bared, dripping foam. Then the cur seized the wildcat on its upper breast and the cat buried its fangs in the dog's shoulder, near its neck. I could almost hear the crunch of bones.

The old brute alligator stayed on the surface, watching us with cruel eyes. We had to reach Daddy Buck before he did. My muscles ached with pain but I knew I must not stop paddling.

We reached Daddy Buck's side, putting the dugout between him and the alligator. Louie bent over and tried to push Daddy Buck closer to shore as I braced the dugout. The snarling and barking continued on the shore, calamitous noise.

Daddy Buck opened his eyes feebly. "Teng Gawd," he whispered. "He ib a mercy."

"We'll get you out," Louie answered.

Back on shore, Old Dirty and Hardtime Swinton had emerged from the woods and had their guns aimed toward the fighting wildcat and cur, who were still rolling on the ground with their jaws locked on one another. Yet they held their fire, for fear of hurting the clamoring dogs who were frenzy around the fight. By this time Uncle Sumter had backed up to the tree, where he stayed, frozen. Then the little cur Sam won out—he killed that wildcat by the force of his grip on the cat's chest. He must have crushed the cat's heart.

When the fight was over, the other dogs tore into the cat. It was a snarling, gnashing storm as they mangled his hide. Old Dirty dismounted, pushed aside the dogs and tenderly picked up the bleeding, gallant dog who lay panting and foaming blood at the mouth. He put him over his saddle and spoke to him low.

Meanwhile, Hardtime Swinton rode down to the water's edge. The old brute alligator was gliding closer to Daddy Buck. I poked my pole out at him, but he paid no attention, so intent was he on nearing the source of all that blood.

Hardtime called in his high-pitched voice, "Ram him in th' throat if he gits close, boys! I'd shoot—but yer jes' too close to that tail!"

I shoved my pole out toward the alligator and braced myself, while Louie swung us closer to shore. The alligator was now at the edge of the pool of blood. Quick as a wink, Hardtime leapt from his saddle and waded into the water waistdeep just as the alligator made a lunge for Daddy Buck. I poked my pole out at the alligator's jaws, ramming him, although it didn't seem to bother him much. He glided back a

The Treasure of Pawley's Island

foot or so, still keeping his eyes on Daddy Buck. Hardtime slipped his knife from its sheath and put it between his teeth. He heaved Daddy Buck closer to shore even as the alligator neared. Since Daddy Buck was a big man, it took quite a bit of struggling to push him up on the slippery bank, through the irises and then pull him up to higher ground. I jabbed the alligator repeatedly on the snout, yet he nosed right into the blood, searching for a stray arm or leg and paying no attention to my pole.

From high on the bank, Hardtime called out, "Hop out, boys!" We scrambled up the bank near Old Dirty.

He was bent over Daddy Buck, stuffing a wad of Spanish moss into the black man's wounds, pressing hard, particularly on his shoulder wound, to stop the gush of blood.

"More moss!" commanded Old Dirty, as he pressed down on the wound with the heel of his hand. We ran and pulled moss from the trees. He packed it in tightly and continued to press.

On the bank with his knife between his teeth, Old Dirty's assistant began to uncoil a few loops of rope tied to his belt.

I realized I was clinging to Louie's arm for support, and he was clinging to my shoulder. I looked up at Uncle Sumter. He had remained under the tree, staring blankly at Old Dirty as he worked over Daddy Buck.

"Louie," I whispered, "Daddy Buck's going to die."

"Don't say that. Dirty won't let him."

When we looked back to the pond, Hardtime had hopped into the dugout and was giving it a slight push toward the nearby alligators. Once beside them, he leaped from the dugout and astride the old brute, just behind its forelegs. At the same time he slipped a noose over and around the alligator's neck. His movements were as smooth as silk, but when the alligator felt Hardtime's weight on him, he seemed to explode.

Hardtime jerked the noose tight and tossed the rope ashore. Louie ran down and grabbed it. The alligator tensed and quivered, tensed and quivered. Its head and tail rose high out of the water. Then it vibrated so violently that water was sprayed high into the air on both sides, even onto Louie. Its warning hiss turned into a deep roar of anger, and its jaws snapped this way and that, throwing up more water as it tried to reach Hardtime, who clung to the beast as if he were glued to it. There was a look of perfect enjoyment on Hardtime's face as he crouched astride the struggling alligator. The 'gator's jaws snapped, and the sweep of that powerful swinging tail threw up mountains of water as it flailed back and forth—but neither jaws nor tail could

Chapter 13

reach Hardtime. The tail hit the dugout with crashing thumps—whack! whack! A bellowing scream came out of its jaws.

Then Old Dirty yelled, "Move 'im on up!"

He left Daddy Buck's side and joined Louie, hauling on the rope as hard as his sinewy arms could. The fighting alligator was pulled closer to the bank, with Hardtime still on its back. Then they hauled even harder, edging the alligator onto the bank. Suddenly Hardtime whipped out his long hunting knife and thrust the shiny blade into the brute's white belly just behind the right foreleg. The alligator fought on, legs thrashing, tail whipping, yet soon it was lying still on the bank. Its life force ebbed as Hardtime once more stuck his knife into the leathery hide, under the neck this time.

A few dogs who had lost interest in the shreds of wildcat padded down the bank to sniff at the dead alligator. 'Gator blood flowed down the bank and mingled in the dark water with Daddy Buck's blood.

Hardtime stood above the creature, looking down. "Dirty," he said, "he been de *debbil*."

I slumped against Louie in exhaustion. The dogs yipped and moved in circles, and I began to realize it was all over.

In a few minutes Grandpa and Uncle Zeke arrived and immediately began taking care of Daddy Buck. They directed the men to put him on Uncle Sumter's horse. then Grandpa climbed up behind him. He called to me, and Louie and I started to follow through the fragrant jessamine thicket and around the pond. Uncle Zeke led Uncle Sumter stumbling along behind.

As I looked back, Hardtime had turned the alligator over and started to skin it. Old Dirty was blowing the "Hunter's Adieu" on his bugle to call off the hunt. Then he chained up the dogs, who were growing more interested in the alligator's carcass. The remaining alligator had moved away toward the other end of the pond where his companions were; now only its nostrils and eyes were visible above the water.

Several hunters on horseback emerged from the woods and dismounted to watch the skinning and learn the news. They bent over the remnants of the wildcat. It was a tale to tell their loved ones.

My heart was still pounding, and I could scarcely breathe. I should have been crying—but, oh no, I was not crying—I had had my first adventure.

The Treasure of Pawley's Island

Louie hesitated, "Now," he said, "y' ain't gonna like this that I'm gonna tell yuh, but here it is."

Chapter 14
De Debbil

When we finally reached home, I pulled away from Mama and fled from Jane Anne's staring eyes to my grandparent's room next to the parlor. I took off my muddy clothes, wrapped myself up in my grandmother's robe, and crawled under a silken patchwork quilt. There I stayed, staring out their window until the sun became a circle of rosy coral at the line of the horizon, above the dark trees on Waccamaw Neck. High in the sky floated clouds of violet, orchid and lavender, their edges painted with coral from the dying sun. The stars slowly lit up in a purple and indigo heaven, and I continued to stare out the window as the clouds lost their glowing edges and the stars grew brighter. A still and quiet night came on, but I could not rest. My mind continued to race through the events of that day.

I thought of our innocent search for treasure, the hours we had spent looking, the 'clues' we had found. Had we manufactured clues for our treasure map where none existed? Did a real treasure exist? Surely, with such peculiar clues, some treasure must be there, waiting to be found.

I thought of the fight between the cur Sam and the wildcat. What a fight that dog had put up, what courage it had shown—only to be carried tenderly back and buried under a myrtle bush near the kitchen door. I remembered the howling of dogs as they tore into the dead wildcat, the rearing of horses, the sound of shotguns, Daddy Buck's scream of terror, the smell of blood.

I thought of poor Daddy Buck, who at that moment lay suffering unto death in his bed. I shed tears for the dead cur and the dying servant, then I remembered my own terror at the alligator's brigand pursuit of Daddy Buck's blood. And in my mind's eye I saw Hardtime Swinton as he confidently rode the alligator and plunged the blade

Chapter 14

into its belly.

Finally, I remembered the astonishment on the faces of my family members when we drove into the yard. My muddy boots, stiffened trouser legs and splattered blazer silenced their usual chatter. Mama alone had not shown surprise as she rose from rocking on the piazza, led me to the kitchen and washed my mudstained face with a cloth dipped in cool lavender water.

Hushed conversation from the parlor drifted under the closed door like smoke—whisper, whisper, whisper. I heard Grandma say, "No, Jane Anne, hush! That poor child needs sleep after her ordeal. Let her sleep!"

And I heard Aunt Alberta declare, "Jane Anne always needs me to calm her down—don't you, Jane Anne? Bessie needs a compress over those red, bloodshot eyes! I've never seen such!"

I heard Aunt Alberta's firm tread toward the door. She seemed determined to take a look at me. Then Mama said, "No, Auntie!" Her voice was trembling but firm. "We'll let her sleep as long as she will."

I smelled the scent of roses and knew Mama was hovering outside the door. I was about to call out to her when I heard Grandma's voice again. "You know you must rest, Sis Mary," she said gently. "Alberta will not disturb Bessie—will you, Alberta?"

The boards creaked overhead as Grandma led Mama to her bed. In a moment, Jane Anne whispered loudly to her mother, "I *knew* Bessie was up to no good when she crept out again this morning! Imagine wearing *those clothes*. Why, they should be burned! And who was that ugly, freckled boy she was with? Mama, what got into Buck to jump out and scare Papa that way? Did Buck go crazy? Papa must *never* hunt again with that filthy man, that Old Dirty!"

They whispered together for at least a half-hour.

Later I noticed how quiet it was. No whispers, no noises, even from the servants. The breeze was gentle, a land breeze. I reached over and slowly ate some food from a tray on the bedside chest.

Suddenly Teaspoon peeked through the door and tiptoed to the side of my bed. According to his news, Maum Polly was kneeling on the floor in the kitchen, calling for God's attention in long prayers and consoling Aunt Hagey, who was moaning and groaning most earnestly, fearful for her husband's life. And rightfully so.

"Ever' minute Maum Polly send me t' Doc an' Uncle Zeke way out in de cabin," said Teaspoon, "wif de hot boilin' water, de white towel, de crack ice, de clean bowl! Holy angel mus' be near, 'cause dey try, try, *try* to save old Buck, but he dyin'—an' Old Dirty he set on de step like a rock, lookin' at de mound ob dirt over dat cur. He spit juice in de tin can lak all forty an' look down at de dirt. Ah stuck my haid through de myrtle an' seen him bow down he haid when he bury dat chewed-up dog. No tear run down he chin, he just bow de haid. An' den Hardtime Swinton set down beside him on de riser, foldin' and rollin' de cigarette, an' de cigarette, an' de cigarette!

"An' ah hear Hardtime talkin' at Tassie when she tek towel an' water t' Doc. 'Hurry bak, gel', he say. 'Yuh know ah pay de ol' conjure woman uh silver dime t' mek Tassie my gel. Come set heah 'side yo' Hardtime.' An' ol Buck mus' be hearin' de bugle, 'cause he ain't got no mo' red blood! Dat blood all ran out in de pond fo' de 'gator t' eat up. An' Hardtime drink smelly stuff fum de jar, an' den he grab Tassie in de bushes, an' she giggle an' mek Maum Polly mad as catfish! She snatch dat Tassie out an' pop wid de wooden spoon an' say to hab mo' respeck f' de dyin'."

Alarmed, I sat up. "Daddy Buck isn't dead, is he?"

Teaspoon looked wise. "Daddy Buck got one foots at de gate."

"Well, you go find out how he is this very minute," I commanded.

He ignored me and prattled on, "Mis-tuh Sumter lock de door up in he room an' gwine neber, neber come out. Ah stand on de Lookout risers an' calls, 'Mis-tuh Sumter! Come outta yo' room! Tell *why* yuh shoot ol' Buck! Come down, yuh *shooter!*' Ah see Mis-tuh Sumter stare uh hole in de ocean. Den he look down t' me an' neber, neber move—an' neber, neber say uh word."

"Oh, Teaspoon, he might beat you if he hears you!"

"Naw. De wind blow de words way, way down de sho', an' he neber, neber hear. But iffen he hear, ah gwine ask him one mo' time."

When Teaspoon left, my throat had a lump in it. He had dared to face Uncle Sumter, something I would never dare to do.

Why had he shot Daddy Buck? Had he sensed that wildcat? Had the "devil" made him shoot Buck? Or had it been God who made him shoot? Was Satan in those hideous alligators when they went after Daddy Buck's blood? And who shot the wildcat up in the tree?

I was about to settle back into the mound of down pillows and come to some decisions about it all when I heard the sound of something hitting the side of the house up high under the eaves. Ping! Ping! Then it skimmed down the side of the house and plunged into the yuccas under the window. Someone was throwing rocks up at my attic window.

I crawled from the quilts and stared into the darkness. The yuccas stood at attention below, their swords rigid and sharp. And there was Louie, weaving his way through them with care. He poised to throw another shell.

"*Louie!*" I cried. "What *are* you doing?"

Chapter 14

"Elbow! Is that you? How's Daddy Buck? Is he dead? I can hear his wife puttin' up a fuss back there in the kitchen."

"He's hanging on. Grandpa and Uncle Zeke are out in his room doctoring him, and Teaspoon thinks he will die any minute. Louie, what are you doing here in the yuccas? Why don't you come in the house?"

"I'm not comin' in that house!" he yelled. "I ain't gonna have all those people starin' at me, wonderin' how I let you get mixed up with all that at th' pond, wonderin' how I could bother you now. I'll talk from *here*!" he maneuvered closer, several times losing a battle with the spear of a yucca. "I'd hate t' fall into a patch of these in th' night," he said. "Why, they'd kill y'. I came t' check on Daddy Buck—uh, an' you, of course. You're not too sick, are y', Elbow? You were so still in th' wagon that I thought y'd passed out. Y' looked kinda sick after Hardtime killed that 'gator and started t' skin it, and then when Uncle Zeke stopped th' wagon an' carried y' into th' saw grass—well, did y' get sick?" I nodded. "So, I didn't know how y'd be . . ." His voice trailed off.

"I've never seen much shooting and killing," I whispered loudly to him. "All that blood in the water with that alligator, and all over Daddy Buck, and on the dog and on the wildcat. And when Hardtime—but I'm fine now. Louie, for the life of me I can't understand why Uncle Sumter would fire at Daddy Buck that way, and why did Hardtime have to hop on the alligator's back? Why didn't he just aim his gun and shoot him?"

We were both silent, thinking about it. I leaned on the sill. Louie moved in closer.

Finally he spoke. "That Hardtime must have had good reason t' ride the 'gator. He must have been after th' skin of th' big bull—an' y' know alligators don't come when y' whistle. Hardtime *had* to lasso him an' get him out of th' water somehow, an' I guess th' best way was t' make him walk out. I just gotta try that! I'm gonna rope me a six-footer and practice on him!"

"What was it like, pulling on the rope that was tied to the alligator?"

"He fought like the devil! Almost yanked my arms out." Louie hesitated, "Now," he said, "y' ain't gonna like this that I'm gonna tell y', but here it is. I know why y' uncle shot Buck—he was pullin on *whiskey* in that flask! That's why he's killed Buck. *He's a whiskey-drinkin' hunter!*"

"No!" I protested. "He'd never drink that! He takes cough medicine for his lungs! I've seen it in his room. Black cherry cough medicine!"

Louie nodded, "An' it stops his cough, all right. Anyways, look, I'll see yuh on th' creek pier at ten o'clock on th' dot in th' mornin'. Can y' be there?"

"Why?"

"Just be there. Do you hafta question everything? I got somethin' special t' tell y'."

"What about Teaspoon? That's his work place."

"Oh, that don't matter. I figure we might need him. I got a plan, an' he's in it. You be there." He turned away and then looked back. "You're under oath now."

◆ ◆ ◆ ◆ ◆ ◆ ◆

It was late in the evening when Grandpa came to the room. Still there under the quilt, I was drifting in and out of sleep. He led me upstairs to my bed.

"How is Daddy Buck?" I asked, expecting to hear the worst.

"That poor fellow lost too much blood—but he's probably going to live, barring infection. We'd have lost him for sure if Old Dirty hadn't stopped that gush of blood after he was shot."

Grandpa held my hand and felt my forehead, "Have you been sick anymore?"

"Not once—I've been toughened up this spring."

"So you have. Now tiptoe into your room, and don't wake Jane Anne. And Zeke is watching after Buck, so don't you worry. I'll see you in the morning."

◆ ◆ ◆ ◆ ◆ ◆ ◆

Early the next morning, Grandpa woke me. Jane Anne's bed was already empty. Outside, we heard Maum Polly's blessing on the house and knew her arms were stretched high above her head. Higher and higher, sweeter and sweeter came her voice. "Amen and ah-h-h-men!" she called out for the family to hear. Then her heavy steps sounded on the stairs as she headed toward her kitchen.

"Thank God for her prayers," said Grandpa. "And how are you this morning?"

"I'm fine. All I need is hot biscuits, hot fried trout and maybe a boiled egg—then I'll be ready to go. Is Daddy Buck better?"

"No, not yet. He's *far* down this morning."

"Grandpa, did the devil make Uncle Sumter shoot him? I can't understand why in the world he would shoot Daddy Buck. Daddy Buck is so *good* to Uncle Sumter—he waits on him, he dresses him—he

Chapter 14

does everything for him. Why would Uncle Sumter shoot him?"

Grandpa stood looking out the window at the sunshine streaming into the marsh. It was a beautiful day, a day for fishing or treasure hunting. Grandpa shook his head. "There's no place on earth I'd rather be than here. Sailor, don't you know Satan didn't make Sumter shoot Buck? And neither did God. Don't you know that?"

"Then why would he do it?"

He gave me a long serious look. "I truly hate to tell you," he said. "Poor Buck, shot by a drunken hunter."

"No, Grandpa! Louie told me that, but I can't believe it!"

"He's right," said Grandpa sadly, "Sumter is a slave to that bottle. But you remember, Sailor, no one *made* Sumter shoot Buck. We all make our choices, and sometimes they hurt others. Sumter chose to drink and hunt." He patted my hand. "That was a terrible thing you saw."

"Terrible, terrible," I groaned. "I'll never forget Daddy Buck's scream. And the blood pouring out of his shirt—I'll never forget that either. And that dog and wildcat fighting—and then Hardtime leaping on that alligator as neat as you please!" Once I started talking about it, I couldn't seem to stop. "Grandpa, how did that dog find the wildcat in the tree without a scent being laid down on the ground? Was that a magic dog? Have you found out who shot that wildcat? Was it Old Dirty? I think those are magic hunters with a magic dog."

Grandpa shook his head and chuckled, "No magic there. That was a special dog, but those hunters aren't magic. Old Dirty and Hardtime know the secrets of the Waccamaw Neck—they know the freshwater rivers and the salt creeks. It seems to me that they know the swamps and freshwater ponds best—the birds and animals, and even where the quicksand lies. The sounds of those birds and dogs—of all the animals—they read as easily as your mother reads sheets of piano music. Zeke says they owe their mastery to 'de debbil.' But I doubt it. It's skill that enables them, not 'de debbil.'"

"I look at Old Dirty, and I can't tell what he's thinking," I said. "He has sad eyes, Grandpa. And I look at Hardtime, and then I shiver."

"Dirty has lived alone for so many years, paddling the swamps and walking those woods, that he doesn't think the thoughts other men think. He's a master hunter, an alligator hunter. He sells those hides. One time he told me that remarkable necklace he wears has one tooth from *each* 'gator he has slain. If you'd like, I'll take you to his cabin sometime, up behind Murrell's Inlet. You'll see about a half-acre of 'gator skulls and bones sitting around where he hauled alligators in and skinned them."

"He's a good teacher, too," I said. "He's taught Louie all the secrets of the woods."

"He has, eh?" Grandpa smiled. "And Louie has been teaching you?"

"Yes, a few of the *most* important secrets. I don't know why Old Dirty keeps that Hardtime with him, though. I think he's a mean man."

I remembered the expression on Hardtime's face when he rode the alligator's back, just before he killed it. It had glowed with an expression of pride and cruelty, with a wildness I had never seen on anyone's face before.

"He keeps him because of his skill as a hunter."

"I wouldn't want Hardtime to be mad at me," I said. "But I'd rather be in the woods with *him* than Uncle Sumter. If Daddy Buck dies, I think the sheriff ought to come get Uncle Sumter. Shouldn't he?"

"Never happen."

"He's a murderer, Grandpa," I said.

"Not yet. Buck may live, Lord willing."

"Well, I think he's a murderer."

"Uncle Sumter is a sick, sick man. I told Zeke I don't ever want any of my family near him in a boat or in the woods. Oh, I know, Alberta wanted me to take him out. She thinks I can make him stop drinking, that I can work a miracle, but drunks don't stop drinking when others ask them to stop. Mostly they drink to forget. I don't know why Sumter drinks, but I do know he's never admitted a mistake."

"Is that why you wouldn't take him out in the boat?"

"About ten years ago Sumter and Buck went out fishing on the ocean. I knew he'd had too much from that flask. They lost their fishing gear, their paddles, Sumter's pocket watch, Sumter's glasses. Zeke and I watched them through the telescope—then when I saw Sumter force old Buck out of the boat into deep water, I feared for his life. Sumter was drunk and angry. We pulled a boat down and went after them. Buck could never have made it in; he can't swim that well. When we reached them Sumter said, 'Rotten nigger! I won't ever come out here with *him* again. He could have reached my glasses before they went down!' Buck never said a word except 'Thank de Lawd!' And when Sumter sobered up, he wouldn't admit to a thing. He's never admitted being wrong—risking himself and Buck out there. I'll never understand it."

"You should have made him leave."

Then Grandpa seemed to be talking more to himself than to me. "I don't quite know what to do about Buck and Aunt Hagey after this," he said. "I don't see how they can stay with Sumter. I'd like them to work for us." He paused, thinking. "Well, we'll see what happens. I could throw Sumter over when I think of what he did to Buck

Chapter 14

yesterday—but we'll see. I'm going to see that Buck isn't mistreated anymore. That's one thing *I'm going to do.*"

We heard Maum Polly cracking out orders on the breezeway, hurrying the maids in with breakfast. Hot buttermilk biscuit smells drifted up to us. Fried whiting, stewed corn that had been canned last year, fig preserves and molasses, fresh milk—that was my breakfast.

The Treasure of Pawley's Island

Sure enough, it was hanging out the corner of the window.

Chapter 15
Secret Signals

At precisely ten o'clock I marched out on the creek pier where Louie and Teaspoon waited. I was wearing summery white linen girl-clothes, for a change. On my head was a wide-brimmed straw hat with an elastic band under my chin, and in my hair I had tied a wide pink satin ribbon—one that Aunt Alberta had given me. My girlish appearance must have jolted Louie, who watched my approach over the pier boards with something near to anguish written on his face. Grandma had told me, "To carry oneself well is half the battle." So I lifted my chin higher.

"Good morning, Louie. Isn't this a nice day? How are you?" I purred. "Teaspoon, have you caught your fish for this morning?"

As Louie stared at me, I inspected Teaspoon's old assortment of fishing apparatus and his ever-present gripsack filled with collectibles.

"No, leetle Missie, not much fish. De storm, she blow de fish t' deep water—deep, deep. An' crabs be stuck in pluff mud dat de rain tumble 'round de salt creek." He rattled a bucket and shifted a cane pole. "Soon de mud settle an' fish swim back."

"Well, good."

Louie took his eyes off me, cleared his throat, and surveyed the marsh.

"You see these cigar boxes, Elbow?" he asked, pointing to two boxes on the pier. "I tell you, it's hard callin' you Elbow when you're wearin' a dress. You see these boxes? Well, they're really *signal boxes*. Leastwise that's what we're goin' t' do with 'em. Did I tell yuh I went back t' th' pond after we brought you home? That 'trunk' full of treasure at th' bottom of th' pond was a big square root from one of them oak trees. I tried to prize it up and couldn't budge it. It has t' be a root stretchin' into that pond."

Chapter 15

"What treasure?" squawked Teaspoon.

I was stupified. Louie had gone back to the *pond*—and he had gone alone. How brave he was.

"But . . . what about the alligators?" I asked.

He was quite casual. "What 'gators? No 'gators there anymore. Now see here, I'm not about t' give up this treasure hunt, are you?"

"I'll never give it up!"

"What treasure?" Teaspoon asked again.

"If nothing else happens, I'm ready to go *tonight*," Louie continued. "Are you? When I was probin' in that pond yesterday afternoon, I looked up an' there was that Hardtime standin' over on th' bank. He said, 'What you doin', boy?' An' I flat out lied. 'I dropped my dead pa's pocket watch in this water, an' I was tryin' t' find it with this pole,' I said to him. An' he squinted at me like he didn't believe a word. Now, we're goin' back to get that treasure afore someone else does. An' if it don't rain or somethin' else happens, at eleven o'clock sharp *tonight*, you look across, an' I'm goin' to signal at y' from my window. Teaspoon, y' go ahead back there a ways on th' pier—I gotta tell Elbow some secret signals." Teaspoon reluctantly walked back up the pier and stood just out of earshot. "Now, y' stand back there, an' don't y' move," Louie called to him.

As Teaspoon kept his eye on us, Louie ripped the top off both cigar boxes.

"Now, here's what we're goin' t' do," he whispered. "If I can go, I'll sneak to my window an' put a candle in th' box with a yellow cloth tacked in front. It'll look like a yellow light from your house. If I can't get outta th' house, I'll put a blue cloth in front, so it'll show blue. When y' see my yellow light—'cause I'm countin' on goin'—then you light yer candle, an' put up yellow if y' can go, blue if y' can't. Then if y' can, I'll meet y' at the end of your driveway ten minutes later. Have y' got it?"

I nodded. "I'll do it," I said, "but where are we going?"

"We're goin' to dig up th' wagon."

"Dig it up? Why?"

"Wagons hold things," Louie declared. "That wagon used t' hold somethin', an' maybe somethin' is still in there, or maybe some *sign* of it is still there. An' if th' treasure ain't there we're gonna dig somewhere else."

"But why do we need *him*?" I asked, gesturing toward Teaspoon. "You made me swear not to tell a soul, and now you want *him* to come along."

"We need help, even if it's Teaspoon. He kin help dig. You kin hold

The Treasure of Pawley's Island

the lantern. Now, you git t' figurin' out how t' git outta y' house tonight—an' how we'll wake up Teaspoon without wakin' up anybody else. I know he ain't never goin' t' sleep outside."

We looked at Teaspoon and he looked at us, still wondering about "treasure." Then he looked over at his fishing lines and sniffed the salt air appreciatively. "Tide changin'!" he called out to us.

"I know!" I said. "We can tie a string to his toe, and he can hang it out the window for us to pull and wake him up!"

Louie looked at me in amazement. "I tell y', Elbow, what you don't got in muscle, y' got in brains."

Then Louie summoned Teaspoon back and explained that we were going to need him late in the night, that he was to tell *no one*, that he would trail a string from his toe out the window, that we would be needing him to *dig* in the dark hours of the night, and that he was to tell *no one* about that either.

Louie looked at him closely, "Do y' understand?"

Teaspoon nodded slowly.

"Elbow," said Louie, "You go on now and git y' stuff ready. Here's th' cigar box. Teaspoon an' I have some talkin' t' do."

Teaspoon looked numb, thinking about what lay ahead later that night.

As I walked off, Louie began talking and gesturing. Teaspoon was listening to every word.

◆ ◆ ◆ ◆ ◆ ◆ ◆

When the clock chimed on the quarter hour, I still had not closed my eyes. I lay staring up at the mosquito netting in the dark. All of the family members had retired early, including Jane Anne, who slept soundly but quietly in her bed. In a minute I rose up in the darkness and without a sound pulled my boy-clothes from under my bed. They were fresh and clean. I had washed them and smuggled them into the house that evening. After I dressed, I dipped the yellow square of cloth in the pitcher of water on the wash stand and draped the cloth over the box in the window. Then I sat on the side of my bed and waited.

Never had time passed so slowly. Never, not even at the pond, had I been conscious of my heart beating so wildly. The moments passed. I was ready.

As the silvery chimes echoes eleven times throughout the sleeping household, I moved the cigar box and candle closer to me and then into the window sill. I looked across toward the dark shape that was Louie's house. Still no light in his window. The island was quiet, and

Chapter 15

only a slight breeze was blowing. The moon had not risen out of the black ocean. I sat and waited, not making a sound.

When I looked out again, a dot of yellow light twinkled in the attic room of the house across the way. Hastily, and with shaking fingers, I lit my candle and dripped tallow on one side of the box, sticking the glowing candle in it. Then I dropped the thin yellow cloth in front, and our signal was complete.

Jane Anne turned over and sat up.

"What are you doing *now?*" she asked.

I did not answer but continued looking at Louie's tiny light, hardly believing that we had really communicated.

"I spoke to you, Bessie. I said, *what are you doing?*"

"Nothing."

"Yes, you are. I can plainly see you have lit a candle."

"No, you go on back to sleep."

"I am going to your mother's room and tell her you are acting crazy again, and you know she shouldn't be disturbed. You better stop that and put out that candle." She made movements to climb out of bed.

I let my candle burn a moment longer and then blew it out. I stepped toward the door in the darkness.

"You disturb my mama, and I'll pinch you so hard you will never lose the spot! Now, turn over and go back to sleep—and you had better not mention one word to Mama about this!"

"You are getting into trouble again," she said angrily, but she stayed in her bed.

"Go to sleep, Jane Anne."

She heard the authority in my voice and slid back under the covers. I heard it too and was surprised at myself.

"Now," I added, "don't you climb out of bed! I'll be back in a little while."

I picked up my boots and crept out the door without a single look back.

Down the narrow stairway from our attic room to the second floor I tiptoed. Uncle Sumter's snores growled at intervals. The rest of the house was silent, although I could feel the presence of the sleeping family.

I hesitated on the landing before walking down the stairs. In that moment of hesitation, a door swung silently open. A nightcapped head peered out into the dark hallway. It was Mama.

She saw me and tiptoed out, holding up the skirt of her voluminous cotton nightgown. The smell of roses instantly surrounded me.

"What's the matter, dear?" she questioned, tenderly.

The Treasure of Pawley's Island

"Nothing, Mama."

"Where are you going? Are you feeling all right?"

"Why are you awake?" I asked her.

"I haven't been sleeping well this evening," she whispered. "Why are you down here?"

I could think of nothing to say but the truth. So there in the chilly hallway we huddled together, her arms around me. I explained that Louie awaited me at the edge of the island road. I told her how we had been searching for a treasure for weeks, and I told her how we had almost found it on the day Daddy Buck was shot.

"We might find it tonight, Mama, *tonight*! Gold, diamonds, rubies, strings of pearls down to my knees! And Teaspoon is going with us to dig!"

She and I looked at each other in the darkness, and although I could hardly see her face, I knew she was looking into my eyes. She nodded slowly, realizing how much the search meant to me.

"I see, Bessie. But must you do this at night, dear? The hour is very late. It must be after eleven. Please, please go back up to bed and find your treasure in the morning." Her soft arms tightened about me.

"But they're waiting for me. I gave Louie the signal that I'd be there, and I'm going! I promise it won't take long, Mama. I'll be back in an hour. When I'm back, I'll knock on your door to let you know I'm here. No one else will even know I'm gone. Louie is very strong, Mama, and he will be careful—and I will, too, and Teaspoon will be along, too. You don't have to worry," I pleaded.

I waited for her answer. I did not want her to be anxious.

"Why, you do sound feverish, Bessie. You had a terrible shock at the pond—"

"But I'm fine now! And it wasn't that much of a shock. If Daddy Buck hadn't been shot—well, it would have been exciting if that hadn't happened."

"How can I let you go out on a dark night, wandering around with a young boy?"

"Mama, I'm determined to go! Louie needs me, and I won't let him wait there for me any longer!" I pulled away from her loving arms.

"Bessie, I just cannot worry at this time—but it would upset all of us terribly if anything happened—wait a moment, dear," she said, but I was already moving away. "Now, I know Louie wouldn't do anything foolish. Louie's mother was a lovely woman and his father a gentleman." She sighed in resignation. "Don't be gone over an hour."

I was already at the top of the stairs. "I won't, Mama, I promise. Please don't worry." I fled down the stairs, through the parlor and into

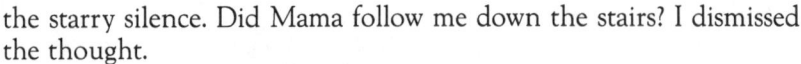

Chapter 15

the starry silence. Did Mama follow me down the stairs? I dismissed the thought.

Oh, how quiet was the night.

But for the surf rhythmically pounding the shore, the only sound was the wind, alive and moving across my cheeks. The darkness was like black sable as I crept from the piazza, past the breezeway and kitchen, past the stable and down the driveway. I waited. The dogs did not awaken. The donkeys were quiet, the horses were quiet, the cow was quiet. No sound came from the chickens or ducks.

Somewhere a twig or leaf cracked.

I inadvertently shivered, from fear or excitement. Suddenly Louie was at my side, keeping our rendezvous. He grabbed my hand, and we crept along the path to Teaspoon's window. The tiny whitewashed house shimmered in the darkness. We searched for the string as contented snores and clicks and hums floated on the air from the window.

"Heavy sleeping in there," Louie whispered into my ear, grinning. "Here's th' string."

Sure enough, it was hanging out the corner of the window. Louie breathed deeply, took a firm hold on it and gave a gentle, long pull. Nothing happened. Then he gave three sharp yanks.

"Eh! Eh!" Thud. Silence. Louie had pulled Teaspoon's leg off the mattress. One more strong yank and another "Eh!" Then we heard Teaspoon sit up, groggy, and stumble his way to the door. Sleep showed on his face.

"Come on, Teaspoon! Git yerself out here," Louie whispered as loudly as he dared. "Time's wastin'!" Teaspoon picked up his gripsack and nearly fell down the steps. Louie eased the wooden door closed behind him. Snores and clicks continued rhymically as we tiptoed away, down the path to the two ruts that formed the island road.

Our only light, faint though it was, came from the stars and constellations above as we trudged soundlessly along the sandy ruts toward South Inlet. With that starry bowl above, the dimness was full of silences, yet also full of sounds—the movement of the bushes, marsh and gentle wind swinging over the high dunes. Silhouetted trees and bushes swayed and danced. They spoke of hints, meanings and secrets. Mystery.

When cicadas sang loudly from some dense bushes, Teaspoon and I moved closer to Louie, who was straining to see in the dark. I noticed then that he had two long-handled shovels slung over his shoulder; I guessed he must have picked them up at the curve of the island road where he had laid them. In his other hand he carried an unlit lantern.

The Treasure of Pawley's Island

"Carry that lantern for him, Teaspoon," I ordered.

Teaspoon took the lantern in one hand, his gripsack in the other, and Louie moved more briskly between the branches of myrtle and fir that seemed to reach out leafy fingertips toward us. We passed no lit houses. We passed no animal life. Still no moon shed its comforting light.

"De signs say we turn back," Teaspoon said.

"Keep walkin', keep walkin'," said Louie.

From deep in the woods of the Neck came the melancholy note of the great horned owl. It carried over the water and marsh with strength. At this "sign," Teaspoon's neck stiffened. His head tossed back and forth as we proceeded through the bushes, along the road, past some dunes. Since I was older than he, I was not as afraid.

"Ah ain't neber been dis far in de dark, an' ah ain't never gwine do it twic't."

"We've passed the house," said Louie. I never saw it. Except for us the island appeared to be sleeping. "Hurry," he insisted. "We're not far from the inlet."

If the island was sleeping, not so the marsh. As we passed along the edge of it, the marsh sounded alive with great flocks of boat-tailed grackles, red-winged blackbirds and cow-birds roosting there. Their twitterings and rustlings were wafted to us on the breeze as the wind poured into the inlet. And in the dimness, the gaseous marsh smell—dense, heavy and much stronger than in the daylight hours—met our noses.

We burst from the bushes onto sea oat-covered low dunes. Beyond, on the crescent of white, white sand, nested black and white-coated terns in multitudes.

Teaspoon and I hesitated, but Louie commanded, "Come on!" We waded among the terns. They were too tired from their daytime frolics to be startled into flight by our passage and allowed us to proceed through their sleepy bird village with but little awareness. Louie urged swift movement among the drowsy birds, but I was entranced by being in the midst of thousands of unafraid live creatures and wanted to linger.

"Git moving," Louie ordered. "We got to go over the water."

I been bit!

Chapter 16
The Treasure

The channel loomed black and swift as the tide rushed in to fill the wide inlet and wind among the salt creeks. When I looked at the dark, moving waters—almost like a living, breathing thing—I closed my eyes. "God, send angels to protect us on this water," I prayed. In all my life I had never explored the darkness, the blackness of the shore.

The bigness and movement, the life of the water seemed to sap the courage out of both Teaspoon and me. Teaspoon meekly looked at the water and heard the ominous hiss of waves as they slapped at the shore. "Praise Gawd!" he said. "*He* know nighttime not de time t' work—*or* de time t' drown fum de boat. Mah pa he die in de water. Ah stay heah on de land an' watch." He sat down.

"Git yourself up!" yelled our taskmaster. "Push out this dinghy! Hold that lantern, Elbow! Git in both of you, git!"

Into the dinghy and over the rushing channel we went. Louie paddled vigorously toward the obscured opposite bank. Teaspoon chattered on and on, discoursing on any subject that came into his head, and I was grateful for the sound of his voice.

The darkness was almost overpowering, and I felt as if the surging water could grab us as Teaspoon feared. Oh, how blessed is sunlight, and how we do not value it. I understood at that dark moment why death and sadness have been described with words like shadow, dead of night, blackness—and how joy and God have always been connected with words like sun, rainbow, candle and light of the world. I could not take it all in, but I knew that the darkness was engulfing me and that I could lose my life in that black and deathly water which I could not even see. I yearned for light. Oh, how blessed is the light!

Louie paddled on, fighting the swift current.

"I need oars!" he gasped. "I need oars!"

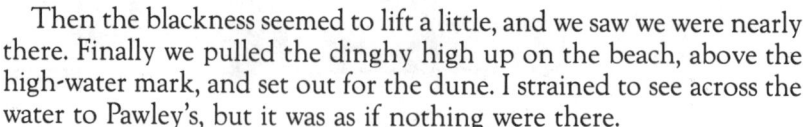

Chapter 16

Then the blackness seemed to lift a little, and we saw we were nearly there. Finally we pulled the dinghy high up on the beach, above the high-water mark, and set out for the dune. I strained to see across the water to Pawley's, but it was as if nothing were there.

"This sure is a dark night," Louie observed nonchalantly as we climbed the shore and circled the dunes. In the gloom as we marched along, the white sand seemed to glow, making it easier to see where we were headed. When we passed behind the first row of dunes, Louie lit the lantern, draping the back and sides with cloth so that light only shone out like a spotlight in one direction.

"That's smart, Louie," I said admiringly.

"Ain't hard t' be smart when there's nothing else t' do," he replied.

In the lantern light, Teaspoon studied me. "*Robbuh buckra*! You dat *robbuh buckra*!" he whispered as he saw me illuminated in my boy-clothes and remembered seeing that same person in the stable. "Why yuh steal from yuh grandpappy?"

"Look! Look!" called out Louie ahead of us.

His lantern cast its yellow light on the hills of sand which rose up on either side of us. Fresh deer tracks picked their way like chicken pox among the dunes toward the ocean. White spider crabs scuttled away as we walked along. The breeze swept in from the ocean, rustling the sea oats and blocking out the sounds of the surf and other noises of the night.

Then there it was—the dune sat undisturbed but for the partially uncovered wagon which cast grotesque shadows in the lantern light. The sword was plunged into the top of the dune with the line trailing from it, over the myrtles and beyond.

"O-o-o-o-h-h, what *hab* ah done?" murmured Teaspoon. "Old Moses, come an' get me an' take me home! Look at dat wagon! A dead an' bury wagon!"

Louie set the lantern down and climbed the dune, trying to decide what to do next. Teaspoon stared at the sky and then at the ominous wagon. The darkness was looking very dark around us, and the area of our lantern light was very small.

"Good thing ah hab de coon foot, de rabbit foot an' de silver dime on de string 'round my neck," he said, casting his eyes upward. "Uncle Zeke gib me de coon foot, Daddy Buck gib me de rabbit foot, and the Good Lawd set de dime on de sand! See dis string 'round my neck, *Gawd*! Put de *eye* on noticin', an' send Old Moses t' get me outta dis land."

Finally Louie made up his mind, "Elbow, I'm gonna dig a bit more just to satisfy that nothing is in this wagon. Now, don't y' say not to,

The Treasure of Pawley's Island

'cause I'm gonna make sure. Teaspoon, stop that muttering. Bring up the shovels an' shine that light this way, up here."

He dug, while Teaspoon held the lantern and I watched. The moving air was laden with the heavy aroma of salt and moisture from the ocean, but I thought I could smell the woods and pond also. I had a sense of wild creatures close by but invisible, beyond the outer rim of our light. Their movements were secret and vanishing.

"Louie, did you hear that?"

"No, an' don't *you* hear nothing that ain't there, either." He threw the sand high, gradually clearing out the bed of the wagon.

Over the edge of the ocean the tiniest tip of a three-quarter moon showed. It hovered on the black horizon like a burning ship far, far out to sea. I watched it sailing there. A few minutes later, it seemed to leap out of the ocean until it hung just above the horizon, like a huge copper penny held in the sky by an invisible string, its light painting a burnished path on the sea directly toward us.

"De red moon up dere be a bad, bad sign," announced Teaspoon, "but ah don't take up no truck wid things lak dat. Ah just goes t' de praise-house an' sings *loud* an' keeps mah charms 'round de neck." He looked around and shivered, adding, "Dat hooty owl an' red-blood moon, an' dem tern birds dat don't fly an' dat swallowin' inlet be signs dat say we turn back."

"If we wanted to," I replied, "we could find a sign in everything. See that ghost crab over there, looking at you with his beady eye? That could be a sign." Teaspoon shivered again. "And the moon jumping out of the ocean, and those animal tracks, and that noise I heard. The sun, the stars, anything. I'd be scared all the time if I lived by signs. I'd be afraid I had missed one of them."

"Now, one sign ain't nuttin', but when dey bunch up, we walk into de mess. Dey bunched, o-o-o-oh dey bunched! See dis *dime*—surely, surely dis dime hold back de badness until we jump outta heah!" Teaspoon clutched at the dime. He was truly afraid.

"I ain't never jumpin' until we dig up a treasure, signs or no signs!" declared Louie. "Signs don't mean nothing to me. The red moon can have stripes, for all I care!" he said, inspecting the wagon. It was almost completely cleared off. No treasure there.

"Grandpa read in the Bible where the moon turns to blood before the Great Day," I said.

"I know this ain't the Great Day," he responded, "and I know good an' well that moon is goin' t' turn to *gold* in a while, but it ain't here!" He threw down the shovel. "We got t' go dig between those trees," he said, pointing decisively toward the pitch-black woods. "Let's go."

Chapter 16

He jumped down the dune, took the lantern from Teaspoon, and began to move briskly toward the opening in the myrtle bushes.

Neither Teaspoon nor I wanted to follow, but we did.

We bent and crawled in a line through the myrtle tunnel, pulling the lantern, shovels and Teaspoon's gripsack. We picked our way through the saw palmetto forest, found our guide line, and followed it past the three palmettos. Only Teaspoon spoke. His words were sounds made to comfort himself in the strange dark forest. We approached the twin giants, looming even mightier in the night.

"Between the trees," proclaimed Louie, "we'll dig between the trees. We'll tie this line between them as a marker an' pace off the center," he said reaching into a pocket and producing more line.

Teaspoon guided us by lantern light as Louie and I circled the trees, one at a time, lashing their thick bellies together.

"I got to satisfy one more problem," decided Louie. He took out his hatchet and directed Teaspoon to shine the light into the rotten cavity where he had found the sea turtle shell. There he gently probed with the hatchet.

"Nothing. Ain't nothing there," he announced, "so let's pace off the line between th' trees." We did, finding the approximate center near where the old rotten tree lay.

"Ain't it good that old tree wasn't in the exact center?" Louie decided.

The rotten tree's base was just about five feet from the spot we had determined to be the place to dig for the treasure. The moments passed as we surveyed the area, Teaspoon faithfully shining the light wherever we wished and muttering to himself.

"Hush, Teaspoon! Louie, did you hear that?" I thought I heard an animal in the woods beyond the arms of the live oaks.

"Sounded like a racoon gruntin' to me," Louie answered. "Those woods are full of animals an' some are sure t' be curious. I guess this is the place, Elbow. We might as well begin."

We still stood there, afraid to begin, afraid that our dream of finding something was only a dream.

Then I grabbed up a shovel and started in to work. Louie did too. We pushed aside the carpet of decaying leaves and began to dig with a vengeance into the rich, spongy soil.

"When de big house say 'wake up!' ah wake up," chattered Teaspoon. "When de big house say 'walk dose feets in de night!' ah walks. When de big house say 'jump in de boat!' ah don't eber want t' jump, but ah jumps wid de eye closed. Ain't neber seen sech big black shadows, but ah holds dis light steady."

"You're doin' good, Teaspoon," praised Louie. "No, give that lantern to Elbow, an' you dig a while."

I was glad to give my shovel over to him. Teaspoon, always willing to work took it over, saying, "When de big house say 'dig!' ah dig—but ah ain't neber seen no treasure, so ah can't spot dat treasure. An' huntin' treasure in de night kill de worker," he said, pausing to look at me. "Robbuh buckra!" he added, under his breath.

In a few minutes they had a deep black hole. No sign of treasure. Louie widened the hole. Still no treasure.

"Dig back toward the rotten tree," I suggested. "It could be that way. It looks to be more in the center, anyway."

They backed up and dug between the hole and the rotten tree. Drips of sweat ringed Louie's face, drenching his straight hair. He threw off his hat and, for the second time since I had known him, his heavy coat. Anxiety drove him to dig faster. Would we find *anything*? Some tree roots got in the way.

"Louie, stop and rest a minute, just for a minute," I suggested.

He was so tired he was shaking. I propped the lantern at the edge of the hole so that the light would shine in and took the shovel from Louie. He fell on the ground breathing heavily.

I climbed down in the hole and dug across from the place Teaspoon was digging.

"See anything, Teaspoon?" I asked, keeping my eye on Louie. He was staring over at the moon which was just above the line of palmettos and myrtles, out over the ocean. He was so silent lying there.

"Nuffing, nuffing, only some white dirt," he murmured. "Bunched up signs, wuk in de night, ridin' dat boat on de killer water—ah ain't gwine t' wuk in de mornin'! Let dem crabs tek de bait. Let dem fishes get clean a-way. Wake me up at dinner," he muttered. "Dis ol' white dirt, what's it doin' heah?" he questioned.

"White dirt? What do you mean 'white dirt?' " I asked, suddenly realizing that he was referring to something in the hole.

I shone the light into his side of the hole. Sure enough he was digging into white sand. Then his shovel crunched down on some shells or something.

"Louie! Louie! Look at this!"

Instantly alert, Louie leaped into the hole and grabbed Teaspoon's shovel. We dug more in the direction of the layer of white sand, clearing off the top few feet of black dirt, wondering at its curious placement.

"A sign, a sign!" babbled Louie excitedly. "Now there ain't no logical reason for a sand and oyster shell-layer to be here, is there? Unless it's a marker for something. Clear the dirt off the top!"

Chapter 16

But old roots kept getting in the way. Louie tried to break through some of them. The sand seemed to be more toward the rotten tree. I handed the shovel to Teaspoon when I couldn't dig anymore. They cleared the black dirt off the layer of white sand. It appeared to be a large white circle of sand over a layer of oyster shells, all entwined with roots of the old rotten tree.

Louie and I looked at each other.

"Dig in the center of the circle," I whispered. Louie nodded. They cautiously dug through the sand, scraping against the rotten roots, sometimes hacking away at them.

"What dis?" asked Teaspoon. I shone the light in that spot. "A log?"

"That ain't no log!" yelled Louie and bent over, scraping at a place with his shovel. "Yeah! Yeah! It's an old box, and old rotten box, with roots growin' all around it, holdin' it fast."

He cleaned it off, and then dug down beside it, trying to see how big it was. He tried to pry it up, but it was held down by the roots.

"Well, I'll be! Kin y' beat that? It does startle up y' eyes when y' see it for real!" His chest was heaving, and he had a hard time catching his breath.

Louie scraped more of the damp dirt off the sides and top. Then together he and Teaspoon tried to pry the rotten lid off with their shovels.

"Stuck faster than a rusted corset!" said Louie. He suddenly lifted his shovel and plunged the blade, leaving a wide gash in one end of the top.

"Bring that lantern closer, Elbow. I want to look down in there."

Louie bent over as I tried to aim the beam of light. His head kept casting a shadow. "Can't hardly see a thing," he murmured. Quickly he reached his hand down in the gash and felt around in one end for a second, then yanked his hand out. "Found somethin'!" In his hand was a little hard leather pouch. We crowded closer, bending down to the light. He pulled it open. It contained gold pieces—ten of them!

"Yow-e-e-e-e! Two hundred dollars in gold!" Louie yelled.

Our gleeful and jubilant laughter rang out. We hopped up and down and shouted.

Louie dropped to his knees. "There's somethin' else down in there!"

He reached in to feel around. Then he screamed a terrible blood-curdling scream and jerked his hand out.

"I been bit!" In the light I could see two round holes in the flesh of his hand near his little finger—it was a snake bite.

"O-o-o-h-h-h, a poisonous snake!" he cried out. "What will I do?"

The Treasure of Pawley's Island

We stared at Louie's hand as a few drops of blood dripped out and the truth hit us. A snake had been sleeping down in that box. How had it gotten in there?

A cloud passed in front of the moon, but I could see Teaspoon shaking all over. To him this was the reason for all the signs to turn back. We drew away from the box. The snake was still in there, although we could not see it, nor hear any movement.

Louie was panting with fright. "What'll I do? What'll I do?" Teaspoon and I were paralyzed with fear. "Give me a knife!" Louie yelled.

I found my breath. "Aren't you supposed to cut the skin and suck all the poison out?" I asked. "But what if you have a cut in your mouth—it'll poison you through your mouth!"

"Find that knife! *This* will kill me!"

Teaspoon fumbled around in his gripsack and found his old kitchen knife, dull and rusted. I wiped it off on the tail of my shirt. My hands trembled. Louie was trembling. Teaspoon was shaking all over. I grasped Louie's hand and on impulse prayed loudly, "Dear Father in Heaven, *please* hear this prayer and save Louie! Amen."

I got ready to cut at the fang marks. Then I knew I could never do it. At that moment, Teaspoon took the knife and prepared to cut. I remembered he often traveled with Grandpa and Uncle Zeke on their medical visits to the community. He had probably seen a snake bite treated.

"Gotta be cut jest so," he said, his voice small. He moved closer to the light with Louie's hand in his.

From out of the shadows came the form of a man, moving quickly toward us. It was Old Dirty, and he had his hunting knife, shiny and slender, in one hand. He knocked the glass tip off the lantern, stuck the knife in the fire and closed my fingers around the handle.

"Hold it there," he ordered. Grabbing Louie, he stroked his arm from shoulder to wrist, shoulder to wrist, then he tied a dirty bandana around Louie's forearm. In one swoop he grabbed the hunting knife and, bending low to the light, deftly sliced at the fang marks. Louie gasped, but in a moment Old Dirty was spitting out the blood.

"Git back!" he growled.

He sucked and spat, sucked and spat, while Teaspoon and I stood there watching, horrified.

"Dirty, it burns! It burns! Am I goin' t' die?" cried Louie.

"Jes' don't get excited, boy," Old Dirty growled again as he spat. Then he sucked again and again, running his hands down Louie's arm over and over as it if to push the blood and poison out.

Finally he barked, "Get that lantern!" Hoisting Louie over his

Chapter 16

shoulder, he strode out from under the giant water oaks with Teaspoon and me running to keep up.

The Treasure of Pawley's Island

I then and there would have danced in the bright sand of that glorious moonlight, with the birds as my audience.

Chapter 17
The Snake in the Box

"Wake up your grandpaw! He's got t' treat this boy!" barked Old Dirty as he pushed past the mahogany sideboard laden with its silver service, flatware and English china. He gently laid Louie on the center of the padded dining table. It was already covered with snowy, embroidered linen in preparation for breakfast.

Only a few steps away was my grandparents' bedroom door. I timidly knocked and stuck my head inside. Grandma raised up at once in the high bed. "Yes, dear?" she said.

"Louie has been bitten on the hand by *a poisonous snake!*" I called out, "and Old Dirty laid him up on the dining table on top of the linen cloth. He looks terrible, and I think he might have gotten some blood on it, Grandma, and he might die. Come quick, Grandpa!"

"I certainly don't care about the tablecloth, Bessie. How is the *boy?*" Grandma's hands moved anxiously as she reached over and hastily lit a candle.

Grandpa was yanking his trousers up over his nightclothes, "Bell, you stay in that bed," he told her. "I'll take care of Louie. Now, don't you worry—Zeke will help me. If I need you, I'll send Bessie for you." He brushed past me at the door.

Old Dirty had lit the overhead lamp above Louie. Its yellow light showed Louie to be pasty-faced and half-fainting from fright. I noticed how his freckles stood out. The hand was swelling and already discolored.

Old Dirty looked down at Louie's pitiful, tear-streaked face. He patted him wordlessly and loosened the tourniquet again. Then Grandpa went to Louie's side and pressed the puffy fingers.

"What kind of snake, Dirty?" he asked.

I spoke out impetuously. "We never saw it—the snake was down in

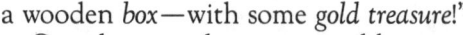

Chapter 17

a wooden *box*—with some *gold treasure!*"

Grandpa stared at me, speechless.

"I'll go see about both of them things, Doc." Old Dirty moved as if to go to the door.

"What were you doing out at night, child?" Grandpa asked me.

"We were looking for the treasure," I said, looking down at the floor, adding, "Mama knew."

"Did you take them out there, Dirty?"

"No, Doc. I didn't take them, but I was there—in case. Do you want me to go get that snake?"

"I do. I've never lost a snakebite patient yet, and I'd appreciate your help. But wait a minute before you go."

Louie's eyes searched mine. He was scared, but beyond his fear he realized the coins were out in the dirt where he had flung them when the snake struck. Louie started to climb off the table, moaning and whimpering.

Grandpa pressed him down. "Lie still, son," he commanded. "Dirty will take care of it. Dreadful viper to strike such a boy."

Then Grandpa looked toward Teaspoon, who stood silent beside the door, and gave orders. "Teaspoon, run wake Zeke. Send him over to tell Louie's uncle, Mr. Haselton, and bring him over here. Be sure Louie's aunt and uncle know that he will be fine. Tell Zeke I need him here to help just as soon as he gets back."

"Comin' up, Doc! Ah run jack rabbit!" Teaspoon disappeared into the night.

As Grandpa and Old Dirty carried Louie to a couch in the parlor, Grandpa asked me, "Sailor, where's your grandma's afghan? There it is. Come put it over him."

Louie fell back on the pillows. When I bent over to tuck the afghan in around him, he whispered, "You got t' get those coins an' th' rest of the treasure. Ain't it something? How did we luck into it?" Then he started breathing heavily as though he was going to vomit.

"Move back, Sailor. Let him have air. Breathe deeply, son," Grandpa said and reached for a bowl on a nearby table.

I followed Old Dirty to the door, meaning to speak with him. I knew I had to follow Old Dirty back to the treasure box. "I'm going with Old Dirty, Grandpa," I said. "I have to pick up those coins." I looked at Old Dirty's face, seeking his permission, but I couldn't read what he thought.

"No, Sailor, you're not to go back out there," said Grandpa. "Dirty will take care of it."

Suddenly Jane Anne appeared, floating slowly down the stairs in her pink cotton nightdress and wrap. She saw me reflected in the light streaming from the parlor lamp.

"Bessie!" she called to me, gesturing. "Your mama came up and woke me. She asked me to come down to listen for you. Why would you worry her by going out in the night? Bessie, if I had told her you were signaling with a *candle* up in our window, she *would* have been worried—what is that man doing here?" she asked, just as if he could not hear her.

She had caught sight of Old Dirty with his hand on the door, staring at her, not speaking. Then Jane Anne glanced through the doorway to her left and saw Louie prostrate with Grandpa on one knee at his side. Her hand flew to her mouth, and she shook her pale flowing hair out of her eyes as if she could not believe the sight.

"What is it?" she gasped.

"Louie's been snakebit," I said, "and Old Dirty is going to bring back the snake. And I'm going with him."

Jane Anne was horrified. She turned ashen.

"Bessie?" Grandpa called out to me, "Are you still there? Go up and tell your mama you're fine. Don't worry her another minute."

"All right, Grandpa," I said and made my way past Jane Anne to the stairs. "But I want to go with Old Dirty," I added.

"Child—" said Grandpa, warning me, then, "Dirty, are you there? Could you go chip off some ice before you go?"

I looked back at Old Dirty, but he had gone, silently closing the door. Jane Anne was still standing at the door to the parlor, her hand over her mouth.

Grandpa caught sight of her and said, "Has Dirty left?" She nodded. "Then you go chip off some ice, Jane Anne. We need to stop this swelling."

Jane Anne stood without speaking.

"Jane Anne? Did you hear me?"

As I went up to Mama, I heard Jane Anne say, "I can't help you." Then she turned and fled up the stairs, pushing me aside. In a minute I heard Grandpa speaking to Teaspoon. I went on in to Mama's room and told her I was fine. Then I tiptoed back down the stairs and past the parlor, letting myself out the door just as quietly as had Old Dirty.

◆ ◆ ◆ ◆ ◆ ◆ ◆

The moon overhead flooded the way with silver-white, transfiguring the sandy ruts, bushes and trees, concealing yet revealing, washing out color but illuminating all with a suspended and eerie quality. Darkness

Chapter 17

shot with silver. The same but not at all the same.

Old Dirty was far ahead of me, his bare feet noiselessly meeting the white sand. I ran to catch up with him on the island road, yet I hung back, too, afraid to let him know I was there. On and on we walked, many yards apart. His pace was steady, and I could barely catch my breath.

When we reached South Point, the terns were still sleeping, and I felt deeply affected by them and by the silver-touched expanse of beauty that stretched from the murmuring, rolling waves to the white sheet of sand, from the bright, glittering inlet over to the clearly visible woods of the neck.

If I had not remembered the yearning and miserable expression on Louie's face, and if I had not seen the coins flung into the dirt, I then and there would have danced in the bright sand of that perfect and glorious moonlight, with the birds as my audience. I could not speak, and my legs, ready to dance, stopped moving. How incredible was the moonlight on the shore.

Up ahead, Old Dirty had neared the inlet water. He suddenly turned.

"Hurry up, gel," he shouted. "Come on!"

Shocked, I ran through the terns—and then he was pushing me into the boat. We went over the rushing waters of the inlet. On the other side, we pulled the boat high up on the bank and headed around the dunes, which could have been great mounds of white sugar in the moonlight.

Old Dirty broke the silence. "This is a deer highway," he said.

Sure enough, there between the rows of dunes, walking sedately among the tracks of other deer, was a doe. She was picking her way to the ocean.

We moved silently behind a dune to let her pass.

"She's goin' to set in the breakers for a while," he said. "She left her newborn back there in the edge of the woods."

We climbed a dune and watched her walk down to the water. The deer was one of those secret and vanishing creatures, I thought, like the spirit of the night with her shy beauty. She sank gratefully into the foam.

"Let's go," whispered Old Dirty.

Before, the trip to the wagon dune had seemed endless, and undoubtedly our apprehensions had made it seem so. Now I was surprised we arrived at the spot so quickly. Old Dirty hardly gave it a glance, passing it by, making for our tunnel through the myrtle. I did not ask him how he knew the way. For the second time that evening I passed through the palmetto forest and under the twin

The Treasure of Pawley's Island

giants, only this time it was flooded with moonlight.

Bending down, Old Dirty lit the lantern which had been left behind. Down in the dirt, near the box, was the pouch of gold. A bright coin lay a few feet from it, half-buried. Old Dirty handed the coin to me without a word. Inside the pouch were more coins.

He motioned for me to sit down on top of the dirt, just above the box but plenty far away from it, too. The box below me, in the hole, looked quite innocent.

Old Dirty pushed a pile of dirt against the box, up even with the top. Then he arranged some twigs and dry pieces of wood, which he brought out of nowhere, lit them and fanned the flames into a small fire. Soon the fire danced and wisps of smoke rose in curls to meet the clear night air. Old Dirty laid a rope noose attached to a stick over the gash in the box. He knelt and started to blow the smoke toward the box. The column of smoke reluctantly turned and ran in a stream toward the hole, where some of it entered but most sprang skyward. I didn't blame it.

He puffed and puffed, blowing more and more smoke over the top of the wooden box. Minutes passed. I felt certain that enough time had passed for the smoke to awaken the snake. And I couldn't help but think that only a while before Old Dirty had been sucking and sucking to pull poison out of an arm, and now he was blowing and blowing to pull a snake out of a box.

We waited. He fed the fire with one hand and continued blowing the smoke. Then he let the fire die down and brought the lantern closer. More smoke dribbled into the hole. Would the snake ever come out? Was it still there?

Then, before our very eyes and before I could comprehend it, a copper-colored head topped with beady eyes poked up out of the hole. Quick as a flash, Old Dirty tightened the noose. He had a snake.

"A copperhead. Well, I ain't surprised," he growled as he pulled out the writhing body of a three-foot snake. In the light, it was pinkish-red with dark hourglass bands around its fat body. I could not take my eyes from it.

Old Dirty took out his hunting knife and chopped the snake's head off. Even as we watched, the snake's headless body writhed and curled on the white sugary sand around the box.

"Their venom don't kill like a rattler or a cottonmouth," he said in his gravelly voice, the voice of a man who seldom speaks. He knelt and blew more smoke into the hole. Perhaps he thought another reptile was down there.

"Old Dirty, what were you doing over here on Debourdieu when

Chapter 17

Louie was bitten?" I asked.

"When children set off in the night, somebody needs to look after them. Leastwise your ma and I think so," he said and continued blowing smoke.

I watched his bony figure bend over the hole, the alligator teeth around his neck rattling. I thought of how his appearance was deceiving. He seemed to be just a smelly old man, a hunter and a hermit, but he was also a man with sympathies and tenderness. As Grandma had often said to me, "Man looketh on the outward appearance, but God looketh on the heart."

After a few minutes when no more snakes crawled out, Old Dirty pried off the top of the box. The lantern light flickered down, and we saw several inches of dirt in the bottom and the impression in the sand where the snake had lain.

Old Dirty dug around with his gnarled, stained fingers and found six more decaying leather pouches. Two pouches contained ten gold coins each. Three others contained five gold coins each, and the last held an old piece of jewelry, a gold cross about two inches long, set with several garnets, one large clear stone and one bluish stone.

I carefully dropped the loose coin into the first pouch, putting all the pouches into my pocket. Old Dirty poured the dirt out of the box, looking for still more coins, but there were no more. He covered the fire, grabbed up the two parts of the snake and tossed them into the box, then hoisted it to his shoulder.

The moonlight flooded down and fell on us as we walked to the inlet. The old man, tattered and weary, was transfigured into beauty by the silver light—and I guess the strange girl in boy's clothes who walked beside him was, too. The moon has an enthralling power, giving views that take us beyond ourselves. That night, the night of the snake, I can never forget.

The Treasure of Pawley's Island

We found Old Dirty sitting on the steps behind the kitchen.

Chapter 18
You Can't Buy Those Things, Old Dirty

When the breakfast bell rang the next morning, I was for once already seated at the dining table with a lacy linen napkin spread across my knees. The tablecloth was immaculate, as usual. Life was back to normal.

The sound of the breakfast bell resounded from room to room, and footsteps were heard from all over the house as family members and servants hurried to the table. The maids came in from the kitchen and breezeway to help serve the meal. Uncle Zeke took his place behind Grandpa's chair, ready to attend. Grandpa helped Grandma into her chair, and she smiled up at him.

Then Mama descended slowly from upstairs. I leaped up and ran to her, taking her arm. She pressed my hand and took her seat next to mine. Her hair was brushed upward, glossy and lovely, her white linen dress newly pressed. She leaned over and looked into my face, tracing half-circles underneath my eyes with her finger. She said nothing, but she must have known I had lain awake for a long time after returning home with Old Dirty.

Aunt Alberta descended the stairs alone, since Uncle Sumter remained in his room, still eating from trays which the servants carried up to him at each meal.

"Good morning, Alberta," said Grandma pleasantly. "I do hope you and Sumter slept well."

"Well enough," replied Aunt Alberta. Her face was pinched, but her chin was high, and she had taken the usual scrupulous care with her appearance.

"Good morning, dear ones," Grandma said with satisfaction as she looked around the table at all of us. She bowed her head after nodding to Grandpa. At that signal the maids stopped milling around.

Grandpa, standing at his chair, lifted his head and prayed, "Kind

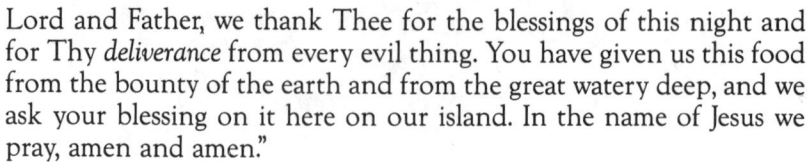

Chapter 18

"Lord and Father, we thank Thee for the blessings of this night and for Thy *deliverance* from every evil thing. You have given us this food from the bounty of the earth and from the great watery deep, and we ask your blessing on it here on our island. In the name of Jesus we pray, amen and amen."

Then the maids passed around the steaming hot food. Maum Polly had fried green tomatoes, tangy and delicious, to be eaten with cheese grits and fried fish. They passed a filigreed silver cake basket heaped with hot biscuits to eat with pale, creamy butter and damson preserves. Fragrant steam rose from two silver teapots filled with mild English breakfast tea.

"Nothing wrong with your appetite this morning, Bessie," said Mama, pleased. "Nothing at all." She saw my plate was heaped full.

"It was a long, long night, Mama, and I'm starved."

"Why hasn't Jane Anne come down for breakfast, Alberta?" asked Grandma.

Aunt Alberta hesitated. "She's not exactly well this morning," she said finally. "I had some spearmint tea taken up to her at dawn when she knocked at my door. The poor thing can't keep any food down, so I excused her from breakfast. I'll send her some toast and weak tea later."

"That girl needs some powdered charcoal," declared Grandpa. "It certainly ought to calm her stomach—never seen charcoal to fail."

"No, no!" Aunt Alberta protested. "I'll take care of her. Don't worry yourself . . ." She looked drained from her cares of the past few days, and for a moment I felt sorry for her.

Then she launched immediately into a conversation about the drummer who had made his way to the island a couple of days before. When word had passed from one end of the island to the other that his cart was at the Haseltons' kitchen door, Aunt Alberta, Grandma and Mama had joined a milling throng of island ladies examining his wares. They returned home an hour later laden with news from as far away as Conway, but they had brought home more than news—spools of thread, shoe paint, ribbons and lace, buttons and flower seeds. Aunt Alberta had bought a new shirt for Uncle Sumter, a fine one, and two bolts of cloth for dresses for Jane Anne.

"That cracker ran on so I could hardly follow what he said. But he did have some cunning lace and ribbons, didn't he?" Aunt Alberta said with enthusiasm. "How could he stay so fleshy in his line of work? I'd be down to skin and bone if I had to drive a wagon all over the Low Country."

Mama's face showed a trace of a smile. "He eats at many a door," she said. "All he has to do is hand a piece of grosgrain ribbon in to the cook, and out comes a hot plate filled with the best food the house has to offer."

"I only wish I had bought a silk flower for Jane Anne's hair," murmured Aunt Alberta.

Both Mama and Grandma had bought picot-edged ribbons and torchon lace for trimming aprons. They had bought shoe paint for the family and some extra for the servants, including Teaspoon, even though he only wore shoes in the late fall and winter. For Maum Polly, they had selected a nice piece of beige lace. For me they had purchased cedar pencils with erasers, ruled pads of paper, embroidery thread and a few Chinese lanterns. They had also bought inexpensive presents for each of the servants.

"We have to look after them all," Grandma said. "We depend on our colored families, and they depend upon us equally." I knew she was thinking of Daddy Buck.

As the conversation continued, I looked over at Grandpa, who always put me on his right-hand side at the dining table.

"How is Daddy Buck this morning, Grandpa?" I whispered. I was scared to ask about Louie. I was afraid Louie had died.

"Some better, although he's still weak. Aunt Hagey isn't planning his funeral any more. And Louie is doing as expected for such a bite."

"*Louie*? What's the matter with the *orphan* Lewis?" asked Aunt Alberta.

All chatter at the table ceased as Grandpa answered, "He was bitten by a copperhead last night. He's in bed and very, very weak. If the boy had been grown, the poison wouldn't have affected him as much as it has."

"How did it happen?" demanded Aunt Alberta.

"Bessie?" Grandpa looked at me. I nodded with downcast eyes.

Grandpa told the tale, briefly, and I was silent.

When Grandpa mentioned the gold coins, I could not contain myself. "Fourteen hundred dollars and a little gold cross set with stones!" I cried out.

Everyone gasped except Grandpa and Mama, who already knew.

"Old Dirty saved Louie," I continued, "and he blew smoke into that hole and caught that copperhead and chopped off its head as neat as could be! He's braver than Francis Marion—or John C. Calhoun!"

"He did all of that?" demanded Aunt Alberta. "Why, I would not allow that man to come near me. It's his fault that Buck startled Sumter. That filthy degenerate. He's incompetent!"

"Don't you say that!" I shouted.

Chapter 18

Aunt Alberta froze.

"Old Dirty *saved Louie*, and he is *not* incompetent! He saved Daddy Buck's life, too! And he would do anything for anybody," I raved on. "Well, almost anything. *His looks don't count.* And Uncle Sumter had no business being out there with a gun!"

"Bessie!" said Mama, shocked at my directness.

"Now, now," said Grandma, putting oil on troubled water, "let's finish this delicious breakfast in peace."

"Pirates buried that treasure," I continued, "and somebody beat us to most of it, or we would have had a million dollars! Then we wouldn't have to take in *boarders!*"

"Elizabeth Lois!" said Mama. "I have heard *enough.*"

And Grandpa added, "Sailor, eat your food."

Silence. I tried to eat.

"Imagine, buried gold, here," said Grandma finally. "I can't believe it. Whatever led you to hunt for it, Bessie?"

"Louie thought it all up. He just decided this would be a good place for pirates to bury treasure and jewels and precious coins long, long ago. We made a map and sorta stumbled on it all. I never really believed—until we found it."

◆ ◆ ◆ ◆ ◆ ◆ ◆

Three days later I knocked at the Haseltons' door and asked to see Louie, who was still in bed. He looked very ill. His terrible swollen hand rested beside him on a pillow, and his pale face stirred me to tears.

I set a present—a banana walnut poundcake baked especially for him—on his night stand where he could see it when he woke up. Uncle Cuthbert whispered that Louie was hardly eating a thing yet, but he knew his nephew would enjoy looking at the cake and might even be tempted to try a piece. I knew Louie was mighty ill when I heard that.

In the past few days, when I had thought of Louie dying, my heart had almost stopped beating. Now, as I watched his rhythmic breathing, I felt that perhaps he wouldn't die. I crept out, nodding to Uncle Cuthbert, for I could not speak.

◆ ◆ ◆ ◆ ◆ ◆ ◆

During those days Louie had lain in bed in pain and shock, vomiting once in awhile. Grandpa had given him doses of powdered charcoal. "Absorbs poisons and stops vomiting," he said. Often, in the first few

The Treasure of Pawley's Island

days, Louie had slipped into semi-consciousness.

Each day I had walked over to sit on the Haseltons' piazza until someone came out with news of him. Finally he passed the crisis point and was fully awake, except when taking long naps.

The next day I went over, and he was glad to see me, even if I was in girl clothes. So I returned often and sat reading and talking to him by the hour. Louie asked me if Old Dirty and Hardtime Swinton were still on the island. He said he wanted to see Old Dirty to thank him. I told him they had gone up to Wachesaw to lead a fishing trip, but that they would return in a day or two.

Teaspoon brought Louie presents of soft-shell crabs and especially fine and succulent whiting, to be fried. He also came in every day with all the news from the island.

Louie and I talked and talked. Sometimes we examined the gold coins and speculated about them. The dates on the gold pieces were 1851, 1852 and 1859. When Old Dirty returned to the island, I cornered him at the kitchen door and asked him about our treasure. He told me that the coins were probably the remains of a small cache of gold sent up from Charleston to Wilmington, North Carolina, before the attack on Charleston by Yankee soldiers in 1864. Bankers had sent what was left of money and jewels out of the city to keep them from Sherman, he said, but the chest never reached its destination. The bearers had been waylaid on the King's Highway a few miles south of Pawley's, toward Georgetown. Two men had been shot to death and another gravely wounded. No trace of the money had been found—until now.

Louie and I asked Grandpa to send a letter to the authorities in Charleston, inquiring into the theft of the money. He did so, saying valuables had been found on Cuthbert Haselton's property. If someone could give proof of ownership, he wrote, we would be glad to surrender the property. Louie and I hoped beyond hope that no reply would come.

For days we waited and planned how to spend "the money." In a thousand ways we spent it in our minds—for sweets, a long telescope, a clay pipe, some Roman candles, a whip—so many items I can't remember them all. When I told Mama, she advised me to stop anticipating and planning or we might be disappointed. But I could not stop dreaming. I was sure it would all come true.

• • • • • • •

One day I visited Louie and noticed that his eyes were red.

Chapter 18

"Have you caught an infection?" I asked. "Or has the snake poison gone to your face? Your eyes have been bloodshot for several days, and the rims are red, too."

He looked away. "When y' git snake bit, y' feel low," he answered, and I realized he had been crying.

"You never seem low to me. And you're going to get back full use of your hand, aren't you?" He nodded. "Aunt Alberta says sometimes snake poison kills the nerves, but she isn't always right."

Louie's sadness turned to anger. "Well, that old lady ain't right about *my* hand," he said. "Anyway, she ain't even been over here to see me—how would she know what my hand looks like? Your mama comes every day or two," he added. "Now, that lady could make a dead man perk up and smile. She can tell my hand is goin' t' be *fine*—she tells me each an' every time she comes. An' she never tells a lie, does she?" I was glad to see his mood changing. "An' Teaspoon brings me a couple of soft-shell crabs every time he comes," he continued. "I'll bet he's brought me a peck by now. I love those soft-shells *fri-i-ied!*"

"He helped us a lot that night, didn't he?"

"Sure, he did. I knew he would. That's why I wanted him t' go along. An' Old Dirty—well, we *got* t' reward 'em. That's a lot of money, and no tellin' how much that little cross is worth. Fair is fair. We gotta re-ward 'em."

"Let's give them each some coins," I suggested.

"No. I though about this a long time. We'll ask 'em what they want most in this world, an' then we'll buy it for 'em."

I thought that was a good suggestion. Again, for the hundredth time, we inspected the coins and the cross. Gold, gold—it was like a dream.

"I only look at the coins when you're here," said Louie. "We can't be too careful. Before we found th' treasure, Teaspoon told me about a 'rubbuh buckra' he caught in your stable. He said he was a big white fellow, an' he would have *killed* Teaspoon if he hadn't had the two setters with him. He said Daddy Buck whipped th' buckra good—in th' woods, so your grandma wouldn't know about it, or she'd have stopped him. That robber was plenty scared, an' he ran off hollerin' through th' trees, Teaspoon said. We can't be careful enough, Elbow. Now you wrap the cross back an' put it in th' secret place."

I wrapped the cross carefully. Louie had cleaned it until it sparkled. And he had polished the coins. I thought all our treasure was worth a king's ransom, or more. I laid everything in the little box that had belong to Louie's mother, then I lifted the loose board behind Louie's bed and tucked it there, out of sight. A perfect hiding place, from the

The Treasure of Pawley's Island

"robbuh buckra."

In a few more days Louie was stronger and out of bed. I was overjoyed to have him up and around. We decided to find Old Dirty and Teaspoon, question them and take the mailboat to Georgetown to buy their hearts' desire.

We found Old Dirty sitting on the steps behind the kitchen. He and Hardtime had returned every day or so to sleep in our stable after leading this or that fishing or hunting party. My grandparents did not seem to mind, but Aunt Alberta saw "no need in *those* men hanging around." I often hid in the bushes, watching and listening to them talk and, although Old Dirty always knew I was there, he never gave any sign.

This time he was alone, except for a black and white dog. Louie and I stood watching for a few minutes as he taught his new dog the cookie trick. The dog knew what was expected of him, but he was having trouble snapping his head around and catching the cookie as it flipped up off his nose. Yet Old Dirty was patient, talking to the dog in a low rumble and stroking his back.

Then he spoke to us while still looking at the dog. "He's smart. Plenty smart—he's even got a couple of things Sam didn't have—but in most ways he ain't near the dog Sam was. He's Sam's brother."

His rough voice was low, yet it carried clearly to our ears.

"Dirty, what do you want most in all th' world?" Louie asked.

"What?" Old Dirty replied, spitting into his tin can and rubbing the dog's head.

I put my hand over my nose. Grandpa had promised Dirty he would buy him a new set of clothes if he would only take a bath. Old Dirty had said he would think about it. Oh, he needed that bath.

"If you could name what you want in th' whole world, what would you name?" Louie repeated, not seeming to notice the smell.

"I want nothing I kin have."

"Aw, come on, everybody wants something. What is it?"

Silence.

"Come on, Dirty."

"I want a wife to kiss me, and a boy your age. And a little girl to set on my knee when I come in from the woods."

We were startled.

"You can't never buy those things, Old Dirty," said Louie.

I spoke up, "Can't you name something we can buy at the store?"

"Nothing. I got it all." He turned and walked into the bushes. The black and white dog, the next best dog to Sam the cur, looked at us and slunk into the bushes behind his master.

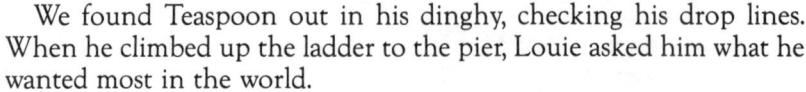

Chapter 18

We found Teaspoon out in his dinghy, checking his drop lines. When he climbed up the ladder to the pier, Louie asked him what he wanted most in the world.

"Eh?"

"I said what do you want most in th' world? In *all* the world?"

"Heh! You kin do my wuk fo' *three* day," Teaspoon replied. "An' den ah kin lie in de shade an' eat. Ah still ain't got ober de night wuk." I tried to imagine Teaspoon lounging in the shade, not working. Since he was always busy, I couldn't visualize it.

Louie tried to be patient. "It's got t' be something that's bought with *money*—from a *store*. I ain't strong enough t' do y' work for three days."

"Den buy me de new suit, de new grip, de new mule ob my own. De new bucket fo' de fish, de new hooks, de new hat—"

"Name *one* thing, Teaspoon," said Louie, impatiently. "*One* thing you want more than any other. One, one, only one."

Teaspoon though about it seriously. "Iffen ah been in de sto', ah might know what t' want'. Ah keep on pullin' up dese drop line an' dese fish, an' de sto' ib over *dere* an' *ah* ib ober *heah*."

"Ain't you got one idea, just one idea?"

"Think a minute, Teaspoon," I added. "Think and don't talk."

He sat down on the pier bench and stared out at his fishing lines, deep in thought.

"We thought we'd buy you a surprise with some of that gold we found," I explained.

"Surprise—dat's what ah wants! Git me de surprise fo' Daddy Buck. He ain't smilin' no mo'. When ah goes in t' see him, ah *needs* t' see dose teeth dats lef' in he mouth shinin'." Teaspoon demonstrated how he wanted to see Daddy Buck smile, and he gave a low belly-laugh in imitation of Daddy Buck. He said, "Daddy Buck neber laugh, an' he don' call Old Dirty a 'po buckra' no mo'—an' he ain't 'Hee-heed' since he been shot. He just turn he haid t' de wall. Git me de surprise fo' Daddy Buck. Git *dat* an' ah be happy."

◆ ◆ ◆ ◆ ◆ ◆ ◆

Within a couple of weeks, a letter arrived from the authorities in Charleston, stating that numerous records had been lost in The War, and they could find no official records concerning valuables buried or lost anywhere near Uncle Cuthbert's property. They believed it to be part of that stolen money sent up to Wilmington during Sherman's march northward, but since the records were lost, they could not be

The Treasure of Pawley's Island

sure. We read the letter over and over. Jubilation! One thousand four hundred dollars, an enormous amount, and all ours. Uncle Cuthbert said that since we had found it, we should have it, even though it was found on his property. When Grandpa told us that it might be worth even more, and that the cross was probably valuable as well, we shook our heads in disbelief. News of our find spread throughout the island. Even Uncle Sumter sent for me to come to his room to tell him the story, which I did.

A couple of days later Grandpa, Uncle Zeke, Louie and I were on the mailboat. It was steaming its way down the wide Waccamaw River to Georgetown. It was a trip I had seldom made. Louie and I watched impatiently as we rounded the turn from the Georgetown harbor into the Sampit River that curves up behind the old city. The Sampit hugs the town, having been its lifeline and outlet to the world for 200 years.

The mailboat gave four long blasts of its horn when we chugged in to the dock. It was the most important sound the sleepy, remote town would hear until the boat's return two days later. From the boat we walked immediately up Front Street toward The Morgan Bank. Dogs idled in the road; we picked our way past them, across the road and around the few people who were headed toward the mailboat. Georgetown was practically empty, for it was early afternoon, dinnertime. A wagon rode past, spitting dust and mud behind it on its way to the dock. A few horses and a wagon were tied in front of Gladstone's General Mercantile. Inside, Louie and I gaped at colorful merchandise piled in glass cases and barrels and stacked a mile high on shelves, only to be reached by climbing a wooden ladder that could be pushed along the walls.

We decided to make our purchases and then deposit the rest of our money in a safety box at the bank. Grandpa and Uncle Zeke left us inside the store, promising to return in an hour or two to accompany us to the bank.

"Don' buy out de sto'," advised Uncle Zeke, grinning.

"Take care of these spendthrifts, Joseph," Grandpa called out to Mr. Gladstone. Then he tipped his bowler and closed us in that bewitching place.

Immediately we asked Mr. Gladstone to cut off a big piece of cheese and count out a couple of dozen crackers from a cracker barrel. Thus fortified, we went to work studying the contents of the store.

Two and one-half hours later, Mr. Gladstone's assistant was wrapping our purchases neatly in brown paper and tying them with string. We had decided on two new umbrellas, a box of fishing hooks, and a large

Chapter 18

box of Roman candles and flares. I had selected an iron penny bank with the figure of a boy and his dog on top (the little iron boy passed the penny to an iron dog who deposited the money below); while Louie chose an iron penny bank with a hammering blacksmith on top (the blacksmith's hammer passed the penny into the anvil). We also bought two volumes of *The Five Little Peppers*; a leather dog collar for Old Dirty, with a brass plate on which we had had "In Memory of Sam the Cur" engraved; and a stiff, fancy shirtfront with attached collar and tie that would perfectly fit Teaspoon (the buttonhole at the back of the neck, attaching the collar, was worked in *silk thread*).

There was a hollow wooden bird that neatly fit into the palm of a hand; when you filled it with water and blew into the pipe in its tail, it trilled magnificently. This was to be Teaspoon's surprise for Daddy Buck. Our packages also included a lace bonnet for the new baby (Louie's idea), a new-fangled mustache trimmer for Grandpa, a pound of rock candy, ten twisted sticks of hoarhound candy, a big red button for Teaspoon, a cameo pin for me and a stickpin of gold for Louie. All these items had cost a total of $29.58, almost four weeks' salary for a workman.

The remaining money we split and deposited in two boxes at The Morgan Bank, to be held there until such time as we needed it.

Louie and I had a long discussion that afternoon. He said that maybe the ricelands he had inherited near Beaufort would not have to be sold if he could pay taxes on them each year. I had not heard about those lands, for he had only spoken a few sentences about his family to me. We asked Grandpa how we should go about selling the gold cross. He said he would think about it and make some inquiries. He also said Louie's share of the money *would* pay the taxes on his land, with a lot left over. Grandpa said he was very proud of Louie.

I told Grandpa I, too, wanted to pay the taxes on our property. He said that we might need to do that, but that if he could get the money together without using the treasure coins, he would certainly do so, and he fully expected the rice crop to pay the taxes this year. Grandpa held me close and kissed my cheek. "To think we might have to use my granddaughter's money," he murmured. "Child, pray for a good harvest."

We spent that night at the home of a relative in Georgetown and caught the mailboat in the afternoon, as it left to travel back up the Waccamaw River. Louie and I trilled the bird whistle all the way home.

The Treasure of Pawley's Island

Well, I thought, one more secret revealed.

Chapter 19
Fair The Day Shine

One morning before dawn, Louie and I sneaked out of our houses and met on the Lookout steps by the ocean. Louie had been gaining strength every day, especially since our trip to Georgetown. We sat side by side, glad to be outdoors, feeling a kinship with the great restless ocean, with the salt air, with the little crescent island—our home—and with the marsh we knew and loved so well.

We reminisced about buying the gifts and the reactions they produced. "Never hear dat bird befo'!" said Daddy Buck when Teaspoon trilled the wooden bird under his window. How he grinned when Teaspoon walked in blowing on the singing bird. In a few minutes Daddy Buck was blowing on it himself. That afternoon he came out of his cabin for the first time and sat on the stoop for a while, blowing on the bird so that the island could hear its song.

Old Dirty had tried not to show his surprise when we handed him the dog collar. "A collar with a genuine brass plate," said Louie. Old Dirty looked at it closely, reading the inscription. "That dog Sam had a proud head," he said, then he buckled the collar on the next best dog.

Teaspoon strutted around in his new shirtfront and tie all day. I advised him to keep it as first best, but he put it on and marched from person to person, house to house, wearing it proudly. That evening he sewed the big red button we had purchased for him on the front of his bowler.

Grandpa had appreciated his new mustache trimmer. I told him that I could tell no difference in the mustache after he used it, and he replied that that was as it should be; if I could tell the difference, then he was using it incorrectly. He said it saved him at least five minutes' work two times a week. I was pleased then.

We waited for the tip of the sun to show on the black horizon. The

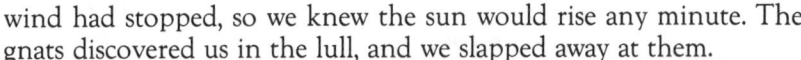

Chapter 19

wind had stopped, so we knew the sun would rise any minute. The gnats discovered us in the lull, and we slapped away at them.

"I'm goin' back to the treasure spot soon," Louie announced. "I been thinkin about that treasure box—how do we know that it was the only box in there? I coulda been settin' right on top of another box which was filled to th' brim with pounds of gold an' diamond crowns an' things."

"Well, I guess I'll go with you and help dig," I told him, "but I wonder if it was all worth it. Are more gold coins worth another snake bite, or perhaps something worse?"

Louie thought a moment. "That snake bite wasn't anything. And anyway, I'm glad I was th' one t' git it, not you. Your puny body couldn't have taken it. Not many boys my age have been bit by a copperhead and lived t' tell it."

At that moment the sun, a brilliant curve of coral-rose, showed above the horizon. It was a welcome old friend after my weeks of rising before dawn to go fishing or exploring. It cast a familiar pink pathway over the water toward us, as hospitable as an outstretched hand.

"I know I pulled some howlers *that night*," Louie continued. "I should never have drug you an' Teaspoon off in th' dark, an' I shouldn't have stuck my hand down in that old box. I just couldn't face goin' over that water by myself." He glanced over at me. "I admit to you that I git t' feelin' alone," he said. "An' I wasn't thinkin' when I poked my hand down in there. I hope I've learned a thing or two. If I haven't, I should take up tattin'."

I thought Louie looked older than he had when we explored the marsh and fished the salt creeks and breakers together. His face was composed now with as much dignity as I had ever seen in a boy his age. His jaw, which had looked so round and babyish at the beginning of spring, was square and firm now; and his eyes, instead of being feverish with sickness, were alight with eagerness. Even his freckles seemed diminished. I liked him. He had been good to me.

Louie turned to me again. "Elbow, you are right. When y' hit it, y' hit it. Those gold coins ain't worth a snake bite—but I'd gladly have paid a snake bite for all the good times we had planning an' looking for that gold. The doin' of all that was th' real treasure to me. An' you might even have built up a little muscle over the last few weeks. I ain't been happy since my pa died last winter," he admitted, "but I got happy when we started huntin' that treasure. It got me plannin' an' goin' again. Now, I know I made some bad mistakes that night. I now turn to y' an' look y' straight in the face an' admit that, Elbow. I did it, an' I got t' take what comes."

The Treasure of Pawley's Island

We looked each other in the eye. Then he put his head down on his arms, and I sudddenly got a picture of what he was going to be like as a man. It thrilled me.

His voice continued low, "I was scared out in the middle of that dark inlet—no moon, no light, that deep water all around, an' you and Teaspoon going along behind me *so-o-o-o* trusting—I thought we'd die. But I pushed on."

"You didn't look scared," I replied. "I'd have bet money you weren't a bit afraid. Besides, I thought you knew what you were doing."

"Well, I didn't, an' I don't have much courage. I just pushed on 'cause I couldn't turn back there in front of y'. Stubborness, I guess. Courage is when y' know something is right, and y' push on when y' don't want to, not when y' know it's wrong. And that was wrong fer me t' do any of it. Courage is what my ma had before she died. And what my pa had too. In me it came out as stubborness, I guess." He shook his head. "When I was so sick, all I could think about was 'What if that snake had bit Elbow? She'd have died for sure.' An' I don't think I could stand anybody else dying for a while. It makes me feel sick t' think about it even now."

Louie reached in his pocket, pulled out a dirty handkerchief and slowly unwrapped it. Inside was that broken piece of wood with our dried blood on it, our oath stick. I reached in the pocket of my suit and pulled mine out. I had carried the wood with me faithfully, every day. We twisted them until they fit together.

"You know," he said, "when I was sick I cried a lot. I think snakebites do that to y'. I worried an' worried, fretted an' fretted, an' felt guiltier an' guiltier. All that poison was runnin' around in my blood, I guess. Anyways, one day I threw myself off my bed an' asked forgiveness from Him," he said, pointing upward, "for takin' y' into trouble, an' a bunch of other things. An' I feel like the weight of a fat mule has been taken off my shoulders. An' it's easin' up some about missin' my ma an' pa, too."

"I didn't have to go with you, Louie," I said. "My Mama didn't want me to go. I went 'cause I wanted to, and she saw I was going *no matter what*. She sent Old Dirty behind us just in case."

Louie thought a minute and said, "If she hadn't done that, where would I be now?" We nodded together.

"Do you think Old Dirty is an *angel?*" I asked suddenly. "You know that angels hover around, wanting to help."

"I know, your Grandma says so." Then he snickered, "She's probably right about angels hoverin' around, but angels don't smell like Old Dirty—an' they don't go around with men like Hardtime Swinton.

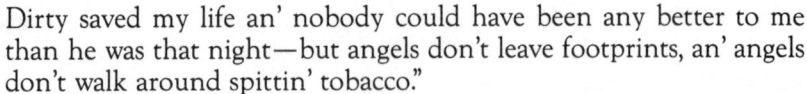

Chapter 19

Dirty saved my life an' nobody could have been any better to me than he was that night—but angels don't leave footprints, an' angels don't walk around spittin' tobacco."

After a minute, he added, "I want you to take this gold cross an' wear it under your shirt, an' I don't want us to sell it unless we hafta. If we gotta, we gotta, but until then—here, you wear it." He thrust the cross at me. He had hung it on a string. I looked at it and then put it around my neck and under my suit.

We sat very still. The sea was restless, wandering, awesome. Porpoise clans passed in review just beyond the gently breakers, gracefully rounding the surface to feel the salt breeze. On the beach, shells lay in heaps as far as the eye could see. The salty air was warm and sweet with the newness of spring at the shore.

We heard a noise and looked up above us. On the Lookout, Grandpa and Uncle Zeke were peering through a telescope toward the South Inlet, where a sailboat with brown stained sails tacked an erratic course. They were chuckling to see it and seemed to know the captain.

At that moment, Teaspoon's voice piped from the Lookout, calling us to a hot breakfast.

"Hot biscuits in ten minute," he announced. "Just ten minute. Comin' up, comin' up!" Then he ran back to the house.

"I still think something more is in that dirt," Louie said, growing excited as he talked. "I feel it. I don't know what it is, but it's there. An' we'll do it right this time—no more people gettin' shot or snakebit. Ain't it good the Almighty gives us another chance, to sing songs again and get them right!"

He grew so excited he could hardly wait for us to start. "Teaspoon will havta go along with us," he said. "He can sure shovel—an' you kin too, if y' want. We got t' get these plans laid."

Grandpa's two setters came bounding joyously over the Lookout, dashing headlong down the steps where we sat. Yipping with exuberance, they raced out on the strand to chase shore birds as they taxied in for breakfast.

"Louie," I asked, "what is that brown stuff you rub on your hands before you touch fishing bait?"

"Awww, it's just chewin' tobacco. The fish don't smell my human smell if I rub some chew on my fingers before I bait th' hook."

Then his laughter rang out over the strand. He was tickled that I could still be curious about his fishing secrets.

Well, I thought, one more secret revealed.

I looked down. Without thinking, I had once again selected my blue sailor suit, probably the last time I could wear it until the killer

The Treasure of Pawley's Island

frost in the fall. Its fine material was stain-free. Suddenly a thought occurred to me: perhaps I could use my share of the coins to attend a year of school in Charleston. Then I was reminded of Cousin Jane Anne. She was like a fragile sea fan that washed up on the shore, iridescent and beautiful, yet shallow and breakable.

Surely, I thought, her weakness on the night of the snake was only momentary. As grandpa said, it's the trend of one's life that counts, not one solitary act. I had wanted her to be like Mama or Grandma, with their character.

But she and I have time, I reminded myself, time to learn.

"I've learned a lot these past few weeks," I told Louie, and I knew he was thinking I referred to the "secrets." Well, I thought, I *have* learned secrets, and I have grown stronger.

I looked up at Louie and smiled, as a wave of relief washed over me. Louie and I have *time*, I thought.

The sunshine on Pawley's was yellow. The sea oats waved in the breeze, and the waves rolled over in curls. We basked in the warmth for a few minutes longer before heading home for breakfast.

Papa had returned from the plantation a couple of day earlier to go "first swimming," another yearly ritual with Grandpa. They had reported the water to be very, very cool. I knew June would arrive before Mama would allow me to put on my bathing costume for a swim. But back at the plantation the rice was almost ready for harvest, a *good* harvest.

The summer days ahead would be full of sun and water, fishing, sailing, tramping in the marsh, horse races on the hard beach, and seashell collections. There would be parties in the dunes by firelight, laughter and tears, balloons and Chinese lanterns, Dickens and *The Five Little Peppers* read by the illumination lamp, layer cakes and white linen dresses swishing through parlors. There would be our new baby, oh wonderful day. There would also be silver lockets and chains, laughter with friends on the piazza, watermelons, memory books, and a great storm. Perhaps there would be another adventure, or even two, while the breeze caressed Pawley's Island, our treasure by the sea.

Fair the day shine as it shone on Pawley's Island in the spring of 1893.

Chapter 19